PRAISE FOR
THE COMFORT FOOD MYSTERIES

Diners, Drive-ins, and Death

"Christine Wenger serves up a delicious helping of comfort food with a dash of mystery and a cast of lovable characters that'll keep you laughing long after the book ends."
—Kate Carlisle, *New York Times* bestselling author of the Bibliophile Mysteries

"A delightful series with colorful characters in a to-die-for setting, nicely seasoned with humor. As down-home and satisfying as the daily special served at the Silver Bullet Diner."
—Krista Davis, *New York Times* bestselling author of the Domestic Diva Mysteries and the Paws and Claws Mysteries

"Sandy Harbor delights with its unique characters. . . . Readers will enjoy ample amounts of humor, indulgent cooking, and the often shady side of the restaurant business." —Kings River Life Magazine

"Boasting a quirky cast of characters, good dialogue, and a comfortable atmosphere, I look forward to the next book in this pleasantly charming series."
—Dru's Book Musings

continued . . .

"Plenty of local color and warm characters add to the investigation with a surprise ending that few will see coming. Readers will enjoy spending more time in Sandy Harbor as Trixie makes it and the Silver Bullet her own." —The Mystery Reader

"A spunky heroine, a handsome cowboy from Houston, a Latino cook, and assorted colorful others make for a fun read." —Gumshoe

"This is the first book in a new series that I hope will be around for a long time. It was such a fun read. It had me laughing and at the edge of my seat. The author knows how to plot a great mystery. I loved the characters." —MyShelf.com

"This is a thoroughly enjoyable mystery with a plot that keeps the reader engaged and very surprised by the reveal, always a joy for mystery-reading veterans. In this debut Comfort Food Mystery, recipes are of course included as are delectable descriptions of decidedly low-fat but down-home cooking. Trixie is a very relatable and likable character deserving of her starring role in this promising and very well-written series." —Kings River Life Magazine

"Culinary mystery fans have a new series to sample." —The Poisoned Martini

"A comfort foodie and cozy reader's delight." —Escape with Dollycas into a Good Book

ALSO BY CHRISTINE WENGER

The Comfort Food Mysteries
Do or Diner
A Second Helping of Murder
Diners, Drive-ins, and Death

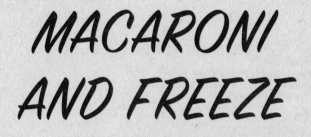

MACARONI AND FREEZE

A Comfort Food Mystery

CHRISTINE WENGER

AN OBSIDIAN BOOK

OBSIDIAN
Published by the Penguin Group
Penguin Group (USA) LLC, 375 Hudson Street,
New York, New York 10014

USA | Canada | UK | Ireland | Australia | New Zealand | India | South Africa | China
penguin.com
A Penguin Random House Company

First published by Obsidian, an imprint of New American Library,
a division of Penguin Group (USA) LLC

First Printing, July 2015

ISBN 978-0-451-47408-7

Printed in the United States of America
10 9 8 7 6 5 4 3 2

*For my lovely sister-in-law, Jean Matyjasik,
and to my sweet and beautiful nieces, Jill Sweeney and
Megan Matyjasik.
And for cozy mystery readers everywhere!*

Chapter 1

I just loved wintery Sunday mornings in my Silver Bullet Diner.

It was organized chaos as families filed in after church, workers came in for breakfast after their shifts, and snow-plow drivers shuffled in to get warm, refill their coffee, and get something to eat.

I loved how the cold weather brought people together and was glad that they came to my diner for good food and to warm their bones. The diner's windows were frosty and gave the feeling that everyone was inside a cozy cocoon.

As I was refilling my mug behind the counter, I paused to listen to the chatter of my customers and the clatter of silverware on plates—another one of my favorite things.

The smell of bacon frying and bread toasting permeated the air along with the strong aroma of coffee brewing. Mmm . . .

Arriving customers shrugged out of their winter regalia and helped their children out of theirs. They stuffed mittens, hats, and whatnot into the pockets of their coats and hung them on the pegs near the front door. If they were lucky enough to find a red vinyl booth right off the bat, they shuffled over to claim it as their own by hanging everything on the brass treble hooks screwed into the frame.

Heads were hunched over my big plastic menus, and fingers were pointing to the colorful pictures as my morning-shift waitress walked around with pots of coffee—regular and decaf—and exchanged friendly banter.

Because Sandy Harbor was such a small village, most everyone knew one another. Joking, shouting, and table hopping were common, much to the confusion of my waitresses. But that was the way of it here. There were plans being made for ice fishing, shopping trips to Syracuse or Watertown for clothing and after-Christmas sales, and a rather in-depth discussion about dairy cows and where to buy hay if there was a shortage.

And as always, weather was a big topic. I tuned in to a conversation between Guy Eastman, who owned a zillion cows and grew the best butter and sugar corn during the summer season, and Dave Cross, who was our area plumber and fishing guide.

Dave stirred his coffee absentmindedly. "My bunions tell me that we are going to have one hell of a blizzard. And that it's going to be bad."

"My right elbow was aching this morning, so I think you're right, but my left knee was calm, so you might be wrong," replied Guy. "My hammertoe was throbbing, and so was this blister I got from my new work boots. I wonder if that means anything."

Dave shrugged. "My right knee was creaking this morning. That's usually a sign of frost, but we're beyond frost. Maybe it's warning me about more sleet coming."

"Creaking? Both of my knees were creaking when I walked in here—it's my bursitis and arthritis. Oh, and I had pain shooting up and down my right leg. That tells me we're in for a couple feet of snow."

"Oh, for heaven's sake, Guy!" Dave exclaimed. "That's not a snow predictor; that's your sciatica."

A big laugh started in my stomach, and it was just about to make its way to the surface. I was in trouble. I had just taken a big gulp of coffee, and I was going to spray it all over my pretty diner if I couldn't swallow both the coffee and the laugh at the same time. Leaning over, I opened one of the cooler doors below the counter and made like I was looking for something until I could tamp down the laugh and the liquid.

These were the sights, sounds, and smells of my diner this Sunday morning in January. And I could think of nothing better in this world.

But both Guy and Dave were right, according to our local weatherperson, Heather "Flip a Coin" Flipelli. She was the daughter of the station manager and had no training in meteorology, and she was too young to have weather predictors like Dave's bunions and Guy's sciatica. Too bad she didn't have them, though. Maybe she'd do a better job predicting the weather.

Heather's morning segment was currently closed-captioned on an ancient TV hanging from the rafters at the end of the counter. I shivered when I saw that she was wearing a sleeveless tank top and denim miniskirt. Heather noted, with a toss of her shiny black ponytail, that it was sleeting outside—a combination of rain and heavy snow and whatever else Lake Ontario was throwing at little Sandy Harbor, New York. Heather named it a "weather event" and identified it as a "lake-effect polar vortex," but I, Trixie Matkowski, just called it another "massive weather mess."

"It's supposed to turn into a blizzard," said Huey Mobley, making a general announcement to everyone in the diner and who, having just walked in the door, had missed the bunion weather debate. Huey was delivering the Sunday edition of the *Sandy Harbor Lure*, our local newspaper, and stocking the paper box. "And this new bout of sleet will make the roads slippery and icy. It says so right here in the *Lure*."

And the *Lure* was sacred in this area.

"Don't you worry. Your friendly Department of Public Works has the icy conditions under control, Huey." Snowplow driver Karen Metonti set her fork down on her plate, which had once held a stack of blueberry pancakes and crispy bacon, and raised her coffee mug in salute. "My hopper is loaded with sand and salt, and I'm ready to go at it again just as soon as I refill my coffee."

"It's on me, Karen," I said, bobbing to the surface of

the counter. "And help yourself to a couple of donuts for the road on your way out."

"Thanks, Trixie. It's going to be a long week if Flip a Coin is right," Karen said, zipping up her insulated orange jumpsuit. She slipped on sheepskin mittens and a matching hat, which were both so stuffed with fur they looked like they lodged a whole sheep. Then she clomped out in snowmobile boots, stopping to get a refill on her coffee from Nancy, my day waitress, and slip a couple of donuts into a white bakery bag.

Spotting several fruit hand pies my Amish friend Sarah Stolfus made revolving in slow circles in the pastry carousel, I walked toward it as if in a trance.

"Beatrix Matkowski, don't you dare eat one of those hand pies, particularly not the cherry one. You just started another diet this morning," I mumbled to myself. I was hoping that maybe *myself* would listen, since I hated to be called Beatrix.

Before the hand pie could jump into my hand, I zoomed past the carousel and hustled back to my usual spot in the kitchen between the steam table and the huge black stove.

Phew. Crisis averted.

I'd been here since midnight, and my shift would end at precisely eight o'clock—in about ten minutes. I enjoyed working the graveyard stint because I always found that the customers who came in to eat then were an interesting group. We had the extroverts who relished the camaraderie in the diner, loners who just wanted to be left alone, and customers who were full of energy and thrived on the night. Almost every shift, I had customers who simply ran out of steam, maybe after a long work shift, and happily snoozed in a booth.

But no matter who they were, they all wanted something to eat—something warm and comforting—and that was my specialty.

Right now I had four different kinds of soup on the stove in huger-than-huge pots: chicken noodle, broccoli and cheese, New England clam chowder, and bean soup. That was quite a variety, but there were a lot of people in Sandy Harbor who worked out in the elements and needed thawing out, and that meant soup—lots and lots of comforting soup.

It also meant chili, mac and cheese, meat loaf. . . . I could go on and on, but before I got carried away by my thoughts, I needed to get some batter started for chocolate chip cookies, for the lunchtime rush.

I looked at the clock on the wall. Juanita Holgado, my morning cook, should be arriving momentarily. She loved to bake, so she could finish them for me. I was dead on my feet and yawning.

Maybe it was the weather. Thank goodness I didn't have any bunions or other body parts that could predict the weather. I usually took my chance on Flip a Coin's predictions.

But today all I needed to do was look outside the diner window—the snow was falling fast in big, wet flakes. I could barely make out the outlines of Max and

Clyde through the plummeting snow. They were my jacks-of-all-trades when they weren't taking long breaks to talk. Right now they were trying, in vain, to shovel and snow-blow the sidewalks around the Silver Bullet so that my patrons wouldn't slip, twirl, and triple flip and get a low mark from the Olympic judges.

But thank goodness for Karen, the first female snow-plow driver in Sandy Harbor, who let the blade down on the village's snowplow and made a couple of swoops in my parking lot.

Karen wasn't supposed to use village equipment to do personal things or for local businesses, but sometimes we close the rule book here in small-town Sandy Harbor. The people here like to look out for their own and help out wherever and whenever they can.

In gratitude, I was going to make sure that Karen was well supplied with free coffee and donuts every time she stopped by the Silver Bullet this winter.

Deputy Sheriff Ty Brisco, a Texas transplant who lived above the bait shop next door, would accuse me of bribing a governmental official. But I'd just call it being neighborly.

Ty was getting too stuffy lately anyway. He needed to loosen up. But then again, maybe he had weather-predicting body parts that were giving him a hard time. Or perhaps he was just grumpy about the snowy weather since he was from Houston.

Just then I saw Ty's big monster of an SUV do a half spin into the parking lot. He easily got the big black machine under control before he ended up in the ten-foot-high snowbank, and he safely parked in a spot cleared by Karen.

I peeked from the corner of the pass-through window, waiting for Ty to walk into the diner. It wasn't because I loved to watch the way he walked or liked to listen to his sexy cowboy drawl or because I enjoyed bantering with him.

No way.

I just liked to talk to him.

I wasn't interested in any kind of a personal relationship with Ty. I was still busy building and cementing a brick wall around myself and my heart—mainly due to my divorce from my ex-husband, Deputy Doug Burnham, slimy cheater. A couple of years ago he'd found a fertile twentysomething-year-old who gave him twins, Brittany and Tiffany, and I became yesterday's birdcage liner.

After all was said and done, I'd left Philly and headed for my favorite place on earth: Sandy Harbor, New York. And then the planets aligned when my aunt Stella decided that the diner, cottages, and Victorian farmhouse she owned weren't going to be the same without her beloved husband, Porky, and she offered to sell everything to me with for a "family discount and easy-payment plan."

We worked out the details on a Silver Bullet place mat. After the dust settled, she handed me a wad of keys and I handed her the contents of my purse, my bank accounts, and all the change I had in the ashtray of my car. Aunt Stella then took off for Florida and an Alaskan cruise with her gal pals, leaving me with balloon payments scheduled through our lifetimes and a diner that was OPEN 24 HOURS A DAY, AIR-CONDITIONED, BREAKFAST SERVED ALL DAY.

Trying to be casual, I took another peek through the pass-through window to see if Ty had appeared yet.

The pass-through window didn't have any glass in it and wasn't used for passing anything through it, but it was my way to see what was going on in the front of the diner whenever I was in the back.

And right now I was hoping to enjoy some cowboy eye candy.

The door opened and there was a collective groan when snow blew into the diner and landed on some of the customers seated near the door.

Sheesh.

Ty should have waited until the outside door had closed before he opened the inside door, but the wind took it. He mumbled a sheepish "sorry" to the folks sitting nearby, took his cowboy hat off, and brushed off the plastic bonnet that protected his hat.

How cute!

The plastic bonnet reminded me of my aunt Helen's living room, with her plastic-covered sofa and chairs. I used to stick to the sofa whenever I wore shorts, and my father loved to joke about the covers as he drove us all home after our visit. But Aunt Helen was proud of how the plastic kept her furniture just like new.

"Isn't it way too early for this kind of weather? When is this stuff ever going to stop falling?" Ty snapped, unzipping his bomber jacket, shaking it out, and hanging it on a peg.

"August," someone shouted.

"I believe it," Ty said.

"Amateur," I mumbled. "It's only January."

But then I remembered that this was only Ty's third winter in Sandy Harbor. It was my second as owner of the Silver Bullet and the eleven housekeeping cottages on the point (there used to be twelve, but that's another story). I also own a big Victorian farmhouse with three floors, a bunch of rooms, and a bunch of bathrooms, because my late uncle Porky loved company and loved porcelain.

I loved it here in Sandy Harbor. I loved my staff, the villagers, the closeness, and the camaraderie. We were a tight-knit community, and if someone needed help, then help they'd get—no questions asked!

Nancy arrived with some orders, interrupting my ogling. "Two cowboys on a raft, wheat. One deadeye with sausage, sourdough. One pig between two sheets, sourdough. And two cows, done rare—and make them cry. And, Trixie, the two cows are taking a walk."

Nancy loves her "Dinerese." And over the years I've come to love it, too. It's like our own special language.

I got the two Western omelets frying and the wheat bread onto the toaster Ferris wheel. I got the water boiling for the two deadeyes—poached eggs—and put two orders of sourdough bread on the wheel. I cut slices of raw onions to make the cows, or hamburgers, "cry" and toasted their buns. When the meat was ready, I plated everything and boxed up the hamburgers for their walk.

Just then the back door opened and Juanita Holgado came bustling in.

"This weather sure is something. I need a vacation, Boss Trixie. Like now!"

"Whenever you want a vacation, just let me know."

Juanita shook off her coat, pulled off a brightly colored hat, and stomped the snow off her boots. After unzipping and removing her boots, she slipped into a pair of rubber clogs.

Today Juanita wore her signature chef pants with red and green peppers on them. My signature pants were covered in red tomatoes. The other cook, Cindy Sherlock, had pizza slices on hers.

I ordered them especially for us because they all had special meanings for us. Juanita loved to eat peppers and feature them in her recipes.

Cindy was a wonder with her crispy-edged pizza dough, and everyone loved her specialty pizzas. Sometimes she couldn't keep up with the pizza orders and one of us would have to help her.

As for me, I loved tomatoes, especially in the summer, when I could pick them right off the vine and eat them. As I looked out at the blizzard, I remembered how warm and sweet they taste fresh from the garden. Yum. I know I shouldn't, but I carry a salt shaker in my pocket for occasions just like that.

And when I do pick the tomatoes, I can them and freeze them. Then, all throughout the year, I make spaghetti sauce, pizza sauce, marinara sauce, and anything else I can think of.

As I loaded more bread onto the Ferris wheel, I thought of my other alleged cook, Bob, who had come with the diner and whom I've never met.

Bob served in the army with Uncle Porky, and it was Uncle Porky who'd hired him as a cook. When I took over, Bob kept calling in sick from Atlantic City, Vegas, Connecticut, and other casinos . . . er . . . I mean specialist physicians.

Bob only ever called in sick to Juanita, but the next time he called, I told Juanita that I wanted to talk to him. Bob was probably in Vegas right now, I thought, sighing to myself. At least he was warm, unlike us.

Juanita's arrival meant that she was ready to start her shift and that mine was finally over. I grabbed my mug of cold coffee, tossed it down the drain, and rinsed it off. I figured I would get a fresh cup in the diner and unwind for a little while before I headed home for my morning nap.

Pushing open the kitchen doors, I paused to take in the scene. The diner patrons were completely silent, which was unusual, but then I realized there was relentless pounding on the roof. It sounded like the place was going to shake apart.

"What on earth is going on?" I asked, to no one in particular.

Ty answered. "It's hail. And they're as big as softballs. I've never seen anything like it before."

"Terrific," I grumbled. "What's next?"

Just as I said that, lightning flashed and thunder rumbled. There was a collective gasp from my customers as the building creaked and groaned.

I hope the Silver Bullet holds up.

Chapter 2

*W*hile refilling my mug with fresh coffee, I replenished everyone's coffee at the counter. Just as I was about to do likewise for those in booths and at tables in the side room, Colleen, another waitress, took the pots—regular and decaf—away from me.

"You finished your shift, Trixie. You must be tired. Go sit down and talk to that delicious cowboy," she said with a pointed smirk, her dark ponytail dancing as she spun on her heel and walked away to make a lap around the diner to refill coffee.

I had to lean in to hear her, though. The hail seemed to be pounding on every side of my diner.

I hoped that Clyde and Max had taken shelter somewhere safe. No sense trying to keep up with the current massive weather mess.

The hail eventually slowed, then stopped, and everyone started to breathe easy again. Pretty soon the cordial din of chitchat and people eating returned.

Ty and I both walked over to the side window at the same time to see if there was any visible damage.

"It turned back to snow," he said, as we looked out. "And it's really coming down again. I'd better get going. I'm sure some crazies are trying to drive in this."

I sighed. I couldn't understand why anyone would risk their life or anyone else's to drive in these conditions. But it happened regularly.

Then Ty's radio went off. And so did most everyone's cell phone or radio. He listened to the static-filled device as Deputy Vern McCoy's disjointed voice came through.

I flashed back to my days with Deputy Doug and the "let's get together code" that he and his young chickie had devised via his radio.

From the grim look on Ty's face, I could see that this wasn't a booty call but something rather serious.

"What?" I asked Ty. "What's going on?"

But Ty didn't have to answer my question. "The roof of the library collapsed" was the response twittered around the diner.

Right about then all my customers stood up at the same time, shrugged into coats, pulled on their gloves, and plopped hats on their heads. That was the thing about small towns—in a crisis, everyone helped one another out, no questions asked.

"Thank goodness the library was closed," Ty said, slipping into his own jacket.

I sighed. "A couple of years ago it was the courthouse. Last year it was the American Legion and now the library. What'll it be next?"

He adjusted the rain bonnet on his cowboy hat. "Maybe we need some roof inspectors to come in and take a look at some of the buildings to make sure they're structurally sound—at least before anyone gets seriously hurt. The weather here is just plain . . ."

"Hideous?" I supplied.

"Yeah." He swung his hat and plopped it on his head, tapping it with a couple of fingers into a comfortable spot.

I glanced out the window again at the fast-falling snow. "Ty, can you at least call Karen and get her or someone else to plow your way? It's going to be tough to drive out there, and all these people are going to drive either down the highway, where there is zero visibility, or into downtown, where there are narrow streets and there is nowhere to put the snow."

"It's already been done. You must have missed that on the radio."

"A police radio is like Dinerese," I said. "You have to develop an ear for it. I never did."

"See you later, Trixie." He put his gloves on and turned to the big line of villagers who were gathering in the center aisle of my diner, ready to respond.

Ty raised a hand for quiet. "Ladies and gentlemen, please listen up really quick. I want everyone to take their time driving in this weather. The village plows have cleared a path for us, but it's still treacherous out there. And from what I understand, no one was in the library, so there is no rush. We'll try to tarp it to save what we can, but first the village engineer, Emmett Woolsey, will decide if what's left of the building is stable enough for us to go in there and do some damage control."

Ty's radio went off again. Same type of mumbling, same static.

"I stand corrected," Ty said. He hooked his radio onto his belt and was ready to rush out the door as if his jeans—which fit perfectly (not that I'd noticed)— were on fire. "I have to go."

"Is anyone hurt?" I asked.

"Can't say."

He never can say.

"Please call me. I have a diner full of people who care," I instructed.

He didn't answer. He was sliding down the sidewalk to his big black monolith of an SUV. I kidded him about it, but a mega truck or an SUV was pretty much mandatory in these parts, especially in the winter months.

"Did I hear the police dispatcher say something about the 'Tidy Trio' on the radio?" Leo Sousa, an EMT, asked, just as his own radio went off.

"I heard that, too," Megan Hunter said, then turned to me. "The Tidy Trio is the town's nickname for Donna Palmeri, Sue Lewandursky, and Mary Ann Glading. They've been cleaning the library for years." Megan owned an antiques shop and restoration business in downtown Sandy Harbor. I hadn't spent a lot of time getting to know her, but from what I knew, she was a bundle of energy, like an elf at Christmas. "I sure hope they're okay."

Everyone's phone went off again. "Tidy Trio" was murmured throughout the diner. And what few customers were left dropped their forks and stood, slipping into their coats, boots, and hats.

I held open the exit door as almost everyone hurried out.

"Be careful!" I said.

My plea was echoed by all the people who had been left behind, with unfinished meals on the tables and the bills.

The Silver Bullet was quiet now. Only a handful of customers dotted the inside of the diner, eating in relative silence, thinking and praying that the Tidy Trio were okay.

It seemed like an eternity before Ty called, and I was buzzed on enough coffee to float a battleship.

"They're all okay," Ty said in answer to my unspoken question. "They were just scared out of their wits by all the noise. The big stained-glass dome is now in shards on the floor. Luckily, they were away from the worst part of it when the roof collapsed."

I looked up to see that every pair of eyes was trained on me. "They're all okay, Deputy Brisco said. Just scared."

There was a round of applause, and a semijovial atmosphere returned to the Silver Bullet.

"How did the rest of the library fare?" I asked Ty.

"Everything's either completely ruined or damaged

with the exception of the archive room and a couple of offices. When this roof decided to cave in, it did a bang-up job. It's too late to tarp the books. They are gone. All gone."

"Oh no! Not all those beautiful books," I said. "And all that marble!"

"The marble is okay. But it's now a marble skating rink."

"Sheesh."

"I gotta go, Trixie," he said.

"Wait! Ty, tell everyone there that I'll deliver hot coffee and sandwiches."

"You're a good egg, Trixie Matkowski."

I smiled. "Good to know."

"Bye," Ty said.

I turned to the patrons again. "Deputy Brisco said that almost all of the books are ruined."

My heart was breaking. I'd grown up in libraries and I loved the sounds and smells of them. As a voracious reader, I loved to touch, feel, and smell a book in my hand and get lost in the world of words.

"I sure hope all that beautiful wood wasn't ruined," Megan Hunter said. "Or those beautiful desks and brass lamps! That would be such a shame!"

Nursery-school teacher Jane O'Connell stood. "We definitely have to have a fund-raiser to repair the library and get replacement books."

"Yeah!" Several fists pumped the air.

"Maybe we should have a chili cook-off contest,"

Lorraine added. "A cooking contest is something we haven't tried lately."

"Please, no." I shook my head, getting into the excitement. "Everyone does chili cook-offs. We need to come up with something bigger—something different and more original, something that will get some real attention."

"What do you have in mind, Trixie?" Megan asked, listening intently.

I thought for a while, then snapped my fingers. "How about we host a macaroni and cheese cook-off? It's a pretty easy dish to make, so a lot of people could participate, and we'll see who can make theirs stand out the most. They'll get first prize. We could have three prizes—gold, silver, and bronze."

"I nominate Trixie Matkowski to be the chairperson of the library fund-raiser," said Jean Vermer, whom I'd hunt down later.

"Wha—"

"Don't worry, Trixie," Megan assured me quickly. "I'll help you out. So will most of the village—whoever's able."

"I second the nomination," said Tess Drennan.

"All those in favor, say aye," Megan yelled.

Oh no! I'd love to take on something so much fun as a cooking contest, but these days I didn't even have the time to tie my sneakers.

"Aye!"

I smiled, grateful that my friends had so much faith

in me. It's not like I didn't want to help, but I had just chaired the Miss Salmon Contest and had housed way too many of the contestants for way too long.

I was simply pooped! But as long as I had a lot of help, I could do it and would have a lot of fun.

"The ayes have it!" said Megan. "You're the chairperson of the library fund-raiser, Trixie, and we are having a macaroni and cheese cook-off."

"I'll do my best, but remember, I'll need help—lots of help."

"Like I said, I'll be your cochairperson," Megan announced to a round of applause. "I'll contact an old sorority sister of my mother's from Sandy Harbor High. They've kept in touch throughout the years. My mother tells me that this certain sorority sister is breezing through town on her way to Ottawa so she can tape her TV show there. I'll call Mom and ask her to contact her for us. Just wait until you all hear this name: Priscilla Finch-Smythe."

There was a general sense of awe around the diner. Add me to the list. I loved watching Priscilla on TV. She was famous for making basic comfort food and was renowned for her many published cookbooks, her latest being *Comforting Comfort Food by the Countess of Comforting Comfort Food.*

"So what do you think about Mabel Cronk coming to town to judge the contest, Trixie?" Megan asked, blowing on her nails and then buffing them on her blouse.

"Mabel Cronk? Who's that? I thought you said Priscilla Finch-Smythe was coming to judge it."

"They are one and the same person."

"I guess you can't be a TV personality with a name like Mabel Cronk," I said with a wry smile.

"Oh, Trixie!" Megan shook my biceps until my teeth were ready to fall out. "You're a scream."

Megan continued chatting. "If Priscilla agrees, and I can't see why she wouldn't, I was thinking the first prize could be a weekend in New York City with Priscilla and an appearance on her TV show to cook the winning mac and cheese recipe—since it's a comfort food. Wouldn't that be incredible? We could get real chefs and wannabe chefs from all over the world by relentlessly using her name. We could charge an enormous entry fee. Good idea, huh?"

"Just incredible," I repeated, and I took a deep breath. "And everyone will help?"

My patrons nodded and clapped, excited to rebuild the library. But I had to admit that I was little overwhelmed. All I said was "macaroni and cheese" and now I was in charge of a national cook-off?

With enough help, though, I thought that, just maybe, I could pull this off. And it was obvious that everyone else felt the same way, too.

So why didn't I feel comforted?

Chapter 3

A week later I was putting out orange plastic cones on the floor of my diner—the ones that said WET FLOOR! DO NOT FALL!—wondering if the warning would actually stop anyone from falling. Midthought, Megan Hunter came bustling through the door.

She didn't fall, but she did slide a foot or two before regaining her balance.

"Geez, it's snowing like crazy again," she said, uncoiling a bright, colorful scarf from around her neck. "Are we ever going to catch a break from all the white stuff?"

"In about August," someone quipped from one of the red vinyl booths.

That joke never got old in Sandy Harbor.

"You got that right," Megan said, then turned to me. "I've got some news about the library fund-raiser, Trixie."

"Great. Let's get a booth in the back and we can talk." I handed Max the mop, hoping that he'd get the message to finish up. "When you're done, maybe you should put the air machine on to dry it."

Max nodded and shuffled to the small maintenance closet near the restrooms, dragging the wet mop behind him. Max had come to visit my uncle Porky way back in the day and had never left, so my uncle had hired him as a maintenance man. The same thing happened with Clyde, incidentally. Clyde and Max are inseparable, and they miss my uncle Porky something awful.

"Cup of coffee?" I asked Megan.

"Please."

She seated herself in the last booth as I went and got two coffees and two of the cherry hand pies I'd been dreaming about the other day. Oh, I was still on my diet. It's just that I didn't think it was polite to let Megan eat alone.

"Trixie, I'm so excited!"

"Spill!"

"My mother got the Countess of Comforting Comfort Food, Miss Priscilla Finch-Smythe, to agree to come and judge and to host the winner on an episode of her show! She'll be returning to Sandy Harbor after an absence of more than forty years!"

"Why has she stayed away for so long?" I asked.

"She's been busy with her TV show!"

"Oh."

I had to wait until Megan finished fixing her coffee and took her first sip to hear more. By then I was just about ready for another hand pie.

"I can hardly believe that Mabel Cronk—I mean,

Priscilla—is going to judge our macaroni and cheese contest. Wait until I tell the Tri-Gams!"

"The who?"

Megan grinned. "Gamma Gamma Gamma. The Tri-Gams. It's a sorority at Sandy Harbor High School that started before my time. The first president was Antoinette Chloe Brown. I believe you know her."

"Antoinette Chloe Brown, or ACB for short, is a good friend of mine. We've had some crazy times together."

"Well, Antoinette Chloe started the Tri-Gams to reach out to the real rural gals on farms. She thought that they needed to socialize more, have more friends, and get more involved in the Sandy Harbor community. The Tri-Gams are actually still active in the high school."

"That's ACB, for you. She has a heart of gold."

"The best thing is that Priscilla was a Tri-Gam herself, and she specifically mentioned that the sorority *must* host a tea for her so she can see everyone again."

"*Must?*"

"Oh yes. Mab—I mean, Priscilla—was very specific. And it has to be at your house."

"My house? Why? I don't even know Priscilla . . . well, except for her TV series, which I watch every Monday night—*Totally Comforting Comfort Food*. Why my house?"

Megan took a loud sip of coffee. "You know, Priscilla used to work for your aunt Stella here at the diner. My mom told me that she always loved the old Victorian.

Over the years she'd constantly nag your aunt Stella and uncle Porky to sell it to her, but then she moved permanently to California for her TV show. I think she still holds a torch for the house."

"I see." I thought about it a bit. "You know, Megan, I suppose it's good publicity for my diner and my housekeeping cottages to have a celebrity chef such as Priscilla Finch-Smythe visiting the Big House."

"The Tri-Gams will help you set up everything, of course. Oh, and Priscilla has some other demands." Megan helped herself to the last cherry hand pie before I could snatch it up.

"Oh?" Something told me that I'd probably need another pie after this conversation was finished. Blueberry this time—or maybe peach. Maybe both.

"We can't call her Mabel. We can call her either Priscilla or Cilla, for short. Or Miz Finch-Smythe. After all, the world thinks she's British, and she wants to keep her TV persona safe."

"Won't they find out that she's from Sandy Harbor? I mean, someone is bound to tell the press," I said.

"Her press kit says that she was born in Sandy Harbor but was raised in England for most of her life— that's why she has the accent. Then she came back to Sandy Harbor for high school."

"Oh, I see. I guess." But I wasn't so sure I did.

"It's not that she doesn't care about Sandy Harbor," Megan said defensively. "Did you know that Priscilla donated her whole cookbook collection to our library?"

"No. I didn't." I did know that the library's cookbook collection had been extensive—I'd visited that section of the library on numerous occasions. I loved going through the cookbooks for new ideas and had copied down several recipes.

Megan's eyes pooled with tears. "We had the biggest collection of cookbooks in the whole county. And now they're all ruined."

"Well, we'll have a successful contest and will be able to restore the library to all its former glory. I'm sure of it, Megan. Try not to worry."

"You're right, Trixie." Megan blotted her eyes. "So, we're having a tea party in her honor, and— Oh, I forgot to tell you this, but she wants to stay—"

"Not at the Big House!" I blurted. I'd had enough people staying at my house lately to last me until menopause and beyond.

"No." Megan chuckled. "And I wish you'd stop calling it the Big House. It sounds like a jail."

I called it that simply because that's what it was—a *Big House*. With its eightish bedrooms, about the same number of bathrooms, wraparound porch, massive kitchen, and other expansive rooms, it was easily one of the biggest houses in Sandy Harbor.

"Actually, her assistant, Jill Marley, told me that Priscilla has a fancy motor home she likes to stay in. It's like a rock-star bus," Megan said, clearly enthralled. "She plans on staying just a couple of days, but she wants to plug in to the Victorian for water and electric, if that's okay with you. She said she'd pay you a stipend to cover the costs."

A stipend?

Megan pulled out a piece of yellow legal paper from her purse, put on a pair of green rhinestone glasses, and pointed to the middle of the paper.

"Priscilla will also need a cottage for her motor-home driver, Peter McCall. Peter is her stepson from her second marriage."

Megan looked over her glasses at me. "I think Peter's father was some Hollywood big shot named Francisco, or something like that. If I remember correctly from what I read in the tabloids, he invested in a few movies and had a couple of hits. He drowned in a hot tub at some party Priscilla didn't attend. Her third marriage was a quickie. After he got back from their honeymoon, he ran off with Priscilla's maid."

"What happened to her first husband?" I wondered.

"That's all been hushed up, but I understand he was a married man who worked with Priscilla in New York City. At the time Priscilla was prepping for another chef. I heard he left his wife and ran away to California to be with Priscilla when she took another job. I think they lived together until he got divorced from his first wife—which Priscilla paid for. Soon after, about a year later, she threw him out."

"Wow! That's so awful!" I knew all about husbands who cheat with other women, from personal experience. I looked down at my dirty sneakers so Megan wouldn't see me tearing up. Deputy Doug's betrayal still hurt, and I was all set to dislike Priscilla for taking up with another woman's husband—although he was clearly to blame, too.

I shouldn't judge. What did I know? Only what Megan "heard," which was probably just local gossip—or tabloid gossip.

Also, I really needed to get on board with all of these plans, at least for the sake of the fund-raiser. But even though Megan was enchanted with the thought of TV royalty coming to Sandy Harbor, I was beginning to think that Priscilla was going to be a pain in my ample butt.

"In addition to a cottage for Peter"—Megan pointed to her list—"Priscilla would like a cottage for her assistant, Jill Marley. There might be some more people in her entourage, but she'll let us know how many to expect as the date gets closer."

Megan pushed her glasses to the edge of her nose. "Trixie, maybe you should reserve all of your cottages for Cilla's entourage."

Entourage?

I motioned to Nancy that I needed more coffee and more hand pies right away. Actually, make that a pot of coffee and a dozen pies!

Barely listening, I nodded numbly as Megan continued with the list of Priscilla Finch-Smythe's demands.

"Wait. What was that last one?"

"She wants you to name a breakfast, lunch, or dinner special after her. She might create the dish or let you do it, but she wants you to feature it in the Silver Bullet a week before she arrives and a week after she leaves."

"That's clear as mud," I mumbled, thinking that no one would judge me too harshly if I began whining. "Just so you know, Megan, if Priscilla does decide to create something, someone should tell her that my customers don't like a lot of fancy stuff."

"Uh, Trixie. She's the Countess of Comforting Comfort Food, remember? She wouldn't cook fancy."

Yikes! In my stress, I'd forgotten that key point.

"Maybe I should name a dessert after her, too," I joked.

"That's a brilliant idea! What a nice touch for Cilla. I can't wait to tell her."

There goes my big mouth again!

"Uh, Megan, could you e-mail me her list of demands so I can keep them all straight?"

She smiled. "Don't you mean her *requests*?"

"Yes, that's what I meant. Her requests."

"I'll write them down for you." Megan clasped her hands in front of her. "Oh no. I forgot to tell you that some of the Tri-Gams and I were talking, and we thought that the macaroni and cheese contest should be held at the Culinary Building at the county fairgrounds. There's lots of counter space there and more than enough stoves for the chefs who will be participating, in addition to plenty of restrooms and chairs for spectators. There's parking, too. It's a perfect venue."

"Perfect," I echoed, thankful that the contest wasn't

going be held here at the point. If the contest were held here, it would be a logistical nightmare.

Is Megan going to eat that peach pie or not?

She continued. "The Tri-Gams will see to it that Cilla has fresh flowers in her motor home and transportation to and from the county fairgrounds. We will also order a corsage for her so she can wear it to the tea. And we'd like everyone to wear hats and gloves to the tea, maybe even period costumes."

Period costumes? They can't mean that!

Was the queen of England arriving or just the Countess of Comforting Comfort Food?

"Period costumes would be a nice touch—don't you think so, Trixie? It would be so much fun!"

Ugh. If there was anything I hated, it was wearing costumes.

I took a deep breath. "I guess it depends on what time period you're talking about."

"Oh, you know, something from the *Downton Abbey* period. Before they started wearing short dresses."

"I see."

I signaled Nancy for another hand pie and dunked it into my coffee. My two favorite vices in one.

"Oh, I'm so nervous, Trixie. Priscilla Finch-Smythe is the first real celebrity I'm going to get to meet. I want everything to be just perfect!"

"I saw Dolly Parton at O'Hare Airport in Chicago once," I told Megan, but she was worriedly looking over her list again. "Megan, please relax. Sandy Harbor will welcome Priscilla with open arms. We won't breathe a word to anyone that she isn't British. We'll have the tea for her with the Tri-Gams and it'll be nice, with or without *Downton Abbey* period costumes. I'll name some kind of dinner special after her. She'll judge our contest at the fairgrounds, and then she'll drive her rock-star bus out of Sandy Harbor and onward to another adventure. Easy peasy!"

"Don't forget her entourage. You need to save room in your cottages!" she said as she pushed her unfinished cherry hand pie away.

Is she crazy? Or just frazzled?

"Oh, Trixie, what if I forgot something really important?"

"I think we have everything covered except a parade," I joked.

But Megan didn't see it as a joke.

"Oh, Trixie! What a fabulous idea! I'm going to call an emergency meeting of all the Tri-Gams who are still local, and we're going to plan a parade!"

Megan jumped up from the booth, rewrapped her scarf around her neck, and slipped her arms into the sleeves of her coat. She ran out of the diner without zipping up her parka, powered purely by the thrill of a parade.

A parade in the dead of winter? Where would everyone stand? In the ten-foot snowbanks that lined the streets of downtown Sandy Harbor?

And just think. It was my all idea.

Chapter 4

It was the day of the parade and Priscilla's tea, and, of course, there was a raging blizzard outside.

It was Friday the thirteenth of February. The awful weather was not due to bad luck—not really—it was just a typical winter day in northern New York.

Despite everything, I was ready to tackle the rest of the events. Ty insisted that I looked tired and should get some more sleep. But no, not me. I promised him I'd relax after this event, but while I was cochair, I would totally immerse myself in my duties and do my best to make the contest as successful as possible.

In the meantime, Ty promised me he was going to train the Tri-Gams' husbands in what needed to done to help with the parade.

We had sleet, rain and snow, which Heather "Flip a Coin" Flipelli said would end before the parade started—unsurprisingly, they didn't. But the streets of Sandy Harbor were plowed to the bone and sufficiently coated with salt and sand. Bravo to Ty again, and to Karen Metonti and Bruce Barker, the other snowplow driver.

Just as I suggested, Karen and Bruce led the parade with the town's two plows, scraping away any rogue snowflakes that dared to fall.

The Sandy Harbor High School's marching band came next. They walked with a banner that said WEL-COME, PRISCILLA FINCH-SMYTHE!

From my position on the bleachers, I could hear the chattering teeth of the poor girls in red sequined jumpsuits. They were sleeveless, no less, and snow was accumulating on the front of their jumpsuits. Poor kids.

They needed winter uniforms! And that was just what I was going to suggest to the bandleader after the parade wrapped up. I'd fund them myself if I needed to, just to avoid being elected chairperson of another fund-raiser!

Then came the Amish horse-drawn wagon with Priscilla Finch-Smythe in it. The two draft horses were covered in blankets of red silk flowers, as if they'd just won some kind of prestigious draft-horse derby.

The parade watchers went crazy cheering, craning their necks and clapping their gloved and mittened hands. It was muffled clapping, but Priscilla got the idea.

She looked thinner in person than she did on TV, and much older. She had on a red wool coat, complete with a wrist corsage, probably from the Tri-Gam Corsage Committee, a white hat and gloves, and a red-and-white-flowered scarf that she knotted stylishly around her neck.

I thought she looked fashionable, though my good friend ACB would say that she was a boring dresser.

Priscilla blew kisses to the spectators sitting in the bleachers and waved her hand like Queen Elizabeth.

Red would be the color of the weekend due to Valentine's Day. Currently, the Big House was decorated in enough red crepe paper, paper hearts, and red twinkle lights to light up the sky for Santa.

I had found several red tablecloths in Aunt Stella's linen closet as well as red napkins. And I had polished enough silver trays, coffeepots, teapots, sugar bowls, creamers, and pitchers to make pawnshops weep.

The Tri-Gam Tea Committee was giddy with excitement over my finds, and they added yet more silver and crystal plates covered with little tea sandwiches, sans the crusts, and delicate pastries.

I don't know where Priscilla parked her motor home. It hadn't arrived in my parking lot yet, nor had her entourage, but that was the job of the Tri-Gam Motor Home and Entourage Committee.

I cleaned the Big House from top to bottom, since there was no Tri-Gam committee for that. And Blondie was under orders not to shed one single hair.

The snow finally did stop and the sun came out just as Heather Flipelli predicted that the snow would fall for the rest of the day and that it would be dark and gloomy. I could see the volunteers of the fire department exchanging money. They probably had bets on Heather's weather report.

The only glitches were a couple of baton twirlers who slid on a patch of ice and skidded on their butts for part of the parade. They quickly got up and kept on twirling.

The parade turned at the Gas and Grab on Route 3, and then it proceeded back the way it had come, basically because there was only one main road in Sandy Harbor's downtown district, and the Gas and Grab had a driveway that went around the building—which was perfect for parades.

Spectators stood their ground, knowing they'd get a repeat performance.

This time the baton twirlers were careful and the Boy Scouts that were sidelined for throwing snowballs were allowed to return to the parade with strict instructions not to make or throw a snowball under any circumstances.

Priscilla still smiled and waved, warming her hands intermittently under a purple velvet lap blanket. When one of the horses took care of business near where I was standing, Priscilla pantomimed a hearty laugh, waving her hand across her nose.

The spectators loved it. And they loved her. And why shouldn't they? Priscilla was going to help save their beloved library.

But I'd decided that Priscilla was too much of a diva for me.

I checked the clock over Bubbles and Suds, the coin laundry. I had to zoom back to the Big House and put the final touches on the tea before the horde of Tri-Gams and Sandy Harbor dignitaries arrived after the parade. Hurrying to my car, I waved to Ty, who was directing traffic, as Hal Manning's antique hearse passed by.

It was easy to pull out, but I had to drive home slowly. The two plows the village owned had really concentrated on the parade route and hadn't paid much attention to the outlying roads.

When I got to the Big House, my friend Antoinette Chloe Brownelli (who preferred Brown these days) was parked in the lot with her radio blaring. Some kind of country song was on, and ACB was singing right along with it. I beeped my horn, and she got out of her car.

As usual, she was wearing a colorful muumuu. This one had big birds-of-paradise all over it, with their orange heads and sharp green beaks, and tropical flowers on a purple background. I shivered when I saw her glittery rubber flip-flops slosh through the snow to meet up with me. Even though Max and Clyde had plowed, there were tracks of snow left from the equipment, and ACB managed to walk through them all.

She'd dyed her hair light blue, for the occasion, it seemed, since it had been flamingo pink last week. And as always, she wore a fascinator on her head. ACB's fascinators were handmade by her and fashioned to whatever event she was attending at the time.

For the tea she sported a pink plastic teacup in a nest of silk flowers glued to a lime-green net. She'd also found a place for one or two faux birds. This time it was two seagulls standing in the teacup. The gulls and silk flowers, too heavy for the net, hung precariously over her right ear.

Her earrings dangled with pink teacups that matched the one on her fascinator.

To keep herself warm from the twenty-degree temperature, she'd draped a red tartan shawl around her shoulders, but that didn't seem like nearly enough protection from the cold to me.

Before I could get steady on my clunky boots, she scooped me into a bear hug, and as usual, I tried not to sneeze from the scent of heavy perfume and cosmetics.

ACB was one of a kind, and I adored her—muumuu, fascinator, blue hair, birds, teacups, perfume, and all.

"I'm here to help," she said. "Let's get this tea out of the way, and then we can concentrate on the mac and cheese contest."

"That's just what I was thinking."

I reminded myself to thank Max and Clyde for clearing the snow and for salting the driveway. The walk was mostly bare.

"Antoinette Chloe, let's get this show on the road."

We hurried into the Big House. I yanked off my boots and put them on the floor of the closet. For the guests, I'd laid out a big throw rug. "I have two huge silver coffee urns set up. All we have to do is plug them in."

"Gotcha."

"Antoinette Chloe, don't take your flips off. I won't hear of it."

She set down her purse, which was actually a beach

bag that read I HEART SANDY HARBOR, LAKE ONTARIO, NY in yellow letters on a fluorescent orange background, and said, "I'll wipe them off."

She pulled a blue flowered scarf from the folds of her muumuu and wiped the bottom of each flip-flop.

Now, that's winter etiquette!

Blondie was a different story. She was loaded with snow. I tried to dry her with a terry towel I kept by the door, but instead she bounded around ACB and shook herself off. Hair and snow flew everywhere.

"Thanks a bunch, Blondie." She licked my hand, then went back to ACB, who didn't mind wet dog as much as I did. Good thing Ty was going to pick Blondie up later and let her stay at his apartment.

"Your house looks fabulous, Trixie. Everything looks so elegant and pretty. Mabel will love it."

"Yikes, Antoinette Chloe! Don't forget to call her Priscilla!" *And Priscilla had better not forget to add the "Chloe" when talking to you, my friend!*

"I'll call her Priscilla when Blondie flies. She's always been Mabel Cronk to me. I started Gamma Gamma Gamma to reach out to her when she was a farm girl without friends. I don't care that she's the Countess of Comforting Comfort Food and a big shot. I remember her when."

Good for Antoinette Chloe!

I preheated my oven and pulled out a plastic bag of cheese-olive puffs from the freezer and positioned the little balls on a tray. Then I slipped the tray into the oven. The puffs were perfect for a tea—or any type of party, really.

After thinking about it, I decided that I should try to convince ACB to call her Priscilla, just because Megan would have a meltdown if she didn't.

"Antoinette Chloe, we promised Priscilla to use her . . . um . . . stage name . . . so just play along. Please? Remember that she's doing the weekend as a favor to Sandy Harbor."

"And for her own publicity! Have you seen all the reporters that have been hanging around town since her arrival? The fairgrounds are loaded with them in their RVs and vans."

I plugged in the coffee and the hot-water urns for tea. "That's my point, Antoinette Chloe. Priscilla is a great draw to Sandy Harbor and the cook-off."

"But so are the other chefs."

I gathered all the fixings for my three punches. One was a mix of juices and wine. The other was made of champagne, pink lemonade, and raspberry sherbet. I made another nonalcoholic punch with just fruit juices and ginger ale, as well.

"The other chefs are a great draw, too, but remember they are all hoping to win first prize to get on Priscilla's show," I reminded ACB.

"Good point, Trixie." She sighed. "But I think it's baloney that Mabel has that fake accent going and she has all her queenly ways. Did you see how she acted at the parade?"

I chuckled. "*Countess* ways. She's a countess."

"Hog poop."

I chuckled again and handed her some ingredients. "Do me a favor and put together this other punch while I check on my cheese-olive puffs. The recipe is by the bowl."

ACB ambled over to the other silver punch bowl. "By the way, are you entering the mac and cheese contest?"

"Of course! It would give me and the Silver Bullet some great publicity if I won. I mean, I'd get to be on TV! And I'd be sure to drop in some comments about my diner and cottages then. Publicity like that is priceless. I could completely pay off what I owe Aunt Stella. Besides, if I got more business, maybe I could put an addition on the diner and build more cottages. I can picture it all now!"

I closed my eyes and imagined my own personal touch on the property I owned—or will own when I finished paying Aunt Stella.

My heart started pounding in double time, and I began to feel overwhelmed. After the tea was over and everyone got out of my house, I would have to clean everything up. Then I needed to make my mac and cheese entry. Then I had to cook from midnight to eight because, unfortunately, Linda Blessler couldn't sub for me tonight of all nights. Then I had to drive to the fairgrounds right after my shift in the morning.

Sleep? Who needs it!

ACB looked at her reflection in one of the silver trays. "Of course, Brown's Four Corners will be represented by my special mac and cheese casserole, which will contain some of the bounty of Lake Ontario—trout, salmon, and perch."

"Sounds fabulous, Antoinette Chloe."

She put the tray down, pulled out a plastic bag full of coconut macaroons from the depths of her purse, and began arranging them on the silver tray. "What's your entry like, Trixie?"

"I'm putting kielbasa, mango-peach salsa, and four cheeses into mine."

"Yum."

"I'm also adding some secret ingredients, which I won't say."

"Oh, for heaven's sake, I'm your friend."

I fussed with getting the sherbet out of the container for the punch, and then I fussed with the red napkins, stalling, knowing it would drive her crazy until I told her.

But I cracked first. "Oh, all right. Quit nagging me! I'm adding sage, marjoram, and oregano, all of which I dried from my herb garden."

"You'll win for sure."

"We'll see," I said.

"I think I hear horns and sirens," ACB said. "It must be her ladyship arriving for tea. I mean, her countess-ship."

Megan and the Tri-Gams had wanted a sheriff's escort for Priscilla with the three members of the Sandy Harbor Sheriff's Department on motorcycles with flags waving and sirens blaring. However, Ty convinced them that it would be just as glamorous with the local deputies warm and cozy and inside their patrol vehicles after spending the length of the parade out in the elements.

"Wait! We have to get into our aprons," I reminded ACB. I pulled out two white aprons and two white mobcaps that looked like they'd come straight out of a Charles Dickens novel for us to wear during the tea.

All the Tri-Gams and I would be dressing like ye ol' kitchen maids during the tea.

"I'll wear the apron, but I am *not* giving up my fascinator. I made it special, just for the occasion," ACB said.

It wasn't *Downton Abbey*, but we'd do.

I hoped that the glue would hold on everything and that the gulls wouldn't dive into the punch.

ACB marched to a different tune from everyone else. That's what made her so unique.

As for me, I'd rather not start another Revolutionary War on the shore of Lake Ontario. One was enough, thank you very much.

Walking to the front door as I tied my apron, I saw a couple of the Tri-Gams rolling out a red carpet from the motor home to my front door. Only it was lacking about thirty feet in length.

Heads would roll on the Tri-Gam Red Carpet Committee!

A six-piece band from the high school played what

might have been "Pomp and Circumstance," but it was hard to tell. If they were going to play it for graduation in June, they really could use more practice.

People lined up on both sides of the red carpet. ACB and I stood inside and watched, not wanting to get cold or wet.

On a certain note during the march, Megan Hunter knocked on the door of the motor home and the Countess of Comforting Comfort Food emerged in all her regal glory. She had changed her outfit a little bit and now was dressed all in red from the top of her pillbox hat to her dyed faux-fur coat. Red palazzo pants ballooned out from bright red patent-leather boots.

Even with the fur coat on, she looked skinnier than she had at the parade earlier. Unlike me, Priscilla Finch-Smythe did not sample her own cooking.

Immediately, I wanted to feed her some protein—like a juicy, rare Delmonico steak with a roast chicken chaser and a side of pork. However, she needed carbs, too. How about a mug of gravy, a vat of potato chips, and butter-soaked garlic bread? Oh, and dairy! There was a salute-to-cheese platter in my fridge that the Tri-Gam Cheese Committee had prepared, complete with a tiny flag of the country—or state—that the cheese had come from.

I'd make her a nice plate of that. In fact, she should have the whole tray.

Halfway up the walk, Megan stopped Priscilla. The

mayor, Rick Tingsley, was making a speech and pinning a huge corsage on her coat. However, her red fur was too thick. Mayor Tingsley got flustered and just handed the red and white flowers to her.

"Another corsage?" I asked. "It's a little big for her."

"I made it," ACB said. "I'm on the corsage committee."

"I guess you can never have too many flowers," I added.

"That's what I always say."

"Why don't you open the door of the Big House, Antoinette Chloe, since you know her? And remember, don't call her Mabel," I whispered.

ACB threw open the door as wide as it could go and pulled Priscilla into the room. "Well, hell, Mabel Cronk! It's been a long time! About time you came back for a visit!"

Blondie appeared out of nowhere, took one look at the red fur coat, and thought she'd found a kindred spirit. She couldn't stop circling Priscilla, sniffing, lunging, and barking. Then Blondie clamped onto a mouthful of the fur and started pulling.

I took hold of Blondie's collar just as Priscilla was about to topple over. Antoinette Chloe steadied her.

The crowd started screaming, led by Megan in high C, who yelled, "A vicious dog is attacking our Priscilla! Someone stop it!"

Out of the corner of my eye, I saw Ty enter the room and hurry Blondie out the back door.

"Was that . . . a . . . a wolf?" Priscilla said, fanning herself with her new corsage.

"It was Blondie, my golden retriever. She wouldn't hurt a fly. I think she just wanted to play with your coat."

"That police officer should have shot the beast!"

"What did you say?" How dare she dis my adopted dog?

ACB sniffed. "Oh, for Pete's sake, Mabel. You know the difference between a dog and a wolf."

Priscilla sniffed back. "Antoinette Chloe, you haven't changed a bit. You are still as blunt and as crass as you used to be."

"You've sure as hell changed. Since when did you become British?"

"Since I got my own TV show," she whispered.

"I heard that you got married four times," ACB said.

"Three, but who's counting?"

I'd better separate those two before things got heated, I thought. But I secretly loved how ACB was handling the diva.

I took Priscilla's coat and hung it in the closet, wondering where the Tri-Gam Coat Committee was. They were supposed to put the coats on three designated beds upstairs.

Then it hit me! I was having boarders staying over tonight and maybe tomorrow night. I'd completely forgotten that I'd volunteered to house Priscilla's entourage at the Big House since my cottages were already closed up for the winter.

Well, I'd get the details later from the Tri-Gam Lodging Committee.

Megan stood on the top step and shouted to the crowd, "Can I have the Tri-Gams committee people come in first to meet and greet Priscilla? Everyone else step aside!"

Soon I was joined by the Tri-Gam Tea Committee. They went to work like little beavers in their mobcaps and aprons and walked around with silver trays, toothpicks, and napkins, serving the guests. Other guests found their way into the kitchen to help themselves.

Megan made a plate for Priscilla, who was too busy meeting and greeting to make it to the buffet in the kitchen. Priscilla was sitting on my uncle Porky's favorite faux-leather recliner with the footrest up.

I stationed myself in a corner of the kitchen, passing out punch.

The afternoon passed by in the blink of an eye. But it seemed that everyone loved the entertainment so much, they didn't want to leave. The Tri-Gam Tea Committee had arranged for a violinist and a soloist from the church to play and sing through the event.

"Do you want to clear out this place quickly, Trixie?" Antoinette Chloe asked me as she replenished a platter of cookies to distribute to the guests.

"You read my mind, girlfriend."

"Watch this!"

She glided over to the violinist, whispered something in her ear, and locked arms with the soloist.

It was then we all heard the strains of "Home on the Range" warbled in a way that only ACB could warble it. The soloist inched herself away from ACB and found her way to the punch bowls in my corner of the kitchen.

"How about a stiff one?" I asked, filling up a cup with champagne only.

"Hit me," she said, taking the cup. "And I need a smoke even though I haven't smoked in two years. Where can I hide?"

"Back porch, but it's snowing, and you shouldn't smoke."

"I'll risk it," she said, chugging the champagne and holding her cup out for another. "I gotta get that caterwauling out of my head."

I filled her cup again, and she walked out onto my back porch, closing the door behind her.

ACB's singing did the trick. In a matter of minutes, I could see dozens of arms checking their watches. The coat committee quickly started fetching coats from upstairs, and as ACB kept on singing old Western songs, people kept on leaving.

Finally, during a showstopping rendition of "Red River Valley," she paused midwarble and asked, "How's that?"

I'd just opened and closed the door for my last guest, the violinist. Then I hugged her. "Better than a smoke bomb."

"So, where's the Tri-Gam Cleanup Committee?" she asked.

"I think we're it. They either ran for the hills or the Adirondack Mountains."

Just then Ty walked in. He shook off his boots and shrugged out of his coat. "The parking lot is clear except for Priscilla's motor home and our vehicles. Clyde and Max are plowing and snow blowing to tidy everything up in the parking lot."

"Good. Where's Blondie?" I asked.

"I left her in my apartment. I thought you might need some help cleaning up."

I looked around at my beautiful house, and it looked worse than the village dump.

"It'll be no problem, Trixie." ACB held a garbage bag open. "We can clean this up in no time."

I was touched. "Thanks. Both of you. I really appreciate it."

We cleaned the place in record time, and then I made the mistake of looking at the kitchen floor.

"Don't worry about it, Trixie," Ty said, reading my mind. "I'll take care of the floor. You just go upstairs and get a couple hours' sleep. Antoinette Chloe, you probably have to get your entry ready, so head for your house and drive carefully . . . and go slow!"

"I have to get my entry ready, too," I reminded him.

"Nope. Not now. Find time at work during your shift to put everything together," he said, bossy deputy that he was.

Just as I was saying good-bye to Antoinette Chloe and thanking her profusely, the door to Priscilla's motor home opened, and I could see three people walk down the red carpet, two of whom were carrying suit-cases.

I'd forgotten about my houseguests—yet again!

"G'night, Mabel Cronk," ACB yelled.

"G'night, Antoinette Brownelli," was the reply as their paths crossed on the sidewalk.

I held my breath. Ty chuckled.

"G'night, Countess Priscilla Finch-Smythe," ACB said.

"G'night, Antoinette Chloe Brownelli."

They both laughed, and ACB flip-flopped her way to her car.

"Hello again, Priscilla," I yelled, waving to her.

Priscilla tossed what looked like a mink coat over her shoulders and paused on my sidewalk. "The tea was quite acceptable. I particularly loved your cheese-olive puffs. You must give me the recipe."

"Sure." I was a little underwhelmed by her opinion of the tea. She didn't have to gush, but she could at least show some gratitude for all the work we had done just for her.

"Trixie, I'd like you to meet my entourage. They will be staying with you in your home. You probably don't know this, but I like my privacy, and my motor home is too small."

Priscilla held out her hand in the direction of a very overweight young man.

"This gentleman is my stepson from my second

marriage, Peter McCall. Out of all my marriages, I liked Peter's father the best. Peter drives my motor home and is a jack-of-all-trades."

I held out my hand to shake his. His grip was limp and lifeless, but I still hung on.

"I'm Trixie Matkowski. This is my house and over there is my diner, the Silver Bullet. I also own the house-keeping cottages behind the house, which you can barely make out in the dark."

Suddenly he came alive, and he pumped my hand hard enough to rattle my teeth. "So glad to meet you. I saw you at the tea, but you were busy making it so wonderful for my darling stepmummy that I didn't want to disturb you."

Did he really say *stepmummy*?

"Nice to meet you, Peter." I pulled my hand out of his grasp to get the blood going in the direction it was supposed to. "And I'd like you to meet a friend of mine, Ty Brisco. Sandy Harbor deputy Ty Brisco, to be precise."

He gave Ty a snappy salute.

Ty offered his hand instead and they shook. "Howdy."

As they made small talk about the weather, I was able to study Peter. I'd say that he was in his late twenties or early thirties and of average height, and he had cheeks with leftover scars from a bad case of teenage acne. He was about fifty pounds overweight. Now I knew who sampled Priscilla's cooking. He had a nice suit on, although he had loosened his tie already. I did remember his face from the tea party earlier. He'd been making the rounds with Mayor Tingsley.

Peter's cell phone rang, and he rudely answered it in front of us and started talking into it, until Priscilla shooed him away.

That left the woman standing in Priscilla's skinny shadow. "Jilly? Where are you?"

Jill walked around Priscilla and stood at her side. "This is my assistant, Jill Marley. I don't know what I'd ever do without her. She does just *everything* for me."

Jill smiled and shook my hand. She had thick chestnut hair with reddish streaks, cut shoulder-length and stylish, and in my porch light, I could see that she had striking blue eyes. Her smile radiated warmth and friendliness.

I momentarily wondered if she and Peter were a couple since they were about the same age, but then I shrugged it off, not wanting to be too nosy. Plus, ACB would find out sooner or later and would tell me.

When I introduced Jill to Ty, she stepped way too close to him, and I noticed he didn't move back.

She stared up at him, beaming a smile that would light up Mars. "It's so nice to meet you, Ty. I hope I see you around a lot this weekend."

Define "a lot," please.

"I'll be around, darlin'," he drawled in the way that only a Texas cowboy could.

Suddenly I wanted to get my lodgers into the Big

House and into their respective rooms. I was tired and my cranky quotient was steadily rising to full tilt.

I could remedy both with a quick trip to the kitchen for leftover chocolate chip cookies on my way upstairs.

Shoot! I'd forgotten my manners!

"Can I offer you a snack? Or are you both good?" I asked, praying for the latter.

"A snack sounds really good," said Peter, smiling at me. "Even though I could stand to lose a few pounds." He chuckled and patted his stomach.

"Nonsense," said Priscilla. "You're fine the way you are." She turned to go back into her motor home, then said over her shoulder, "You two, get some sleep. I'll need you in the morning. I have to be up very early tomorrow. The Tri-Gams are taking me to breakfast."

"Oh, really? Where?" I asked.

"Why, at your diner, of course, Trixie. I understand that you created a breakfast dish in my honor. I have to sample it."

Wait. That's not right!

"Priscilla, there's a *dinner* special named after you. It ran all this week. It ends on Monday," I said, trying to remember the checklist detailing Priscilla's demands Megan had given me.

"Isn't that nice of you!" she replied. "I'll have to sample that, too. But I'm definitely sure about the breakfast special tomorrow at breakfast, so I'll be expecting it. Good night, everyone."

Crap. Now I had to go to the diner and make something unique for Priscilla for breakfast and incorporate it into the menu . . . or maybe just the chalkboard. How about a poster? Yes, a poster. Delores, one of the night waitresses, is pretty creative. She'd be able to make it look nice and not like it was an afterthought.

As I looked at Jill, who was still grinning at Ty, I remembered my manners. "Jill, how about you? Would you like a snack, too?"

"Oh, I definitely found the snack I want," she said, taking Ty's hand and guiding him toward the parking lot. Ty looked over his shoulder at me and raised an eyebrow, but he still let Jill lead him away.

Jill certainly knew what she wanted, and she wanted Ty.

I was going to go to Ty's rescue but then decided that he could handle her himself, if he wanted to. He was a grown man, after all.

That left Peter and me.

"I have chocolate chip cookies and milk."

Good Lord, I sounded like a mother.

"I'll make you up a plate, but I'm not going to join you. I have to get to my diner. I have a zillion things to do, and it's my shift."

I put the cookies and milk on a tray and showed him to his room down the hallway. I pointed to where Jill's room was located in case she came back anytime soon.

"Good night, Peter. If you need anything, just give

me a call at the diner. The phone number is on a pad on the nightstand next to your bed."

"Thanks, Trixie."

He seemed like an okay guy, for the most part. I wouldn't open my house to anyone I didn't get a good vibe from, celebrity chef's stepson or not.

I hurried to my room, washed my face, and ran a brush through my hair, thinking the whole time what kind of breakfast dish I could create for Priscilla. After all, the place was crawling with media. Maybe my diner could get some of that attention, too.

But first I had to fix the breakfast mistake.

Hopefully the Tri-Gams wouldn't kill me.

Chapter 5

"Priscilla, welcome to the Silver Bullet," I said, greeting her with my hand out.

She didn't shake my hand but instead looked around intently. I thought she was going to give my diner the white-glove test, but instead she pulled off her white gloves and handed them to me along with her matching leather hat.

Peter was already assisting her in removing her coat.

"I've been here before, you know. I used to be friends with Stella and Porky. We had some great times on this property, especially during the summer. Now, where is my breakfast special?"

I pointed to Ray's poster and let her read it.

"Potato pancakes? With kielbasa?" She grimaced. "How very . . . uh . . . old-fashioned, but I'll give them a try. I haven't had potato pancakes in years—the grease and the starch, you know, they just kill my stomach. We won't even talk about the kielbasa!"

Oh, you're very welcome! I wanted to say, but instead

I said, "I'll have Nancy bring the horseradish and mustard with it."

I escorted Priscilla to one of the tables in the side room so the rest of the Tri-Gams could enter and take off their coats. Then I turned to Peter and Jill, who had followed closely behind, and gestured to seats on either side of Priscilla.

Just then I noticed Ty Brisco walking into the diner, and the crowd separated like oil and water. With a couple of "Hello, darlin's," the Tri-Gams were eating out of his hand—and not ordering off my menu.

He walked over to me, took Priscilla's garments from my hands, and pulled out a chair next to her. I thought it was for Jill Marley, like I was planning, but then I felt it on the back of my knees.

"Have a seat, Trixie, and get to know Priscilla. Besides, Juanita told me that you needed some time out of the kitchen. She said that she and Cindy have it covered."

"Oh, no. I couldn't," I protested. Besides, Priscilla and I had nothing to talk about.

"Sit and relax. That's an official police order."

Priscilla laid her hand on mine. "Do what the handsome man says, Trixie. Talk to me."

"Are you enjoying your stay here, Priscilla?"

"I am. One of the highlights of my trip is being able to spend so much time with my dear stepson, Peter, of course."

Jill coughed on the other side of me and quickly chugged down her water.

Priscilla turned her head toward Peter, who was holding up Priscilla's coffee mug for Nancy to fill. "Isn't he just so thoughtful?" Priscilla said.

"He certainly is," I said, wanting to point out that it was Jill who'd given Peter the idea by reaching for Priscilla's cup earlier. Peter had snatched it from her hands.

"Jill and I are going to teach Peter the ins and outs of my business," Priscilla said. "It's about time he finally took an interest. Isn't that right, Jill?"

"Oh, yeah . . . sure. Whatever you think is best, Cilla."

"Oh, Trixie? Just so you know, I'm expecting a very important package today. I had it addressed to you here in Sandy Harbor, since I wanted to make sure it was delivered quickly. It's being overnighted from New York City. Will you please see that I get it immediately when it comes?"

"Of course," I said.

Priscilla took a sip of coffee. "Oh dear. This is much too bitter," she said, reaching for the creamer and sugar. "When are we going to be served, Trixie? I don't have all day."

"Soon," I replied. People from her party were still being seated, and I thought it was only right to wait for them before I gave the okay.

"So, Priscilla, when do you plan on leaving Sandy Harbor? Right after the contest?" I asked, hoping.

I knew what the Tri-Gam Departure Committee had said, but I wanted to hear it right from the TV chef's mouth. *The sooner, the better*, I thought.

"It depends on the weather," she said. "I don't have to be in Ottawa for . . . um . . . I forgot when I was supposed to be there." She turned to Jill. "Darling, when am I supposed to appear in Ottawa?"

"In three days," Jill said.

"No. That can't be right. Are you sure?"

Priscilla's voice had become a little thin, and she was definitely getting upset.

Jill put her hand on Priscilla's. "I'm sure, Priscilla. Three days. Don't worry. I'll take care of you."

"I'm glad I can depend on you, Jill."

Priscilla stared at the roof of my diner until I asked her, "So, you have to leave in three days?"

"Yes. Three days, just like I told you," she snapped. "So I have a little time to spare. If Peter is too tired to drive, we can stay for a while longer with you, Trixie. I assume that won't be a problem."

I wanted to say, *You assume wrong, Countess,* but instead I said, "No, of course, it's not a problem at all."

Since everyone who was having breakfast with Priscilla dared not order anything else but the special named after her, we were all served breakfast rather quickly. Coffee was set out in carafes as well as hot water and tea bags for tea. As planned, bowls of sour cream and applesauce were placed on the table at various intervals. A jar of horseradish and mustard joined them.

Nancy and Chloe, who were serving us, were efficient and friendly. The breakfasts came out of the kitchen hot and delicious.

I thought it was a pretty nice event until Mayor Rick Tingsley got up to give another welcome speech to Priscilla.

Priscilla leaned over to me and whispered, "Richard Tingsley always was a windbag. Likes to hear himself talk. I can't believe you people elected him to be the mayor."

"Don't count me in on that one. I wasn't living in Sandy Harbor when that happened."

"Oh, and, Trixie? Your potato pancakes, although a little unimaginative, are tolerable. If you give Jill the recipe, I'll put it in my next cookbook." She waved her hand as if she didn't care what I did.

Unimaginative? Tolerable?

Sheesh. I'd given up sleep to give Priscilla her breakfast special.

I swallowed my coffee before I choked on it. "How nice of you, Priscilla. I'll be sure to keep that in mind."

After breakfast was over, I thawed out my car and drove the three hundred yards from my diner to the Big House. It seemed ridiculous, but there was no way I could lug the heavy cooler full of my mac and cheese supplies through the foot of ice and snow that had accumulated from yesterday's storm.

I left everything in the car and hurried inside to take a shower. Kicking off my boots and shucking out of my heavy coat, scarf, hat, and mittens, I tossed them on a chair and hurried upstairs.

Finally, after a nice hot shower and a blow dry, I was as presentable as possible, with my moussed hair and my puffy, sleep-deprived eyes, which I tried to hide with concealer and purple eye shadow.

Just as I was about to pull out and head to the fair-grounds, an overnight-delivery truck pulled up and parked right behind my car. It had to be Danny Morrison. He normally had the Sandy Harbor route.

"I have a package addressed in care of you, Trixie. It's for a Miss Priscilla Finch-Smythe," Danny said, handing me a large vanilla-ice-cream-colored bubble mailer. He was dressed all in brown, and his words came out in puffs of vapor. "Sign my machine, would you?"

He held out an electronic clipboard–looking thing and offered me a stylus. I handed him my purse, as well as the carafe and mug I was carrying, for him to hold while I signed.

"See you at the contest?" he asked.

"Yup. I'm on my way there now."

"The way you cook, I bet you'll win first place."

"Thanks, Danny. Too bad you're not a judge!"

He nodded, shivered, and climbed the stairs to his delivery truck. He drove off, leaving a cloud of gas fumes in his wake.

I looked at the thick mailer. It's not that I'm nosy, but the return address seemed to jump out at me. It was from a bunch of New York City lawyers.

It must be really important for Priscilla to send it in care of me with instructions to get it to her immediately.

I tossed the package and the rest of my stuff into my frozen car and started it. After a couple of sputters, the engine finally came to life. Back outside, I chipped off the ice and brushed the snow off again. It looked like one or two inches had fallen since I'd driven here.

I started to worry about the turnout for the contest due to the weather. There would be a massive Tri-Gam breakdown if a lot of people didn't come.

My car slowly chugged through the slushy muck on Route 3. Every now and then the wheels would grab and pull the car to the right or left. I didn't want to end up in a field or whatever was under certain bridges, like a river, so I drove slowly.

The drive, which was usually less than a half hour, since the fairgrounds were a straight shot from the Big House, took about forty-five minutes.

When I arrived, it looked like the husbands of the Tri-Gams, clearly outfitted in their lime-green vests, were assisting Deputies Vern McCoy and Lou Rutledge in parking cars. Then I noticed the huge snowbank that was as tall as some of the Adirondack Mountains. On both sides of the snowbank were cleared areas for parking. A couple dozen RVs looked like they had spent the night there.

I pulled up next to Deputy Rutledge. "G'morning, Lou."

"Morning, Trixie. Hey, if you're unloading your car, go behind the Culinary Building." He motioned to a semiplowed area behind the building. "Then move your car over to that cleared-off area." He pointed to his left. "Park over there as soon as you're done. We have to keep the area around the building clear for emergency vehicles."

"Of course."

"I'll bet my paycheck that you'll be happy to get this weekend over with," Deputy Rutledge said with a sly smile.

"You have no idea, Lou. Priscilla is such a difficult diva, and I really, really dislike having her around. I can't wait to get rid of her."

He nodded, and I drove around to the back of the building as instructed.

I was impressed with the efficiency of the Tri-Gam Parking Committee, although it was way too early to really judge if they had it all under control. The bulk of the people wouldn't arrive for another hour or more.

I knocked on the back door of the Culinary Building so someone could let me in. It was a bustle of activity when the county fair was in progress, but now I could barely hear a murmur of volunteers talking.

Connie Benson, a Tri-Gam, opened the door. "Thank goodness you're here, Trixie. A busload of crazy ladies showed up a little while ago looking for Priscilla Finch-Smythe. I'm not sure where they went, but they seemed like they wanted her head on a platter!"

"Yeah, well, so do I. I can't wait to get rid of her once and for all, after this fund-raiser is over." I handed Connie my purse, mug, and carafe of coffee.

"I phoned Megan," Connie said. "She said that Priscilla and her entourage are in her car and that her husband, Milt, is driving them around, showing Priscilla some of the beauty of our village first and what improvements we've made since she lived here back in the day."

"Well, Megan has to bring her here sooner or later," I said. "Priscilla is the final judge of the mac and cheese contest. And I really hope I win. I want to be on TV and get the publicity for my diner and cottages!" I was getting excited, not just for me, but I wanted success for the whole contest.

"And, Trixie, have you heard the buzz? Chef Walton DeMassie is here from New York City. Can you believe it? I have his line of cookware." Connie was positively giddy. "I watched his show all the time, until it was canceled. Apparently he's been telling everyone that he wants to make a comeback and that winning this contest is just the way to do it."

I doubted that our little contest would help in his comeback. But what did I know?

"Kip O'Malley is here, too. He's the head cook over at the Watertown Jail." She rolled her eyes. "He told me that he's dying to quit and be on TV. He said that he wants to share his culinary artistry with the world and that he didn't go to correspondence cooking school just to cook for prisoners."

Correspondence cooking school? I chuckled, wondering how that worked.

"Teacher, my guests ate my homework."

"Well, then, Mr. O'Malley, you get an A."

"Oh, and Chef Jean Williams is here from the soup kitchen in Syracuse. Looks like she wants some TV glamour, just like you, Trixie. And she wants to work with Priscilla. She said that Priscilla is her heroine, and she wants to follow in her footsteps," Connie said, helping me set my things down on a table. "What about you, Trixie? Do you want to be a TV chef, too?"

I shook my head. "Nah. I'm pretty happy being the chief cook and bottle washer at my own place. But if I did get on TV, I'd talk up the Silver Bullet and my cottages and hopefully the money would increase. Then I could expand. Put on additions. I could even franchise! Man, the sky's the limit." I was getting carried away again. "Anyway, that's what I'd do."

"Sounds like a great plan, Trixie."

Quickly, I unloaded the rest of the things I'd brought and put everything at my table, which was clearly marked with my name and contest number. There was a name tag, too, which I picked up and clipped on to the collar of my jacket.

Nice job by whatever committee was in charge, I thought.

Then I parked my car where Lou had indicated, avoiding a fire hydrant that was dug out next to my car. I prayed that there wouldn't be an avalanche from the snowbank during the cook-off, or my car—and all the others that would have to park there—would be buried.

Two hours later, the contest was organized chaos and the building smelled divine. Sixty-two chefs had made it to Sandy Harbor, which meant a gross of sixty-two thousand dollars. We'd have to pay out the prizes for first, second, and third place and give a cut to the state fair to rent the building, but that wasn't too shabby.

Finally Priscilla Finch-Smythe arrived with Megan and Milt Hunter and her entourage, which consisted of Jill and Peter. Reporters surrounded her, shouting questions. Flashes flashed and cameras rolled as the audience stood and clapped.

Megan and Priscilla walked up onstage together. And then Megan called me up to the stage. I balked. I just wanted to stay behind the scenes. But many hands propelled me up to the stage, and reluctantly I climbed the stairs and waved to everyone.

That was enough for me. But it wasn't enough for the Tri-Gams. I was presented with a dozen long-stemmed red roses. Much to her surprise—*not*—Megan was presented with the same.

After a long welcoming cheer from the Tri-Gams, complete with choreography in spite of some of their walkers and canes, it was Priscilla's turn to speak.

"What a wonderful reception I've received from Sandy Harbor. It is a pleasure to be among such warm and dear people. I am so honored that you asked me to judge your macaroni and cheese contest. The winner will create his or her winning dish on my TV show, which will be broadcast throughout the United States and Canada. And don't forget to check out my newest cookbook: *Comforting Comfort Food by the Countess of Comforting Comfort Food*. Thank you. Now let's get started, and best of luck to all the participants."

"Cheater! Stealer! Priscilla steals recipes for her cookbooks and claims them as her own!" said a woman with a walker.

Oh, no! I'd forgotten all about the ladies Connie had mentioned to me before. Priscilla wasn't going to be happy about this.

"Priscilla Finch-Smythe stole from our church!" said a woman wearing a royal-blue parka. "The Church of the Covenant of Saint Dismas in Poughkeepsie, New York!"

"Thief! Cheater!" A woman with orange earmuffs pumped her fist.

I looked at Priscilla, and she was frozen in place. Then she turned to Jill, her assistant, and whispered something to her.

Jill was furiously shaking her head, and I could hear her saying, "No. No way, Cilla. No way. I don't know what they're talking about."

Covering the mike with her hand, Priscilla motioned for me to come over to her. "Shut them up, Trixie, or I'm leaving."

"What's going on, Priscilla?" I asked.

"How the heck would I know what those hicks are bellowing about?"

Hicks? Bellowing? Priscilla certainly had a gracious way with words.

I took the microphone from Priscilla. "Ladies, please sit down and be our guests. The contest is going to begin soon."

"We're not going to go quietly! Priscilla, we want to talk to you first!" the lady in the purple full-length parka yelled. "Don't you dare ignore us!"

Right then Ty Brisco appeared. He had gotten rid of his coat and was dressed from head to toe in all navy blue with the exception of a colorful shield-shaped patch and various insignias. A black belt circled his waist, which held a variety of cop regalia—a Glock, bullet clips, pepper spray, handcuffs, and other stuff. A black radio was clipped to his shoulder. He didn't have a hat on, and his dark hair was disheveled in a sexy way.

I wanted to run my fingers through it in an effort to make it a little tidier.

Although, it looked kind of cute the way it was.

Ty got the church ladies all seated and quiet. He was in cop mode and had turned on his Texas charm; they didn't stand a chance.

Neither did I.

After everyone quieted, Megan nudged me and handed me a typewritten piece of paper. I took a deep breath. "I'd like to thank Gamma Gamma Gamma, along with their husbands and significant others, for all of their help before and during this event. Without them, this weekend wouldn't have been possible. And I'd like to thank the entrants—chefs from all over the Northeast—who braved these horrible weather conditions for a chance to re-create their signature mac and cheese dish on TV with our final judge, Priscilla Finch-Smythe."

"Boo! Hiss! Plagiarizer of cookbooks!"

Ty sent the ladies of the Church of Saint Dismas a stern look, and they quieted instantly.

I read on, wondering why Megan didn't want to read her speech herself. "Our prizes are two thousand dollars for first place, eighteen hundred dollars for second place, and twelve hundred dollars for third place. Our preliminary judges are: Mayor Rick Tingsley, Fred Henderson of the Gas and Grab on Route 3, and high school senior and computer expert Ray Meyerson, representing the younger crowd. Pause for laughter."

Huh? Oh! Oh, no! Did I really read "pause for laughter" out loud?

With the exception of Priscilla, everyone in the room started laughing hysterically, and I actually *did* have to pause and wait until it subsided. As I stood there, I had to laugh myself. Then I was laughing so hard, it took me a while to be able to talk again.

Thanks to my gaffe, the sticky situation between the church ladies and Priscilla was forgotten for a while. And the tension in the room eased dramatically.

Megan hesitated, looked at me, and then added, "While our preliminary judges are tasting the entries,

Priscilla will be autographing her latest cookbook, *Comforting Comfort Food by the Countess of Comforting Comfort Food*. Please form an orderly line for purchase and autographing."

The ladies stood up, looked at Ty, but didn't say a word. Instead they formed an orderly line as instructed, but not one person picked up Priscilla's cookbook.

Ty moved next to them. So did the media. One of them interviewed the woman in the purple coat, who spelled her name for the reporter twice and repeated it twice: Marylou Cosmo. The lady with the orange earmuffs was right next to her and said her name was Dottie Spitzer.

Those two seemed like the ringleaders of the church ladies.

Priscilla held out her hand for the microphone. "No one asked me if I'd like to say a few more words before they put me to work." She laughed, and it sounded like a rusty hinge. The audience remained silent, not suspecting that Priscilla had attempted a joke.

At least, I thought it was an attempt at a joke.

"I'd like to thank the lovely people of Sandy Harbor for inviting me here. Everyone has been so nice. And thank you to everyone, especially to the wonderful Tri-Gams. Now, I'd like to proceed without any more immature heckling."

Ty and I made eye contact across the room, and we both raised an eyebrow. It seemed that we were both thinking the same thing—that Priscilla shouldn't antagonize the ladies who were already unhappy with her and who'd driven here on a bus in a blizzard to confront her about stealing their recipes.

The church ladies were lined up and waiting for Jill Marley to finish setting up her equipment for credit-card payments and whatnot. Peter McCall was arranging piles and piles of Priscilla's books.

Judging by the lack of interest from at least the church ladies, Peter would soon be putting all those books back into their cartons.

Priscilla waved one of her arms in the air. "Without further ado, let's get started with the book signing while the preliminary judges begin tasting."

She turned to me, and I thought she was going to shake my hand. Instead she handed me the microphone and adjusted her red silk scarf.

Oops! I looked at the microphone and took the opportunity to remind everyone that the judging would take a while with the number of entrants we had. "So feel free to wander around the building and visit the booths that our organizations are sponsoring. You will be notified when the finalists are going to be announced so you can return to your seats."

Peter McCall was walking around, shaking hands and talking to the entrants. First he was engaged in a quiet discussion with Jean, the soup kitchen chef. When I looked over a little bit later, he was hunched over with Kip, the prison chef. Still later, with another person, whom I didn't recognize. Then he moved on to Walton

DeMassie, the chef whose show was canceled. Then I lost track of where Peter went.

Ty stood near Priscilla, listening to what the church ladies were saying to her.

Priscilla looked uncomfortable after each discussion and kept on turning to Jill with an angry look on her face.

It looked to me like Jill was getting the blame for everything.

Jill looked around, probably for Peter, because she made a face and unloaded another box of cookbooks by herself. Sales were picking up due to those in line behind the church ladies.

One of the ladies held a bubble mailer in her hand, and it jarred me.

Oh, fudge! I had forgotten to give Priscilla the package that had arrived from the New York City lawyers.

I ran to my area—well, I walked fast—plucked the mailer out of my tote, and hurried over to Priscilla.

Jill saw me coming, package in hand, and hurried over to meet me. "Trixie, is that the item that Priscilla was expecting?"

"Yes, it is. She wanted me to give it to her immediately, but I forgot about it due to all the excitement."

"I'll take it," Jill said, pulling it from my hand. "I'll see that she gets it. She's quite busy signing her cookbooks, as you can see."

Priscilla was in another heated discussion with a church lady. They had two cookbooks open, Priscilla's and the church's, and it appeared that they were comparing recipes.

Jill glanced at the return address on the mailer and smiled. With a bounce in her step, she went back to Priscilla's side, put the package in a navy blue tote bag, and then returned to handling money.

I noticed that Dottie was waiting in line again to talk to Priscilla and watching every move the diva made.

I walked back to my station. The preliminary judges were nearing my area, and I needed to take my mac and cheese out of the oven and let it cool for a while.

Gathering up my potholders, I lifted my dish out and put it in line with my contestant number. It looked gorgeous, and it was perfect timing on my part!

The cheese on my entry was aromatic and bubbly, and I could smell a hint of garlic from the kielbasa. I would bet one of my cottages that the medium salsa I'd drained and mixed into the melted cheese would be the perfect touch, along with my assortment of dried herbs.

This was going to be good! I could just picture myself on the TV set!

Then the preliminary judges moved to Antoinette Chloe's entry. There was a lot of smiling and additional sampling. ACB looked very pleased. So did the judges, right up until the gray plastic mouse and the plastic yellow cheese that she had glued to her fascinator dropped into her entry.

The judges moved on.

When they came to me, they seemed to like my mac

and cheese with salsa and kielbasa. They didn't say much, but I did get a couple of nods, and three out of three judges proclaimed it "Delicious!"

Although I didn't think it was fair to the other contestants that Ray Meyerson, who worked for me as a dishwasher and computer geek, should have judged my entry. When I'd pointed this fact out to Megan, she talked to Ray, and he assured her that he could be fair.

I'm sure he could be fair, but he'd better vote for me! Oh, I'm kidding—mostly!

After another half hour, the preliminary judges huddled together intently. They were supposed to come up with ten finalists.

Then Priscilla was supposed to decide first, second, and third places out of those ten. Right now she asked if she could go on a break "to compose herself after her book signing."

I took that to mean that she wanted to go to the bathroom.

Priscilla's red silk scarf dropped off her shoulders, and I picked it up. "Hold that for me, Trixie. I'll be right back."

After a while Megan announced that everyone should gather back at their seats. She had to say it three times before anyone began to move toward their seats. Finally they did.

Then Mayor Rick Tingsley revealed the final ten contestant numbers.

ACB and I were included in the ten.

So were the big three contenders: Kip O'Malley, the

prison chef; Jean Williams, the soup kitchen chef; and Walton DeMassie, the chef from New York who was trying to make a comeback.

Megan instructed us to dish out more portions of our entries into a coffee cup, put them by our numbers on the table, and then take a seat away from the table.

By this time Priscilla had returned, escorted by Jill on her right and Peter on her left. Megan led the procession around the room to the finalists' tables. The Sandy Harbor High School's marching band, which stood in place, played what might have been "Happy Days Are Here Again" or it might have been their salute to Cher.

Pricilla nibbled, huddled with her entourage, nibbled and huddled more. She made notes on the "official results ballot" Ray Meyerson had made. She smiled, nodded, and dabbed her mouth with a white linen napkin and nibbled more.

Then she removed the page from the clipboard and handed it to Megan. Waving, she left the stage. I held out her red silk scarf, which I was still holding, and she took it from me and quickly draped it around her neck.

Megan took a while to translate the contestant numbers to contestant names. While she was doing that, the audience was treated to a rendition of the Boy Scout pledge and "God Bless America" from our local troop.

I always love watching the Scouts. They looked like little angels, although we all knew that at any second they'd be done singing and would be darting around the building like fire ants.

I noticed that Marylou and Dottie's chairs were empty. Since I didn't see Priscilla, I wondered if I should look for her, assuming that she was being yelled at by them again. I was just getting up to look for all three when Megan called me up onstage to help her announce the winners. I waved no, that she could do it.

After all, Megan liked the spotlight.

ACB and I both got honorable mentions. And my dreams of TV were over.

Third place went to Kip O'Malley of the Watertown Jail. He wasn't happy and reluctantly walked up onstage to get his prize. Later everyone could hear him tossing his equipment into a container. He kicked open the doors and left.

Everyone looked at one another and shifted uncomfortably at the childish display, but the best was yet to come.

Walton DeMassie came in second place. He uttered a colorful expletive that had the church ladies covering their ears. He stormed onto the stage, plucked the check from Megan's hand, and exited the building, yelling that the contest was rigged.

Jean Williams, of the soup kitchen in Syracuse, came in first. She was so happy that she did a cartwheel on the stage. The spectators were so thrilled to see a positive response that they gave her a standing ovation.

After closing remarks were made by Megan, Ty Brisco took the mike. He told everyone to drive slowly and to take Route 3 for as long as they could, especially if they were connecting to Interstate 81 north or south. He said that it had stopped snowing and that the roads were all plowed and salted, but the snow had been blowing and drifting across the roads, causing icy conditions that might grab tires and spin cars.

I decided that I'd better round up Priscilla and her entourage and drive them back to the Big House. Milt and Megan Tucker lived the other way, so it made more sense for me to drive everyone back.

The Saint Dismas ladies filed out. I walked up onto the stage because of the higher elevation and looked for Peter and Jill. Where was everyone?

I spotted Jill coming into the building from outside. She looked very distraught and wet. What was up with that?

Peter wasn't anywhere inside the building, as far as I could see. I asked Ray Meyerson, who was heading into the men's room, to see if Peter McCall was in there.

After what seemed to be an eternity, Ray returned. "Peter's not in there, boss. Oh, and the two chefs are in there whining that the contest was rigged. As a judge, I took offense at that, and I told them so."

I shook my head. "Sore losers. Right, Ray?"

He shook his head, muttered something under his breath, and walked away. I didn't want him to be offended. He was just doing his job, and he took it very seriously.

"Looking for me, Trixie?" Ty said, walking toward me.

"No. I just like hanging around the men's room."

"Picking up sailors?"

"As usual." I grinned. "But right now I'd really like to gather up Priscilla, Peter, and Jill and hit the road back to the Big House. I'm pooped. I saw Jill walk in from outside, but I don't see her now."

"Let me give the guys a call on the radio and have them look for them."

"Priscilla can't be far, Ty. Her hat, gloves, and boots are still here. She might be wearing her coat—it's red wool—and she has designer red heels on, so I'd guess that she wouldn't go outside."

I walked around the building again, looking for everyone. Then I saw Jill packing up Priscilla's books.

I yelled to her, "Jill, I'm going to drive you, Priscilla, and Peter back to my house."

She nodded. Then I walked over to my cooking station to get my equipment, deciding to load my stuff into the car so we could hit the road when Priscilla and Peter finally showed up. I put on all my winter paraphernalia and shuffled outside through the back door, carrying some of my things.

It was as I approached my car that I saw Priscilla Finch-Smythe sitting with her back against the fire hydrant in the snowbank beside my car. Her coat was unbuttoned, and I could see that her red skirt and sweater were all disheveled. Snow had drifted on her and against her right side.

Oh, no! She must have slid on an icy patch with those fancy heels on and couldn't get up.

But what was she doing outside?

"Oh my goodness, Priscilla. You must be frozen!" I knelt beside her to see how badly she was hurt and brushed the snow off her. I didn't know if I should help her inside or call 911.

Before I had to decide, I heard the roar of a snowplow on the other side of the snowbank. A crush of snow tumbled over the top of the snowbank and onto us both. Priscilla tipped sideways onto my lap.

It took a while before I could register what I was seeing. Her red silk scarf was so embedded into her neck that I could barely see it. And there was a thick patch of blood frozen onto the back of her head.

"Priscilla? Priscilla? Talk to me! Please! Priscilla!"

I sat her up and brushed the snow from her face. I pulled off my mitten and felt for a pulse.

Nothing.

Then I screamed and screamed until Ty found us.

Chapter 6

"*D*on't you dare get out of that bed, Beatrix Matkowski. That's an order!"

"No one calls me Beatrix and lives to tell about it," I whispered, feeling like a dense fog had settled in my bedroom.

Antoinette Chloe Brown had her hands on her hips. She'd just delivered a steaming mug of chamomile tea and a piece of banana bread to my nightstand.

I couldn't eat a thing, but the tea was calling my name. It would shout my name if it were accompanied by a couple shots of something stronger.

I didn't remember taking off my clothes and slipping into my pink Minnie Mouse nightshirt and matching fuzzy socks. Or sliding underneath my plump down comforter.

The events before that were all a blur, but I tried to bring them into focus.

"How long have I been sleeping?" I asked.

"About fourteen hours."

"No way!"

"Way."

"Priscilla is dead." I hoped that ACB would contradict me and the awful scene I remembered was just a nightmare.

"Yes, she is," ACB said grimly. "It appears she was choked to death with her red silk scarf and then left to freeze like a Popsicle."

I vividly remembered the scene, and shivered. There'd been so much red—her outfit, her coat, her shoes—and all that blood. I don't think I'd ever be able to forget the horrible image that had been burned into my memory.

ACB propped the pillows behind my back, and I sat up against the headboard of the sleigh bed.

"She must've slipped and hit her head on the fire hydrant," I said. After taking a sip of tea, I enjoyed the warmth that spread through my body. Then I remembered the scarf around her neck. "Do you think she hit her head on the fire hydrant before or after she was strangled?"

That was a dumb question. I didn't even know why it mattered. It wasn't like it would change what had happened.

ACB plopped herself on the edge of my bed and helped herself to some of the banana bread. What a shame. I had started feeling much better and could have gone for some of that. "Are you asking which injury came first?"

"I . . . Yes, I guess that's what I'm asking."

"Hal Manning is working on figuring that out right now."

Hal was Sandy Harbor's resident coroner and funeral home owner. In fact, his Happy Repose Funeral Home was the only one in the area.

"Maybe someone pushed her and stunned her. Then strangled her," I speculated.

Antoinette Chloe chewed thoughtfully and then spoke. "Or maybe they choked her, and then she fell backward and hit her head."

"Well, no matter what order it happened in, the poor woman was murdered," I said. "In little Sandy Harbor."

ACB nodded. "And the press is having a field day. More and more reporters are showing up and sniffing around. The Silver Bullet is media headquarters central due to the fact that they can get reliable Internet hookup there better than anywhere else in town. Juanita called in more help to feed them, the gawkers, and the regular customers."

"Juanita probably didn't know how long I'd be sleeping."

"You've had a rough time of things lately. Seemed to everyone that you needed the sleep."

"I did a good job of it." I didn't even remember waking up to get a snack or to take any bathroom breaks.

Antoinette Chloe patted my hand. "Seeing Priscilla like that was the final straw in your stress-o-meter. I think you might have fainted."

"And Ty wasn't even around. You know how I like to faint in his arms."

"I do." She laughed. "You actually fainted while holding on to Priscilla. An avalanche of snow almost buried you both."

I shivered; then we sat in silence for a while, which was unusual for us. ACB broke the silence first. "Ty told Jill and Peter not to leave town."

That meant I still had houseguests. Crap.

"Where are they?" I asked. "I would have heard them moving around or talking."

"Jill moved into Priscilla's motor home. I moved Peter into my guest room, and I moved in here to nurse you back to health."

I could handle ACB. I didn't want to handle Jill and Peter at this time, so I guess I lucked out.

"Well, I'm fine now, Antoinette Chloe. I just needed some rest."

"And more rest is what you are going to get. Then Ty wants to take your affidavit. Apparently you weren't in the best condition when he first found you. You were in shock, half frozen yourself, and sleep deprived."

"I just can't do all-nighters like I did in my college days. And I think seeing Priscilla like that pushed me right over the edge."

"By my calculations, you did two all-nighters in a row. It's a wonder you didn't collapse sooner."

"I feel great now. Time to get out of this bed and find out what happened to Priscilla. You know, there must be a suspect list a mile long. I mean, I knew her only a few days and I thought she was a diva. I didn't like her demands, especially how she insisted on the specials and the tea and all. And she wasn't very nice to anyone. And she could have thanked us for the tea and for breakfast and naming the specials after her, but she seemed to expect it."

"And she didn't come from wealth in the least, so it must have been all her TV and cookbook success that changed her."

"Still, no one deserves to die like that, and the least we can do is bring her murderer to justice."

I started to get out of bed, but ACB gently pushed me back.

"What?" I asked.

"There's a couple of other things you should know."

"Like?"

"Like there's talk about you. They're saying you entered the contest for publicity for the Silver Bullet and because you lost, you were . . . well, you were rip-roaring mad at Priscilla. Did you say that you'd do anything to get on TV?"

" 'Yes' to the publicity thing, but a big, damn 'no!' to the rip-roaring-mad part. I wasn't mad at Priscilla in the least."

"What about the part that you'd do anything?"

"I didn't mean that I'd kill Priscilla to get on the show. That would defeat the purpose of me being on TV with her, wouldn't it?"

She shrugged. "Yeah, it would. And, Trixie, a lot of people heard you trash Priscilla after she dissed Blondie, saying that Ty should shoot her for yanking on her coat. And that you had complained about Priscilla saying that your potato pancakes were only tolerable."

"I was just complaining that I didn't get any sleep in order to prepare the potato pancakes for her. And of course I didn't like her talking about Blondie the way she did. Blondie probably thought that Priscilla's faux-fur coat was a new species of dog. She didn't mean to yank on Priscilla's coat."

I slammed my fist down on the pillow. "Oh, for heaven's sake, I hate to be the subject of gossip, especially when it's overexaggerated to make me look bad."

ACB chuckled. "I'm *always* the subject of gossip. I heard a couple of the Tri-Gams talking about my muu-muus and my fascinators and that I dress 'over-the-top.' I know I do, but I enjoy it. I think they're just jealous of my fashion sense."

"Then wear what you like, Antoinette Chloe. Don't listen to them." We were off topic, which usually happened whenever I talked with my friend. "Um . . . what else should I know about Priscilla's murder?"

She looked at her fake glittery fingernails. They had little rhinestone bows glued on each one. "Ty told the second- and third-place winners not to leave town. They both had been angrily spewing that the contest was rigged right before you found Priscilla's body and that the first-place winner—sweet Jean Williams from the soup kitchen in Syracuse—shouldn't have won. Ty let Jean go because she lives close by."

"How could they think the contest was rigged?"

"It was probably just sour grapes on their parts."

"That's pretty much what I said to Ray Meyerson. He'd heard them talking in the men's room right after the contest." I thought for a while. Then it hit me. "Um . . . you know . . . with Priscilla's passing, Jean Williams doesn't have a cooking show to appear on now."

"Megan Hunter is aware of that. She's trying to work out something with another TV chef. Priscilla's assistant, Jill, is using her connections to help, too."

"That's nice of both of them. Megan is totally efficient."

"Oh, by the way, Connie Benson is the one who told Ty that you wanted publicity and that you were hopping mad that you weren't picked for first place."

I racked my brain. What on earth had I said to Connie to give her that impression?

"And Megan said that she hated to cast suspicion on you, but she said in her statement to Lou Rutledge that you called Priscilla a difficult diva and that you really disliked her."

"True, but that doesn't mean that I wanted her dead."

"Megan also told Lou—again, she was very regretful—that she saw you holding Priscilla's red scarf."

"Priscilla handed it to me. I was holding it—for her!"

"And then, coincidentally, you were both together and she was dead when Ty appeared."

My stomach sank as if I were dropping on a roller-coaster ride at the state fair.

"Trixie, I know you're innocent, and Ty probably knows you're innocent. But we have to find the person who really did it. And soon. You can't leave town."

"*What?* I can't leave town?" Then I thought about it. "I *never, ever* leave town except for the occasional shopping trip anyway."

"Yeah, but you *officially* can't leave town."

"Isn't this just . . . peachy?" I said. "Okay. So the people who can't leave town are Kip O'Malley and Walton DeMassie. And then there's Jill Marley and Peter McCall, the doting stepson. Who else?"

"The two church ladies can't go either: Marylou Cosmo and Dottie Spitzer. They were the most vocal of the bunch, but Ty, Vern, and Lou took down everyone's name on the Saint Dismas bus, along with their addresses, phone numbers, and other pertinent contact information. They'll probably run record checks on all of them and see what *pops*." She chuckled. "I think I heard that on *Castle*. You know, the TV show with that really gorgeous hunk Nathan Fillion. I love how he relates to his mother and daughter. It's so refreshing and sweet and funny. If I had kids, I'd want a daughter just like—"

My friend was veering off track as she sometime does. I decided I had to rein her in.

"If the bus driver, Marylou Cosmo, had to stay here, then how did all the church ladies get back to Poughkeepsie?" I interrupted.

"Ty got one of our local bus drivers to drive them all home. It took a lot of finagling and some waiver signing, but the church went for it."

"Where are Marylou and Dottie staying, then?"

"In Megan Hunter's guest room."

I closed my eyes and said a quick thank-you prayer to the powers that be. I was grateful they weren't staying with me.

"What about Kip and Walton? Where are they staying?"

"In their trailers or motor homes at the fairgrounds."

So far I was doing great! No guests at the Big House except for ACB. For a person in the hospitality business, I wasn't feeling very hospitable lately.

"What else do I need to know, Antoinette Chloe?"

"I don't think you're ready for the best part."

"Tell me."

"I'm your warden. I have to see that you don't move from your property." She chuckled. "It's like everyone is on house arrest."

I wanted that slice of banana bread. Right now. No, make that a big bowl of chocolate fudge ice cream with rainbow sprinkles. "Did Ty really say I couldn't leave town?"

"Yup. He wants to sort everything out first."

"I guess you can say that you're in my custody." She

giggled and the bed shook. She was loving this. Really loving this.

"But, Trixie, I'm also here to see that you get a lot of bed rest and that you don't volunteer for anything in the near future."

"I never volunteered for the whole Priscilla thing in the first place!"

"You're still new here. Fresh meat!" We both laughed. She stood and smoothed my comforter. "Would you like some more chamomile tea, Trixie?"

"No, thanks. But, tell me, who's working my shift at the diner?"

"Linda Blessler, as usual. And she's doing a great job, so you just stay in bed. Get more sleep," she said, pointing a finger at me.

"Sure. Whatever you say."

I waited until the sounds of her flip-flopping faded as she walked to another part of the house. Then I yanked the comforter off myself and stood. Yikes! I got a little dizzy, but it soon passed.

"Stay in town?" I mumbled to myself. "You gotta be kidding me, Sheriff Ty Brisco. I don't go anywhere anyway. But I'm not going to stay chained to ACB in the Big House while the real murderer is on the loose."

I tossed my clothes into the hamper. Then I jumped into the shower.

I was a woman on a mission. I needed to find out who had really killed Priscilla—and fast!

Chapter 7

"Well, if it isn't Trixie Matkowski sneaking out her back door."

My heart did a cartwheel and then pounded so loud they could probably hear it over the border in Canada.

"Well, if it isn't Ty Brisco, keeping an eye on the perimeter."

"You're supposed to be resting."

"And you're supposed to be investigating Priscilla's murder."

"Who says I'm not?"

I bit back a smile. I could banter with him all day. He was quick, but I was quicker.

"Are you investigating me, Deputy Brisco?"

He pushed back his cowboy hat with a thumb. Yeah, okay, I loved it when he did that.

"I'm investigating everyone on my hit parade of suspects."

"What number am I on your hit parade?"

"That's confidential information."

"You always say that."

"It's always true."

"I have to clear my name, you know. That means I'm going to have to investigate on my own, Ty."

"The heck you are!"

"I have to."

"Haven't we had this conversation in the past? Actually, haven't we had several?"

"And in spite of your multiple warnings that you were going to arrest me for my own good, I did what I wanted."

"And almost got yourself killed a couple of times. Or did you forget about that?"

"You sound like you care!"

"Of course I do, Trixie. Who's going to cook me dinner at the Silver Bullet if you're gone?"

"Go home and microwave yourself a TV dinner."

He laughed, and therefore, crumbled first.

"If only we could work together and find out who killed Priscilla, Ty."

"If you worked as a deputy or a cop for a dozen years, then maybe we could work together. Or if you got a degree in criminal investigation and were employed by the state police."

"I almost had a two-year degree from Onondaga Community College in liberal arts. Isn't that close enough?"

"Let me think." He snapped his fingers. "No!"

"As much as I'm enjoying this conversation with you, I'm getting cold. Would you like to continue this at the Silver Bullet? I want to see how things are running, and

I'm dying for a meatball sandwich with melted mozzarella on it."

"With a side of fries?"

"Onion rings."

"I'm in! Let's go."

I felt a slight brush on the back of my purple parka, and I guessed that Ty might have put his hand on the small of my back. It was hard to tell due to the puffiness. I couldn't help but wish that it was the middle of summer and that I was wearing a blouse or a T-shirt. That way I could actually feel his touch.

No. No way. I must be still recovering from my recent meltdown to think of something so sixth grade. Or else I needed nourishment.

We walked to my diner. It was seven o'clock in the evening and completely dark with the exception of the lights around the packed parking lot and the brilliantly lit neon signs of the Silver Bullet. In the distance, I could see customers through the windows. They were moving and talking . . . probably about Priscilla's murder and putting together their own list of suspects.

I didn't tell Ty, but I was anxious to hear the chitchat. Sometimes there was a kernel of wisdom that might be of help. And I was curious to hear what the reporters were saying, not to mention all of the people who were confined to Sandy Harbor until they were ruled out as suspects.

Oops. I should have told Antoinette Chloe that I was sneaking off to my diner for dinner.

But I needn't have bothered. When I pushed through the front doors of the diner, I spotted ACB sitting at the counter.

"To think I trusted ACB to keep an eye on you," Ty said.

"ACB has ADD."

"Clever, Trixie."

"I know."

When Antoinette Chloe saw me, she stood up and turned to the patrons. "We owe Trixie a round of applause for the successful library fund-raiser. All the figures aren't in yet, but we raised in the neighborhood of sixty-five thousand dollars! Isn't that incredible? It's our most successful fund-raiser in the history of Sandy Harbor!"

ACB started clapping, and Ty enthusiastically joined in. Soon the whole diner was applauding—probably not for me, but for the sixty-five grand.

But I knew what my friend was doing. She was trying to tamp down the bad gossip that had been going around about me.

I received several handshakes, lots of good wishes, and pats on the back.

I felt so welcome, so warm and fuzzy, that I almost forgot I was a suspect due to my verbal diarrhea and other circumstantial events.

I'd do anything to get on TV.

What had I been thinking when I said that? Clearly I hadn't been.

Ty and I took a seat at the counter. Through the pass-through window, I could see Cindy Sherlock doing the Silver Bullet Shuffle preparing orders. She waved to me and grinned.

Cindy was in her early twenties and worked hard both here and at home, taking care of her brothers and sisters when her mother was working at the box factory in Oswego.

I was relieved that Linda was going to take the grave-yard shift for me. The break was welcome, and it would give me time to hang out and listen to the gossip. Maybe do a little sleuthing.

The media presence had doubled since I was last here, and they were holding court in the area off the main part of the diner, where we'd had Priscilla's breakfast.

And I was seated at the perfect spot to listen in and observe.

"I did some investigating, and it seems that Ms. Finch-Smythe was actually from Sandy Harbor. Her whole TV persona is pure fiction," said a stocky man with a gray beard. "All that crapola about the English moors and frolicking through the heather is a figment of her publicist's imagination. I have her real name here somewhere. Oh yeah. Get this! It's Mabel Cronk."

"I'm looking into her stepson, Pete McCall," said an older man in a leather vest with a toothpick hanging out of his mouth. "I haven't found anything exciting about him, but Priscilla's assistant, Jill Marley, told me that he came back into her life only about a year ago.

I'm looking into his financials. There must be a reason for his sudden love of Priscilla."

Now, that was interesting!

I waited for them to talk about Priscilla's assistant, Jill, but the conversation shifted to who might play in the Super Bowl and the baseball strike that occurred years ago.

Jill . . . I wondered how she was doing. Priscilla's death must have been a real blow to her. She seemed very fond of her, even though I couldn't imagine how.

"Ty, do you know how Jill Marley is doing? She seemed to be the closest to Priscilla."

"I talked to her on a couple of occasions today. She's doing okay. Kind of shell-shocked, and she's pretty much been holed up in Priscilla's motor home, hiding from the press."

"She's probably been handling a lot of loose ends and making arrangements for Priscilla's funeral. Has Hal Manning released Priscilla's body yet?"

"Not yet," Ty said, taking a sip of the coffee Nancy poured for him as she breezed by.

When Nancy returned, she placed a glass of ice tea in front of me. She must've read my mind. I was craving exactly that.

"Trixie, would you like something to eat?"

"I'm dying for a hot meatball sub with melted mozzarella and a side of onion rings," I said.

"You got it, Trixie." She turned to Ty and smiled brilliantly.

"How about you, Tex?"

Ty chuckled. "I'd like a bowl of the split pea soup first. Then I'll have the same as Trixie."

"You got it, cowboy." Nancy sashayed to the kitchen. It was an over-the-top exaggeration, and she got some wolf whistles and chuckles from the reporters.

She turned back, laughing, and curtsied.

Ty and I laughed. When my staff had fun, so did the customers.

Just then the front door opened, and all eyes locked on Jill Marley as she came in. It was just one of those things—when the door opened, everyone automatically looked up to see who it was. But this time the media mobbed her. Her eyes grew wide, and she looked like she was ready to bolt or cry or both.

"I shouldn't have come here," she said in a wobbly voice.

Ty stood and made his way over to Jill. "Let Miss Marley into the diner, ladies and gentlemen."

I got up, put my arm around Jill, and led her to a booth away from where the media was holding court. I motioned her toward the window seat, and I slid in next to her. Ty sat across from us.

"I—I just wanted to get something to eat, Trixie," Jill said, her eyes misty. "There's really no food left in the motor home, and I didn't want to drive to the grocery store because I thought that Deputy Brisco—" She looked at him and blinked. Tears trailed a path down her cheeks, and she dabbed at them with a couple of napkins from the dispenser. "Well, I thought that you might think I was leaving town. I don't know how long I have to stay here, but I really need to get back to California to take care of things for Priscilla."

"Miss Marley, I'll let you go just as soon as I possibly can," Ty said warmly.

"And I'll drive you to the grocery store," I volunteered. I felt really bad for the poor girl. "That's not a problem. Is it, Ty? I mean, even prisoners get a meal now and then."

"And what are you doing here now? Playing tennis?" He tapped a finger on the table. "It's not a problem for you to get groceries. The Gas and Grab is in Sandy Harbor, not in South Dakota. And I need groceries, too. We can all go together."

I waved my hand. "What absolute fun. Not!"

He grinned. "We'll all go anyway. Tomorrow morning. I'll pick you both up at about ten."

I made a motion with my eyes for him to leave the booth so Jill and I could be alone. Maybe she'd open up to me. Finally he took the hint.

Even though I didn't have any formal training, according to Mr. Wyatt Earp over there, I did have a knack for making people talk, and I wanted to talk to Jill. Or rather, I wanted her to talk to me.

"Excuse me, ladies. I have a couple of things I need to take care of," he said, finally leaving the table.

Ty took his seat back at the counter. I went over and

moved my meatball sub from the counter to Jill's booth, and along the way I whispered to Ty that I'd wanted Jill to be able to talk freely without him being there.

And he mumbled back, "Trixie Matkowski, you leave the investigating to me."

I shrugged and gave him my best innocent smile. "Of course."

So now it was Jill and me alone until Nancy came over to the table and took Jill's order: a salad with Thousand Island dressing, a Western omelet with rye toast, and a glass of ice tea.

I worked on my now-cold meatball sandwich. I was tempted to pop it in the microwave to bring it back to some kind of life, but then Nancy set a cup of hot spaghetti sauce in front of me.

Perfect.

"Jill, with the exception of nothing to eat, are you doing okay in the motor home?"

"I'm okay. I'm just getting tired of being alone in there and hiding from the media."

"Would you feel more comfortable in my house?"

Say no. Please say no. I love being alone.

But then I remembered. Antoinette Chloe was there with me.

"No. I'm fine, really. It's just that wherever I look, I see things that remind me of Cilla."

After reaching for her hand across the table, I patted it. "Of course you would."

"I don't understand why Peter hasn't been arrested." She glanced over at Ty. "I hear that his cell phone was found at the scene."

"Really? That's odd. I didn't see a cell phone when I found Priscilla's body."

"It had fallen in the snowbank somewhere. The cops found it after they cordoned off the area where you found her."

"Oh." I took a deep breath, remembering how I'd found poor Priscilla. "Did they find anything else?"

"The cell phone is all I know about. And I know that Peter was talking to Deputy Brisco for a long time, because I was in the waiting room of the sheriff's department, waiting to give my statement."

"You and Peter don't quite get along, do you?" I asked, remembering how Jill always seemed exasperated whenever he was around.

Nancy delivered her salad, so we stopped talking for a moment.

"I don't particularly like how he came back into Cilla's life all of a sudden after not calling her or seeing her for years. Then suddenly there he was."

"I wonder why," I said.

She ate a forkful of salad. "My guess is that he probably ran out of money. Cilla was his cash cow. She always was."

"Really?"

She nodded. "Yeah. Peter is a parasite."

"I wonder what's going to happen to Priscilla's empire now that she's passed. Does Peter get it all because he's related?"

She set her fork down and stared at me. More tears traveled down her cheeks and landed on her salad. She pushed it away as Nancy delivered her Western omelet and rye toast.

"I shouldn't have asked that, Jill. That was very rude of me. I was just thinking out loud. I'm sorry."

I'm sure I looked apologetic. However, in my vast experience watching cop shows on TV and being married to a cop with loose lips—in more ways than one— I knew money was almost always a factor.

And this information had moved Peter to the head of the line in the list of suspects that I was mentally preparing. As soon as I could, I was going to find out if he had any more beefs with Priscilla.

There was no way I was going to stay out of this investigation. I had to clear my name.

"I'm really sorry that I asked you about Priscilla's money." And then switching tacks, I asked, "What can you tell me about the ladies from the Church of the Covenant of Saint Dismas?"

"Well, they call it the Church of the Covered Dish due to all the potluck suppers they have." Jill smiled, and I laughed out loud.

"I love it!"

"They're fruitcakes." She took a bite out of her omelet. "To think that they would accuse Priscilla of stealing from their amateur cookbook, which they typed on an old relic on someone's kitchen table ages ago, is just crazy. How would Priscilla even get a copy to steal anything from?"

I shrugged. "Well, she used to live in Sandy Harbor, and those types of cookbooks for charity do get around. Maybe Priscilla bought one, or maybe someone from the New York area sent it to her as a gift. Maybe she found it in a used bookstore out in California. Who knows?"

Jill took a sip of water. "She did love collecting cookbooks from all over. When she ran out of room, she had me send boxes of them to the Sandy Harbor Library."

Jill tapped on the table with a manicured nail. "And be assured, Trixie, that as long as I'm still taking care of Priscilla's finances, I will see to it that the donations continue. I imagine now that she's deceased, the Sandy Harbor Library can have her entire collection just as soon as the library is repaired."

"Really?"

"Really. Not only did Cilla want to come here to lend her name to the contest, but she also wanted to contribute money to the library personally."

"That's incredibly nice of her," I said. "I mean, *was* nice of her. And totally out of character, if you know what I mean."

"I do know what you mean, Trixie. Sometimes Priscilla was hard to take. She had . . . uh . . . some personality quirks."

"She sure did," I said. "But getting back to the

church ladies, they were awfully mad, particularly Dottie and Marylou. They showed their cookbook to Priscilla at the contest and they complained that it was taken mostly word for word. Copied, in fact. The whole thing."

"I haven't compared the two, but Priscilla wouldn't plagiarize. She was a cooking and baking icon."

"Are you sure, Jill?" I asked, holding my breath for the answer. If Jill Marley was Priscilla's assistant, she might know the answer to that.

Jill shifted in the booth and didn't meet my gaze. "Could I have some coffee, please? I'm just dying for a cup of coffee."

I waved at Nancy and mouthed the word "coffee," pointing to Jill. Nancy hustled over.

I decided that I wanted to compare the two cookbooks for myself and find out just how mad Marylou and Dottie were at Priscilla.

Chapter 8

*N*ancy shook her head. "Trixie, you barely ate any of your meatball sub. Let me get you another one, a fresher one."

"Box it to go, please, Nancy. As long as everything is running smoothly here, I think maybe I'll take another nap."

"I'll take care of that sub, boss, and give it some legs. Take it home and relax," Nancy said, then turned to Jill. "Jill, can I get you a fruit hand pie? They're divine. We have apple, cherry, and peach."

Mmm. Peach was my favorite . . . well, one of them.

As if she'd read my mind, Nancy looked at me with a smile and said, "Don't worry, Trixie. I'll get you a peach hand pie with some legs, along with the sub."

"Thanks, Nan," I said.

"Jill, can I tempt you, too?" Nancy said, pen poised above her pad.

"I should watch my waistline, but what the heck? I'll have a cherry hand pie to go also," Jill said.

We both got up. When Jill reached for her purse to pay, I shook my head. "It's on the house, Jill. My treat."

"Thank you, Trixie. See you tomorrow for grocery shopping with Deputy Brisco." She rolled her eyes. "As cute and as charming as he is, I don't feel that I need an armed deputy to watch me."

"Just think of it as an outing to one of Sandy Harbor's most interesting grocery stores with some local guides. Okay?"

She smiled. "Yeah. Okay."

Nancy handed us our items "on legs," and Jill and I bundled up. Then I opened the door for her.

"Oh, sorry, Jill. I forgot to tell my cook about tomorrow's special," I lied. "Go ahead without me. Just be careful walking. It's probably icy."

She left, and I sat down next to Ty.

"So what's the scoop, Sherlock?" he asked me.

"Nothing exciting, really. Though she changed the subject when I asked her who wrote the cookbook the church ladies have a beef about."

Ty took a sip of coffee. "I don't know if Dottie and Marylou are that crazy to kill over a cookbook—although stranger things have happened. Anything else?"

"Jill doesn't like Peter McCall."

"I know."

"That's about it, Ty. I'm going to call it a night."

"Aren't you forgetting someone?" he asked, pointing to Antoinette Chloe's booth.

"Oh, yes. My warden."

Mmm . . . maybe, just maybe, ACB would want to take a ride with me to her house to visit Peter McCall.

I was sure he'd like a nice meatball sub, a peach hand pie, and a little conversation about Priscilla Finch-Smythe.

"Wait for me, Trixie! I'll walk with you," ACB yelled as I got ready to brave the frigid winter night.

Her flip-flops sounded like the beat of a rap song as she hurried toward me.

I handed her coat to her, and she shrugged into it as we walked into the frigid outdoors. We both gasped at the below-zero temperature and the frosting of ice on everything.

"I wish you'd get some boots!" I'd told her the same thing last winter, to no avail.

"You know I don't like boots."

"Then put on sneakers or moccasins—something to cover your bare feet and keep your toes from freezing solid! You can decorate them with sequins and glitter to make them your style."

"I'll think about it."

It was hopeless. She wouldn't give up her flip-flops any more than she'd give up her muumuus or fascinators.

"Antoinette Chloe, I'm headed to your house to talk to Peter McCall."

"You are?" She grasped my arm when we came to an

icy patch, and we both held on to each other. If one of us slid on the ice, we'd both go down together.

"I want to hear what he has to say. I don't like to be considered a suspect just because I shot off my mouth and was seen holding the infamous red scarf. Besides, as much as I like you, I don't want to be stuck on you like a piece of lint. I have to get to the bottom of what happened."

"I'll go with you. I need to get a couple of things from my house anyway," ACB said. "Let's see what Peter has to say. We could always play good cop/bad cop."

"Uh . . . we could just play ourselves."

"That's no fun, Trixie."

I hope I wasn't going to regret taking ACB along, but a lot of times she surprised me. Actually, we worked well together—like a squeaky, nonoiled machine.

We walked to my car, and I yanked on the car handle, but the door wouldn't open. It was frozen shut.

ACB tried the passenger-side door, and it opened. I knew it was really winter when I had to get into the passenger side and somersault myself over to the driver's seat.

Which is what I did.

And got a perfect ten from the French judge!

I started the car and it groaned to life. We had to sit in it for a good ten minutes before the windshield defrosted and I could see out the windows. So we talked about everything under the sun to kill time, and, of course, the main topic was Priscilla.

"She'll always be Mabel Cronk to me. I told her that, too." ACB liked to repeat herself.

"You know, Antoinette Chloe, she probably had to take a fancier name for her business. That's all."

"But why the phony accent? Puh-leeze."

ACB was quiet for a while, which allowed me to concentrate on driving. I was always worried about black ice—the kind of ice that you couldn't see but would send you doing wheelies down the highway. I drove down Route 3 with the defroster blaring.

"I shouldn't speak ill of the dead," she said, interrupting the silence. "I'm sorry, Trixie."

"Oh, sweetie, you didn't say anything awful, and you were always a good friend to her. She knew that. You invited her into the Tri-Gams so she could have some more friends, too, and look what happened. She became a famous chef."

"She always did like to cook. She had to. Her mother was usually too sick and her father was a farmer. She cooked for them both and all of their helpers. One of her first jobs was at the Golden Age Home. She ran their food service, and she was only eighteen."

"Wow. That says a lot about her."

"Did you know that she used to work at the Silver Bullet, too?"

"Seems like I heard that before."

"It was only one summer, but your uncle Porky and aunt Stella taught her everything they knew. I think she was sixteen. And she made it pretty clear that she wanted to own the point someday. I think that's why she wanted the tea at the Big House and wanted a special named for her at the Silver Bullet. It was like she was pretending she finally owned it."

"You think?" That was food for thought.

"Yeah, I do."

"And here I thought she was just acting like a diva. I feel awful, Antoinette Chloe. Priscilla had a lot of important things she was dealing with."

Speaking of important, I suddenly remembered the envelope from the law firm in New York City and was curious. It had been important to Priscilla, whatever it was.

Whenever I thought of important legal documents, I immediately thought of criminal issues. Maybe that was just because I'd lived with Deputy Doug, my ex, for so long. But mail from lawyers could easily be about real-estate matters. Maybe she was buying or selling property somewhere. Or maybe it was a new contract related to her business or one of her new cookbooks. Or maybe Priscilla was making out a will or changing one that she already had.

Oh, who knows? Maybe it was nothing, but maybe it would shed some light on what had been significant to Priscilla at the time of her death.

But who on earth would kill her? Priscilla didn't seem to be over-the-top awful. She was just obnoxious and totally lacking in expressing gratitude.

Maybe Joan Paris, the editor of the *Sandy Harbor*

Lure, had some insider scoop about the suspects who weren't allowed to leave town—minus *moi*, of course.

Joan was living with Hal Manning, the Sandy Harbor coroner and funeral parlor director. In my experience, Hal's pillow talk usually netted top-notch information, which Joan passed along to her fellow book club members, particularly ACB and me. This was usually information that Ty Brisco would never give up in a million years.

I'd have to put Joan on my list of people to talk to after Peter.

I was about to pull into ACB's driveway but found that a snowbank was blocking my way.

"You'd think Peter would shovel," she grumbled. "But I guess that I should have taken care of that, since he's my guest."

"He's not a guest, Antoinette Chloe. He's a suspect."

"True. And Peter does seem a little . . . smarmy. But we don't know if he had any reason to want to hurt his stepmother," she said.

"Well, that's what we need to find out. Honestly, I'm still wondering about the whole cookbook thing," I said. "The church ladies from the Church of the Covered Dish were pretty insistent at the cook-off that Priscilla stole everything from them—their recipes and the little family stories that accompanied them. Maybe we should compare the two cookbooks to see if it's true."

"Well, I bought Priscilla's cookbook at the fundraiser," ACB said. "So, we just need the other one."

"We'll make a stop to see Marylou and Dottie and get one from them."

"No need," ACB said. "I knew you'd want to talk to them, since they were on Ty's suspect list, so I invited them to the Big House for lunch tomorrow. I'll make sandwiches and a pot of split pea soup."

I grinned. "You're the best."

"Someone had to do something to get the investigation going while you were acting like Sleeping Beauty."

I chuckled. ACB wasn't everyone's cup of tea, but she was mine.

Right now we needed to climb over that snowbank and get to ACB's very colorful Victorian. Her painted lady looked like something out of a Wild West house of ill repute compared to the others on her block, but it showcased her flamboyant personality perfectly.

Shutting my car off, I turned to Antoinette Chloe. "Ready for some snowbank climbing?"

"Ready."

We sank in past our thighs. Now the trick was getting our legs to take the next step.

"On the count of three, grunt!" I ordered. "One. Two. Three! Grunt!"

"Ugh!" we said together.

ACB's right flip-flop got stuck in the snow. Like I hadn't seen that coming from a mile away. Now she had one bare foot, at about eight degrees below zero. I reached my hand into the hole she'd vacated and pulled out her flip-flop.

"Don't lecture me about boots, Trixie," she warned.

"I won't. I've given up on you." I sighed.

Finally, after some stunning acrobatics, we were on level snow and able to slog through it to the front door.

ACB rang the doorbell. Peter McCall didn't answer. Then she pounded on the door. Still nothing.

"Do you have your key, Antoinette Chloe?"

"Yup." She was already inserting the key into the lock. The door opened, and we both yelled his name.

Nothing.

I pulled off my boots and ACB walked out of her flip-flops. I stopped myself from looking at her feet, not wanting to see blocks of blue ice, size eleven.

"Where could he have gone?" I wondered. "He doesn't have a car. And even if he'd rented one, there aren't any car tracks in the driveway."

"Maybe he's asleep." ACB herded me to the stairs going to the second level. "I have to go to my bedroom closet to get some things. Come with me?"

"Okay." It crossed my mind that ACB didn't want to happen upon a sleeping Peter McCall alone. "Where did you put him?"

"In my guest room. Where else?" she said.

"Of course."

As we got closer, I could hear a masculine voice.

"I hear him," ACB said. "He's on the phone."

"Do you still have a *real* phone?" I asked.

"No. I canceled it. No sense having a landline here at the house when I have a cell phone."

"Peter must have bought another cell phone, since his was found in the snowbank by Priscilla's frozen body, according to Jill. I'm sure that it's in evidence down at the sheriff's department."

"Should be."

As we passed, I heard bits of a heated conversation: "Priscilla's will," "my share," "what's next?" and "no arrest has been made yet."

ACB sneezed, and Peter's conversation stopped abruptly and the door to ACB's guest room flew open.

"What the hell? Who's here?" Peter McCall stood in front of us, blocking our way, his cell phone glued to an ear. He was wearing nothing but a floral towel and a scowl on his face.

"We both yelled your name so we wouldn't surprise you, but you didn't answer," ACB said. "I came to pick up a few things I need."

"I'll call you back. Don't go away. Stay right there," he hissed into the cell phone. Then he snapped it shut.

"I'm very sorry for being so abrupt," he said, suddenly remembering his charming manners. "I apologize, ladies. Let me just go put some clothes on."

"Maybe we can enjoy a cup of tea together," I suggested, feeling about as British as Priscilla. I wasn't a committed tea drinker, but I didn't feel like coffee this late. Besides, it'd be a great opportunity to get some information from him.

"That sounds cool."

I walked past him. Taking a quick peek into his

room, I saw beer cans on his nightstand and an open twelve-pack. It seemed like Peter McCall was enjoying a secret stash of Bud Light.

Not that it mattered to me. I just thought it was interesting that suddenly he was switching to tea for our sake. Actually, I could go for a can of Bud Light.

"Oh, Peter, I almost forgot," I said. "I brought you a meatball sandwich and some dessert, but it's in my car. If you are interested, you'll have to get it. I needed all my appendages for balance or I would have brought it with me. The walk to the front door was an Olympic event."

"Which reminds me, Peter," ACB said. "I'll get Hiram Glazer from Residential Plowing and Lawn Service to keep the driveway plowed for you. I should have thought of it before."

Now would have been the perfect time for Peter to volunteer to keep the driveway shoveled, had he been well mannered, but he just nodded. I hoped Antoinette Chloe was charging him for staying at her house, but she was so kindhearted I knew she'd never take any money from him.

Which reminded me . . . With Priscilla gone and her estate unsettled as of yet, how was Peter going to earn a living? For that matter, how was Jill Marley going to earn a living?

I decided to fish. "Peter, I hate to sound . . . uh . . . nosy, but with Priscilla gone . . . well, do you need some money to live on? I could loan you some money for food and essentials."

He hesitated just a bit, clearly thinking about it. Yeah, he was broke.

"Let me get dressed, and we'll talk," he said.

"Certainly," I said. I had actually forgotten that he was half naked. Peter wasn't exactly eye candy.

It'd be much more interesting to see Ty Brisco wearing nothing but a towel. . . .

"I see you got a new cell phone, Peter. Did you get it at the Spend A Buck in town?"

"Yeah." That was all he said before pivoting on his bare feet and going back into ACB's guest room. The door slammed shut behind him.

That was rude, but he obviously didn't like the fact that we'd interrupted him. Or maybe he was just uncomfortable lying. I happened to know for a fact that the Spend A Buck didn't carry cell phones. In fact, if you wanted a cell phone, you had to drive to Syracuse, Oswego, or Watertown to get one.

He could have bought one online, but he definitely couldn't have received it this quickly, and he hadn't had a shipping address until ACB had offered him her guest room.

So where had Peter gotten a cell phone? And it wasn't a newish smartphone like the one I'd seen him using before. It was the old gray clam type.

"Let's all meet downstairs," ACB shouted to his closed door. "I won't be long."

In her bedroom, I sat on the edge of ACB's burgundy-and-purple-brocade, gold-tasseled-to-the-max fainting couch. I had a hunch. Since Peter's cell phone was taken into evidence and there weren't any cell phone stores in Sandy Harbor, I'd bet that Peter McCall was using Priscilla's cell phone.

But how had he gotten her phone?

Maybe from her purse or her coat pocket? Or Priscilla's motor home? Or maybe Jill Marley let him borrow it while his was in evidence. Or maybe Priscilla had asked him to hold it—like she'd ask me to hold her red scarf—and Peter had forgotten to give it back to her.

The possibilities were endless.

I wondered if Ty Brisco and his gang of deputies knew Peter had her cell, if it even was her phone.

Maybe Ty had released Priscilla's phone. Maybe he didn't think of looking for it at all.

No. That couldn't be. Ty was good at his job. In fact, he probably already had the list of numbers stored in Priscilla's phone. That would contain a treasure trove of people she knew—one of which might be the person who killed her.

Since Ty would never share that kind of information with me, I wanted to check out the phone Peter was using!

ACB was humming some tune and piling up muu-muus and matching flip-flops on her bed as if she were going to Hawaii for two years.

Thank goodness there were a good dozen closets in the Big House along with clothes racks in the attic. ACB would need them all.

"Antoinette Chloe, do you know if Ty released the contents of Priscilla's personal property? You know, like her cell phone and her purse and whatnot?"

"Gee, I don't have a clue. You'll have to ask him—not that he'd tell you. But what are you getting at?"

"Priscilla's cell phone. I think that's the phone Peter is using right now."

She shrugged. "So?"

"So, there'd be a lot of information stored in it. Right?"

ACB let out a long whistle. "I see. So, like, let's get it."

"Just what I was thinking. But how?"

"Leave it to me," she said.

"Do you have a plan?" I hoped.

She smiled innocently. "Of course not."

Hmm. This wasn't going to be good. I swallowed hard, glad I was already seated on the fainting couch. I didn't have far to go.

Just in case, I'd come up with a plan, too. Basically, one of us had to steal the phone from Peter.

I took as many muumuus as I could carry as ACB was stuffing flip-flops into suitcases.

"I'll put the water on for tea," I said.

After draping the muumuus over a chair, I went to the kitchen, filled up an orange teapot, put it on the stove, and cranked up the temperature.

I set the table with cups and saucers, milk from the

fridge, sugar, and tablespoons. If only I'd thought to bring an assortment of hand pies.

No. I had to kick the hand pie habit.

After a while Peter McCall and Antoinette Chloe came down the stairs. Peter was loaded with luggage and some of the muumuus.

ACB was chatting up a storm. I noticed that Peter had a death grip on his cell phone.

"Antoinette Chloe, where is your tea?"

"I have an assortment in a tea box. It's in the cabinet on the top right side."

Peter took a seat and put his cell phone down in front of him. I got the tea box out, put it on the table, and poured hot water into everyone's cup. ACB scoured her pantry, and after much noise and rearranging, pulled out a package of Oreos.

"Found 'em!" She pulled opened the cellophane with the tab and placed the cookies in the middle of the table. "Help yourself."

Peter reached for the Oreos and lifted a perfect row with his thumb and index finger, as if they were a stack of poker chips.

I admired his skill.

"So, Peter, have you heard from Jill Marley? How is she doing?" I asked. It was time to get some information.

He shrugged. "Beats me. We don't really talk."

"I noticed that you guys don't seem to get along. What happened?" I asked casually.

"I think she was jealous of my relationship with Priscilla."

I stirred sugar into my tea. "But Priscilla seemed to depend on her a lot. How long was she working as Priscilla's assistant?"

"Twelve years, I think."

"I was kind of surprised that you didn't want to stay in Priscilla's motor home, too," I pressed on.

"I did, but the charming Jill beat me to it. Which is a shame. This . . . uh . . . place is better suited for a woman," he said. "You know, because of how it's decorated."

At least he was being diplomatic about how he described ACB's avant-garde, clutter-is-me house decor. There wasn't a bare spot on any wall. If it wasn't heavy with pictures or paintings, there were swags of silk flowers and faux ivy trailing over hill and dale. The furniture was early funeral parlor—filled with velvets, brocades, tassels, and pom-poms. Every botanical flower was represented either in the wallpaper or on the curtains and furniture.

It was Antoinette Chloe, through and through.

Like a nervous twitch, Peter picked up his gray clam cell phone and opened and closed it. *Snap. Snap. Snap. Snap.* I almost prayed that he would get a phone call just so he'd stop doing that.

"Peter, why don't you go out in my car and get those takeout bags that are in the backseat? We'll heat up that sandwich for you. And you'll just love the fruit hand pie. It's peach." I needed to send him outside for my plan to work.

He didn't blink and didn't move.

"My car is unlocked, and we already made a path for you. It'll be a quick trip," I said. "Right, Antoinette Chloe?"

"Oh, yes. And Trixie's meatball subs are to die for. She makes the best sauce in the county."

"I don't think so," he said. "I'm fine with the Oreos."

Say what? No one in their right mind turns down one of my famous meatball subs.

"Then be a dear and get the sandwich for me. I'll eat it," ACB said. "I'm famished."

"But you'll both be leaving in a while, won't you? You can eat it at Trixie's," he said. "No sense in me getting cold, too. I just got out of the shower, and my hair is still wet."

Spare me. He was as much of a diva as Priscilla!

Antoinette drummed her fingers on the table. I could tell she was changing channels in her mind, contemplating what she was going to do.

Her next move was to reach for the bag of cookies in the middle of the table as she was drinking her tea. She slid the bag across the table, and in one slick move, Peter's cell phone came with it and both dropped to the floor.

Antoinette Chloe bent over to pick everything up from the floor. She plopped the cookies and his cell phone back onto the table.

Huh? Why didn't she take it? Well, actually, on second thought, she probably couldn't. Given the way Peter was attached to the phone, he most likely would've asked for it back immediately.

ACB gave me a quick wink. I guess she wanted to leave now.

Peter moved the phone toward him.

Oh well. Maybe I could think up a plan. I could ask Peter to borrow it, and perhaps I could quickly study the contact list and phone numbers.

Antoinette Chloe got up and pushed in her chair. "Well, Trixie, I changed my mind about our tea. I think we should get going before the snow starts falling again. I heard that we are supposed to get another foot of snow tonight. We'd better hit the road."

So much for our tea party and getting more information.

I was getting cranky and anxious to take back my house, my parking lot without a motor home, my freedom, and my good name.

So, what should I do next?

Chapter 9

"Peter, could you give us a hand with Antoinette Chloe's stuff?"

I thought I'd ask, but I didn't hold out much hope that he'd help us. The man was a slug.

"Sorry. My hair is still wet."

He ran a hand through his thick, wavy hair. Looked like it was as dry as a bone to me. "I'll stand on the front porch and hand you the items from there."

What a man!

"By the way, do you know how long I have to stay here in Hicksville?" he said as we stood.

ACB furrowed her brows. "Hicksville?"

"Yeah. Podunk. Cabbage Patch."

"You must have forgotten the name of our delightful village. It's called Sandy Harbor," I said slowly and clearly. "And we would have no idea how long you have to stay here. Only the sheriff's department can tell you that."

"I thought that you might know," he said, looking at me.

"Why would I know? I was told not to leave town, too."

"I hear that you and Sheriff Ty Brisco are a couple."

My mouth went dry. "What? I . . . No. We aren't a couple."

"Sorry. My mistake." His lizard-lipped grin told me he wasn't sorry at all. He was enjoying making me squirm.

And squirm I did.

"Well, the sooner I get out of here, the better. I need to sell Cilla's company. I need to settle her estate," Peter said. "She appointed me executor. There's a million things I have to handle."

"Isn't Jill handling all of that? She's Priscilla's assistant, after all," I said.

"She'd better *not* be handling Cilla's estate! Cilla designated her lawyers to do that and me! I'm her sole heir and executor, too. Priscilla told me that herself a while back," Peter said. "Plus, I have debts to pay."

Interesting, I thought as I stepped into my boots and shrugged into my coat. ACB stepped into her flip-flops. She had her coat draped over her arm.

"Antoinette Chloe! Put that coat on or I'm not going anywhere with you. I hate to have to be the one to tell you this, but this isn't Hawaii. You're my friend, and I worry about you."

"I've never had a friend who worried about me. Sal and Nick worried about me, but I'm not counting husbands who tried to kill me or boyfriends who are deceased. You're my best friend, Trixie."

She gathered me into a big hug. "Aww, Antoinette Chloe, you are my—"

Peter sighed loudly, opened his arms, and walked toward us. He was ushering us out the door. "Ladies, can we adjourn the girlfriend talk? I have several important calls to make regarding Priscilla's business."

"What kind of calls, Peter?" ACB asked.

"Obviously, I have to settle her estate."

"Are you going to try to straighten out the cookbook mess?" I asked.

"I could care less about that disaster. I told Jill that she needs to handle it with the least possible disruption. She was Priscilla's assistant, not me. I'm just going to take care of selling everything off as fast as I can and for the most money possible."

"I'm sure Jill must have loved you giving her instructions—instead of Priscilla, I mean." I hoped that would encourage Peter to keep talking.

"Jill knows better than to cross me."

Sheesh. That sounded creepy.

Before I could ask him what he meant, ACB interrupted by banging him in the shin with a suitcase.

"Yeow!" he yelled, rubbing his leg.

"Oh, Peter, I am so sorry."

As Peter was whining and ACB was apologizing, I was itching to talk to Jill about Peter's claim that he was Priscilla's executor. Being her executor didn't mean that he was necessarily the beneficiary, but it would mean that he'd get at least ten percent of the money for his trouble.

No wonder he wanted the most possible money for Priscilla's estate. Well, I'd get my chance to ask Jill about it when we went grocery shopping in the morning.

True to his word, Peter stood on the front porch as we shuffled back and forth across the driveway to my frosty car to load all of ACB's stuff.

I started the car and blasted the window defroster to let the car warm up.

On one of the trips, I grabbed the take-out bags from the backseat and handed them to Peter. It was only right.

"Thanks, Trixie. You're the best!"

And you should have helped us, slug-o!

We got settled in my car, and I turned to ACB. "Wish we could have snatched his cell phone."

She held up the gray clam. "Got it!"

"What? How?"

"I made a switch when I dropped everything on the floor. Peter has my ex-husband's old cell phone now. I realized they looked the same. Fortunately, it's not charged, so Peter will think he needs to charge his phone, and by the time he realizes that he has the wrong one, we'll get everything we need from Priscilla's phone. Right?"

"Antoinette Chloe, you are totally and undeniably brilliant!"

"I know."

"Let's get back to the Big House and see what we can find on it."

"The sooner we can solve this case, the sooner I can move back home and the sooner your name will be cleared."

"Sooner is good," I agreed. "But I do enjoy your company."

She held up the phone. "Right back atcha."

We rode together in silence for a while. "Trixie, what are you hoping to find on the cell phone?"

"I don't know. Maybe see what calls Priscilla made before she died. Who is on her contacts list. I want to see if there is a pattern. And I might as well check out the calls Peter made in the last twenty-four hours."

"Okay. I'll make some tea for us," she said. "We never really got to enjoy our tea party at my house."

I drove down the narrow streets of downtown Sandy Harbor, made even narrower by the snowbanks on both sides of the road.

"No tea, not unless you put a shot of something stronger into it," I said, thinking how glad I was that Linda Blessler was covering for me for a while.

Then, of course, the Polish-Catholic guilt that had been my constant companion for thirtysomething years took its position over my head like a storm cloud about to rain on my parade.

"I feel guilty letting Linda work for me when I'm supposed to be sleeping," I said, hoping that ACB would tell me to knock it off.

"Oh, don't worry about it, Trixie. Linda wants the extra money. She's lusting over a red Mini Cooper she saw for sale in Barney Pardo's roving lot. She has to hurry before the lot—and Barney—roves again and she can't find him."

Barney's used-car lot was always roving because no sooner did he set up business than someone shut him down. Barney didn't believe in paying taxes for property or staying in one place for any length of time. He said that it was the gypsy in his soul. So once you found Barney and a car you liked, you had to act fast or risk losing out.

"Okay, then. That makes me feel better."

As I turned down Route 3 and got closer to the Silver Bullet, I noticed a lot of cars in my nonroving, snow-plowed lot. I could see how fast the snow was falling by looking up at the tall lights positioned around the lot.

"Looks like another blizzard is on the way," Antoinette Chloe mused, taking the words out of my mouth.

"Check out all the customers at the diner. Must be all the media still churning up stories about Priscilla's death."

"Or . . . maybe something hit the fan."

I'd just pulled into the driveway when I saw Ty Brisco walking toward me. He was wearing his uniform jacket, gloves, and hat, and by the glow of my headlights, he looked madder than a bear.

"Uh-oh. Looks like we've been caught," ACB said. "Do we have to tell him where we've been?"

"I think we can just tell him that you needed to pick up some things from your house. Maybe he won't remember that Peter McCall is crashing there," I hoped.

Yeah, right.

Holding my breath, I got out of the car, trying my best not to look guilty.

"Good evening, Antoinette Chloe . . . Trixie."

"Hello, Ty." We both sang it in unison, like schoolgirls caught hiking up their skirts by Sister Mary Mary.

"Where've you been? What have you been doin'?" he asked in a singsong tone, imitating us.

"Antoinette Chloe needed some things from her house, so we took a quick ride," I said.

"Oh, yeah?"

"Yeah," I replied. "And since you're here, you can help us lug it all inside."

"Of course I'll help," he said, opening the back door and pulling out muumuus on hangers. "And since you haven't been here, you probably haven't heard the news."

"What news?" ACB asked. "Tell us!"

He smiled. "Jill Marley walked into the Silver Bullet and asked for a press conference. She issued a statement that the cookbook was indeed copied almost verbatim and that Priscilla Finch-Smythe shouldn't have done such a thing. She said that Priscilla was under a lot of pressure from her network and her publisher to do another cookbook, and she never thought anyone would find out that she used recipes from a little-known church cookbook."

He closed the door to my backseat. Looking like a sales rack from Muumuus 'R' Us, he began walking up the sidewalk to the Big House.

Antoinette took the handle of one of her suitcases and began rolling it behind Ty.

"Peter McCall said that he instructed Jill to handle the cookbook fiasco, and she did," ACB mumbled.

"What?" Ty turned toward ACB. "You talked to Peter McCall?"

"Oh . . . oops . . . ha . . . ha . . . ha . . . um . . . uh . . . um . . ." That was my friend, quick on her frozen toes.

"What else did Jill say at the press conference, Ty?" I said, trying to change the subject. "Don't keep us in suspense!" Ty was purposely dragging out the punch line.

He shrugged. "Jill said that Priscilla's estate will give all future profits to the Church of the Covenant of Saint Dismas."

"That's a good compromise," ACB said as she dragged her suitcase down my sidewalk.

I dragged the other one. "Although that'd be money that Peter McCall won't see if he's the heir, like he claims."

"Trixie Matkowski!" Ty snapped. "You'd better not

be interfering in another one of my cases or I will lock you up right now."

My mouth suddenly went dry and the snow was looking nice and cool under the glow of the moon . . . all except for the yellow areas Blondie had visited.

"Why, Deputy Brisco, what on earth makes you think that I'd ever interfere in one of your cases?" I sang the words. In fact, we all were singing tonight. "And by the way, if it weren't for me, you'd have a backlog of unsolved cases!"

He knew exactly how to press my buttons.

Oh, what the hell? I made a snowball and let it fly. It hit him right in the back of his hard head.

I don't really run, and it's basically impossible to run on an icy sidewalk anyway. So I did the next-best thing. I hid behind Antoinette Chloe as Ty formed his own snowball.

"This has your name on it, Trixie," he said.

"Don't stand behind me! Take it like a woman," ACB said.

I was being a chicken. I peeked out behind ACB, moving just as Ty whizzed the snowball at me. It hit me in the thigh—a heavily padded area—but it still stung.

"Sheesh, cowboy. Did you pitch for the Houston Astros?"

"They recruited me, but I joined the force instead. I pitched for the Police Benevolent League."

"Unfair advantage!"

He grinned. "Do you want to go again?"

"Children, time-out!" ACB shouted. "I'm getting cold out here."

"Oh, all right. It's a time-out, Ty, but I reserve the right to get you back."

"Anytime you're ready. I'll be waiting."

We trudged up the sidewalk with ACB's suitcases and muumuus, careful not to fall. Ty, the gentleman that he was, helped us up the stairs even while loaded down with muumuus.

When we were all inside the front porch, I scooped up a coffee can full of ice melt from the handy bag in the corner and shook it down the stairs. By the time Ty left, the stairs would be in better shape.

Blondie greeted us by twirling around our legs. I knelt down and petted her. She had been alone too long today. I should have taken her with us to ACB's.

I opened the door, and she hurried outside to do her business.

"Coffee or tea, Ty?" I asked as we deposited Antoinette Cloe's stuff near the stairs.

"Coffee, if it's not too much trouble."

"Not at all," I said. "How about you, Antoinette Chloe?"

"Coffee. I'm done being British for a while."

Ty raised an eyebrow. "I want to hear more about your conversation with Peter McCall."

"There's not much to tell other than there's no love lost between Peter and Jill," I said. "Jill thinks that Peter is after Priscilla's money, and Peter thinks that Jill was taking advantage of Priscilla's trust."

"I know that already."

"And Peter is a lazy sloth," ACB added.

"But that doesn't make him a murderer," Ty said.

"Probably not," I said regretfully. "But it doesn't look like he's mourning for Priscilla at all. In fact, it seems like he wants her estate settled as quickly as possible. He's very eager to get out of town—or 'Podunk,' he called it. 'Cabbage Patch.'"

He raised a perfect black eyebrow.

"Yeah, I know. I don't like anyone trashing my adopted town," I said. "Antoinette Chloe, while I'm thinking of it, will you come into the front room and try on a pair of boots I have for you?"

"But, Trixie . . ."

She was going to fight me about boots, but this wasn't really about boots. It was about getting the gray clam cell phone from her.

But she picked up on my clandestine wink.

"Oh, okay. If it stops you from nagging me, I'll try on the darn boots."

"Ty, we'll be right back. When the coffee stops chugging, help yourself."

We hurried to the front room and talked about boots.

"Here you go, Antoinette Chloe. If you like them and if they fit you, they're yours."

She got the phone from somewhere in her cleavage and passed it to me. I pointed to the stairs, where I planned to get a piece of paper and copy as many recent contacts as I could.

"Would you excuse me? I have to make a trip to the ladies' room. Ty, will you let Blondie back in?" I shouted in the direction of the kitchen.

I took the stairs two at a time. By the time I got to the landing, I couldn't inhale enough oxygen. No more hand pies! I got a pen and a piece of paper from my nightstand and started pushing buttons and writing.

The more recent phone calls in the phone's memory were ones Peter had made and were mostly to the same number—and the same number, it seem, had called him multiple times as well. The number corresponded to someone named Stan Booki. Peter had also called Jill Marley a couple of times and someone by the name of Jake Orlando, who had a New York City area code.

Hold on! I knew that name. It was a last name on the package that had been sent to Priscilla in care of me. I remembered the name of the law firm because Orlando was one of my favorite places in Florida: the home of Mr. Mickey Mouse.

Orlando, Biltmore, Orlando and Fischer, Esq.

I copied everything down furiously. Luckily, there weren't that many contacts and the same numbers were called again and again, not only by Peter, it seemed, but by Priscilla, too.

Finally I had to quit before too much time went by and Ty started to wonder where I'd gone off to. I pocketed the phone and went back downstairs.

Ty and ACB were sipping coffee. Antoinette Chloe found some shortbread cookies that Sarah Stolfus had made for me to try to see if I'd like to sell them at the diner.

Of course I would!

The two of them were making small talk and Ty was absentmindedly scratching Blondie's chin. She was sitting in front of him and gazing up at him adoringly, as most women did.

Sheesh, Blondie.

I winked again at ACB to clue her in that my mission was accomplished.

Ty pulled out his phone and punched in some numbers. "I don't mean to be rude, but I've been calling this number periodically, to see if anyone answers it."

His finger paused and hovered above the glass. I held my breath and broke out into a sweat. This wasn't good!

"Huh?" ACB asked eloquently.

"I've been trying to locate Priscilla's cell phone. Neither Jill nor Peter could find it. I've been calling in the hope that someone found it and will answer. We've been trying to locate it via GPS, but the phone company said that it's too old. So I just keep calling it."

I hurried to my freezer, pulled the phone out of my pocket, discreetly slipped it in, and shut the door.

Why hadn't I left the darn thing in my dresser drawer? Why hadn't I figured out how to shut off the ringer?

Ty's finger continued punching the buttons on his

cell, and Priscilla's phone rang in my freezer. It was faint, but we all could hear it.

ACB and I exchanged glances. We were dead women walking!

Ty's eyes grew as wide as one of the old rodeo belt buckles he sports when he wears jeans.

He stood and followed the ringing right to my freezer.

Opening the door, he found the clam, right where I'd put it—sitting on a carton of marshmallow chocolate walnut ice cream.

"Are you kidding me?" Ty said, pulling it out.

"We were *going* to give it to you," I said.

"When? When it was frozen and wouldn't work?" he shouted. "You two are more dangerous than I could have imagined. I hope to heaven that you haven't tampered with evidence."

"Of course not!" I said, getting mad and realizing that I had no good reason to get mad.

"I won't ask how you got it. I don't want to know," Ty said.

"Peter McCall had it," ACB blurted. "He was using it. It fell on the floor of my kitchen with some Oreos. When I picked up everything, I got that phone mixed up with Sal's phone. They are identical."

ACB wasn't a great liar, but I was impressed. Well, it wasn't a lie. It was mostly the truth.

"Peter lied to me, and I don't like people who lie to me," Ty said, pressing in numbers on the clam's buttons. "Looks like he started making calls about an hour after Priscilla died and has been doing so ever since then. At about two in the afternoon when we searched Priscilla's motor home, about two hours after she died, both Peter and Priscilla denied that they knew where her phone was."

"And his own cell was found at the scene," I pointed out.

"He claimed that he had lost it and doesn't know how it turned up there. He insisted that it was planted in the snowbank."

"Whenever I saw him, he always had a phone in his ear," ACB said. "And if he was sitting, he always put it down in front of him or to the side. Someone could have easily picked it up and planted it at the scene to cast suspicion on him. As a matter of fact, he was looking for it at the time of Priscilla's book signing. I remember that he had a phone in front of him on the table as the church ladies went through the line. One of them could have easily picked it up, strangled Priscilla, and then planted the phone."

"Or Peter McCall could be the murderer," I pointed out. I refilled our mugs with coffee.

Ty didn't move a muscle or say a word. ACB raised her royal-blue eyebrows.

"Maybe we can help you investigate the contacts," I volunteered.

"Forget it, Trixie. This is a matter for your friendly local sheriff's department."

"It's not been that friendly lately," I said.

"Well, at least it's not putting you both in jail for interfering with a pending criminal investigation." He took another sip of coffee. "At least not yet."

Wow. I've never seen him so mad.

Blondie flipped over on her back to have her tummy rubbed.

Traitor!

He scratched her tummy and behind her ears, pulled out a couple of dog biscuits from his jacket pocket, and made her sit for them.

I had to smile. Blondie just adored him, and we both adored Blondie. I had primary custody of her because Ty knew how much it meant to me to have her in my life. I'd never had a pet before we found Blondie half frozen by the Dumpster behind the restaurant.

Besides, it was kind of lonely here in the Big House by myself.

I had to remember that feeling when I had a houseful of guests I didn't want to entertain.

Ty took a gulp of coffee. "Is there anything else I should know about Peter McCall?"

"I believe we told you everything," I said. "But he really thinks he's going to inherit Priscilla's estate and all the money that goes along with it. That's a great motive for killing her."

"There's nothing else that I can remember," ACB said.

"Tell me more about Sal's phone," Ty ordered.

"The battery's dead, but I suppose he'll try to charge

it. He could always dial Sal's old gambling contacts."
ACB laughed.

Ty's lips moved into a brief smile. Anyone else would
have missed it, but for some reason I look at his lips—a
lot.

Then I remembered one of the names on the clam.
Stan Booki. Wait. Was it supposed to stand for Stan the
Bookie? "Uh . . . Ty . . . did you happen to find out if Pe-
ter McCall has a gambling problem?"

"Why do you ask that?"

"Um . . . just wondering. I thought it would explain
why he needs Priscilla's estate settled fast. Doesn't that
make sense?"

He stood and drained his coffee cup. "I gotta go."
He squatted down and gave Blondie several pats on
the head and some back scratches.

"But you didn't answer me," I pushed.

He shook his head. "You know I can't talk about an
ongoing investigation, Trixie. I'm bound by law."

That was what he usually said, and I really understood that. I didn't like it, but I understood. After all, I
wasn't law enforcement. I was a civilian. And as he recently reminded me, I don't have a criminal investigation degree either.

And ACB wasn't law enforcement. However, it was
due to her bait-and-switch skills that Ty was walking
away with Priscilla's phone.

ACB, Blondie, and I walked Ty to the door.

"Thanks for the coffee," he said. "I'm sorry that I got

so mad with both of you, but I need you to leave things to me." He took a deep breath. "Now, get some sleep, Trixie. Linda Blessler is doing a great job holding down the fort at the Silver Bullet, so don't worry. I had dinner there tonight. Her macaroni and cheese dish is fabulous."

I raised an eyebrow.

"It's not as good as yours, of course—or yours, Antoinette Chloe—but it's still fabulous."

I wondered what Linda's secret was. I'd make a point to stop in at the diner again and see her. First to thank her for subbing for me, and then I could ask her about her mac and cheese recipe.

I'm always up for new recipes for the Silver Bullet's menu!

I like to keep the menu fresh and exciting with new dishes.

And although I wanted to take Ty's advice and get some sleep, there were some things I needed to do.

First I was going to talk to Antoinette Chloe about what I'd found on Peter's phone. And then maybe I'd call Stan the Bookie and place a bet myself.

I'd bet that Peter McCall was in hock to Stan up to the roots of his wavy black hair.

Chapter 10

*W*hen Antoinette Chloe came back downstairs from another change of flip-flops, she poured herself an iced tea and sat down at the kitchen table. I was unloading the dishwasher.

"I'm convinced that Peter McCall has a gambling problem. There were a lot of calls on Priscilla's phone to a guy called Stan. Stan the Bookie."

ACB's eyes went as wide as platters. "You're kidding? Stan the Bookie? I haven't heard that name in a long time."

"You know him?"

"Unless there's another Stan, he was my husband Sal's bookie. I think he lives in Salmon Run Corners, about twenty miles from here. They did a lot of business together."

"Small world," I said. "Let's arrange a meeting with Stan."

"Yeah, sure."

"I think I'll place a bet." I got a spiral notebook and a pen from a drawer. "Do you know how to do it?"

ACB shrugged. "I haven't placed a bet in a long time. I always left that kind of thing to Sal. We can figure it out. Do you have his number?"

"I do. I copied it down from Peter's phone." I picked up my cell and my notes.

"Punch it in."

"Wait. What do I say?"

"Say you want to place a bet. Aqueduct. One hundred on number six in the ninth."

"Then what? I give him my credit-card number?"

She laughed. "No. It's an honor system."

"Honor system?" I made an unladylike noise. "I think I just figured out how Peter got in trouble gambling. He kept placing bets and then never paid up."

"Yup. And now apparently Stan probably wants to break his kneecaps."

My thumbs got to work calling Stan.

"Speak to me."

"Uh . . . um . . . Aqueduct number six in the ninth. One hundred."

"Who is this?"

"Uh . . . Trixie."

"Do I know you?"

"No. But you know a friend of mine, Peter McCall."

"He's cut off. If you see him, tell him that I hope he enjoys his . . ."

"Kneecaps?"

"Yeah."

"Stan, you seem like an okay guy. Can I just ask you a question?"

"Depends. Try me."

"How much does Peter McCall owe you?"

"Why? You going to cover it for him?"

"Maybe. How much?"

"Half a mil."

"Uh . . . actually, I don't think that's a possibility."

"Yeah, I didn't think so."

"How can I find you to pay you for my bet?"

"Where do you live, Trixie?"

"Sandy Harbor."

"I know the place. Meet me at the Silver Bullet Diner tomorrow at eight in the morning. Know it?"

"I've heard of it."

"The food is good there."

"How will I know you, Stan?"

"You'll know me."

Click.

I shut off my cell. "Antoinette Chloe, I think I just placed my first bet with a bookie. We're having breakfast with him tomorrow. Eight o'clock at the Silver Bullet."

She laughed. "How did that happen?"

"Beats me."

Next I called Ray Meyerson, who was busing tables and washing dishes over at my diner.

"Ray, after you're done with the dishes, would you mind coming over to the Big House? There are a couple of people I'd like you to look up for me, if you don't mind."

"I have my laptop with me, Trixie. I'll be right there."

"That'd be perfect."

He knocked on the door about fifteen minutes later. He knew the drill. Kitchen table, open laptop, boot it up, and help out Trixie, the computer klutz.

After a while Ray said, "Okay. I'm ready to go. Shoot."

"Now, remember: Anything you do for me is private and should be kept under wraps. Okay?"

"Of course. You don't have to keep telling me that, boss."

"Okay. Sorry for nagging." I put a bottle of lime-green Gatorade in front of him along with a large glass of ice. "Will you look up Kip O'Malley for me?" I asked. "He works in food service over at the Watertown Jail."

Ray typed and pecked on his keys as ACB and I sipped our coffees and talked.

"Kip is also known as Christopher," Ray said. "He has a criminal record. He's been arrested three times for forgery, assault, and failure to pay child support. It's a recent arrest for child support, and he was arrested just a couple of months ago. He's in arrears thirteen thousand dollars."

"Sheesh!" I said.

ACB put her cup down. "How can he work in the jail if he has an arrest record? I thought that was a civil-service job, and I happen to know that you can't have a criminal record if you're hired for a civil-service job. My sister's older kid—she named the poor thing Clarence after her husband's rich uncle she hoped to get money from—and then she found out that the guy's real name was William, but he liked the name Clarence for some reason, and—"

"Antoinette Chloe, focus!" I ordered.

"Anyway, poor Clarence was arrested for chaining himself to some historical monument in a park. Apparently he heard the city of Syracuse was going to take it down, and he really loved this Civil War guy on a horse. He was arrested for criminal mischief, criminal trespass, and defacing governmental property due to the chain marks on the guy's sword, and—"

"Antoinette Chloe, is there a point?"

"Well, the point is that the city of Syracuse was just going to restore the guy to his former luster. That's all. Clarence got his wires crossed."

"Is there another point?"

"Well, yeah. He passed the civil service test to be an Account Clerk I and was offered a job at the Onondaga County Comptroller's Office, but they couldn't hire him because one of those crimes was a felony. At least, I think that's the story. I really can't remember the details."

Ray kept typing, and Antoinette Chloe kept drinking more coffee and was getting even more buzzed as the time went by.

Ray looked up. "Kip's position is not a civil-service

position, actually. The jail's food service is contracted out to USA Foods and Catering," Ray said. "But according to their work rules, Kip *cannot have an arrest record to work in any kind of quote state, county, or municipality with a criminal record, unquote. See footnote three.*"

ACB sighed loudly. "If he owes that much in support for his kids, then why did he pay one thousand bucks to enter our little contest? He could have put it on his tab for his kids. What's wrong with him?"

"He probably thought that with the TV appearance, his career would soar and he could get another job before they found out. After all, he took a correspondence cooking class," I said sarcastically.

Ray kept typing. "Ray, can you find a link between Priscilla and Kip?"

Click . . . click . . . click . . .

"Kip took a culinary class with Priscilla Finch-Smythe in New York City—the Academy of Culinary Production."

"So they knew each other," I said. "Interesting."

"Wait a minute," Ray said. "Peter McCall, who I remember from the contest, was in this class also. He happened to mention it to me and the other judges for some reason, like we cared."

"Interesting again," I said. "Maybe he was trying to learn more about what Priscilla did." I leaned over the table to see Ray's screen. "Can you tell how they did in the class? Any grades or comments online?"

"Let me see if I can access their grades," Ray said,

typing away. "Nope. Oh, yes! This is what Priscilla said about Kip: 'This individual should never pick up a cooking utensil ever again.' "

I grinned. "What did she say about Peter?"

" 'Peter McCall is a very promising chef who will soar in the culinary world.' "

"Hmm . . . think she's a little slanted?" I asked.

"Oh, yes. I didn't think he knew a thing about cooking when I spoke with him at the contest," ACB said.

"Okay. Let's recap," I said, feeling like Jessica Fletcher talking to Seth in Cabot Cove. "Kip has a criminal record. He's in the hole for child support. He was in a class that Priscilla taught, and Peter McCall was in the same class. So what does all that mean?"

ACB called for more coffee for us.

I wished I had a pen on me so I could doodle on the notepad as I thought. When I draw daisies, I really think.

"Do you have a pen, Ray?"

He handed me a thin-point permanent pen. Perfect!

Around a circle, I started on the petals of the daisy. "Do you guys think that Peter knew about Kip's record?"

"Maybe Peter found out and told Priscilla at the cook-off, and she threatened to call and turn Kip in," ACB said. "Priscilla was very . . . uh . . . *what's the word?* . . . *condescending* to chefs who weren't top-notch and as pure as the snow falling outside. I can see her dropping a dime to the jail or to the food service. And Kip would probably have lost his job over it."

"That would give Kip a motive to stop Priscilla."

"I agree," ACB said. "But how on earth would we ever find out if Priscilla or Peter was going to snitch? Kip can't make child-support payments if he doesn't have a job, and he didn't win. Now he's probably ruined financially."

I drew the leaves on my daisies. "Somehow we have to get Peter to tell us if Priscilla was going to tell the authorities about Kip's criminal record."

Later, in my kitchen at the Big House, I was making a ham and cheese on rye and a phone was ringing. This time it wasn't muffled like Priscilla's clam cell in the freezer. It was mine, and on the charger where I'd left it.

"Hello?"

"Trixie, it's Linda Blessler," she whispered. "I hate to bother you, but I think you should know something."

Immediately, my heart started racing. "What's that?"

"Jill Marley is here, in the kitchen. She's crying in the diner, and she seems very distraught. The customers are getting a little uncomfortable."

"I'll be right there, Linda. Hang on."

"She also wants to look at your recipe book. She said she was sure you had one and that you wouldn't mind."

"Be right there!"

Throwing on my coat, boots, hat, and mittens, I stomped, slid, and skated my way up my driveway and through the parking lot that led to the Silver Bullet.

Seeing it at night always amazed me. The windows glowed and the light spilled over to the blanket of snow on the lawn and on the snowcapped bushes around the diner. As I got closer, I could see the shadows of people enjoying their meals, and I could hear the din of the diners and the clink of silverware on china.

Remembering what had summoned me here, I prepared to see what I could do for Jill.

I swung open the door and closed it quickly behind me so as not to let out the warm air. I wiped my feet and hurried to the kitchen.

The first person who waved at me was Carlee Churchill, one of the Tri-Gams who'd worked on the tea committee.

"The library is being cleaned up," she said. "And Mayor Tingsley hired a roofing company."

On that note, I smiled and waved to everyone and disappeared into the kitchen.

I found Jill and Linda engaged in a tug-of-war with my recipe binder.

"Jill, what's going on?"

"I want to finish the new cookbook Cilla started. The publishers want me to hurry."

"Why didn't you ask me, Jill? I would have helped you."

"I couldn't find you, Trixie. I tried, but you didn't pick up your phone. My publisher said that I need to get moving on it while there's a lot of publicity about Cilla."

"I see." My face flushed, and not from the heat in the kitchen. "They are going to capitalize on her death."

She shrugged. "It's going to be publicized as Priscilla's last cookbook. The one she was working on at the time of her death. It'll sell like crazy."

If I'd been softening about giving some of my recipes to Jill, I was absolutely going to refuse now. "I won't participate in exploiting Priscilla's death. Forget it."

"It's not as if I can go to the library here and get recipes, can I? The library is underwater. It's not as if I can leave here and go to another library because I can't leave Sandy Harbor. And your Internet here is hit-and-miss. And my printer won't work."

Her face was redder than my tomato plants.

"And Peter has the absolute gall to promise the publisher that it'll be done in a month. Can you imagine that? He's got a lot of nerve, that big overgrown *stepmummy's* boy."

Peter didn't miss an opportunity to trash Jill, and vice versa.

"You two don't get along, huh?" I knew the answer, but I wanted to hear it from her.

"Of course we don't get along. He didn't bother with Priscilla for years. Then he appears from nowhere and suddenly is the son she never had, and she's giving him a lot of money." She shook her head. "I don't want to talk about it."

"Do you know for sure that she was giving him a lot of money?"

"I know for sure. I keep track of her income and expenses for tax purposes. I balanced Priscilla's checkbook because she couldn't handle it."

I see. "Peter seems desperate to have her estate settled. I wonder why he needs the money."

Nudge.

Jill twisted her mouth in a scowl. "Ask the bookies. Ask the loan sharks." She chuckled. "He's borrowed money from just about everyone in North America."

"Why?"

"To support every bookie who handles sports parlays. Peter is a terminal parlay player."

"Say that fast a couple of times."

She laughed. She sure loved bashing Peter.

"Did Priscilla know that Peter played parlays?"

"Yes. And she told him to stop, that she couldn't keep bailing him out. Then he'd stop for a while, but that was only the lull between hot games."

I shook my head. Gambling was a bad vice, but so were a host of others.

"As for my recipes, Jill, the answer is no. Like Juanita suggested, someday I'll do my own cookbook. So you don't have my permission to use them. And, Jill, I have to ask you to leave my kitchen. I can't have anyone but my staff in here. It's diner policy. You understand."

Linda Blessler looked up from her cooking and seemed relieved that our conversation was winding down.

I escorted Jill to the back door of the kitchen. "I'll walk you home."

"I'll be fine by myself. There's probably no crime in this little town."

I looked at her as if snakes were crawling out of her ears. She had the good sense to lower her eyes and look ashamed. "Oh. I forgot about Cilla for a moment."

"And that means that there's a murderer on the loose, so we can never be too safe. I'll escort you to your motor home. I'm on my way back home, too."

I opened the back door, gave Linda a wave, and waited as Jill walked out.

"Linda, call me if you need anything. And thanks for working for me. You'll get that Mini Cooper yet!"

"Take as much time as you need," Linda said. "I mean it."

"Thanks." It was good to know I didn't have to rush back to work so I could concentrate on finding Priscilla's murderer.

Jill and I walked mostly in silence. I decided it was a good time to ask about the package from the lawyers in New York City.

I chose my words carefully, so I wouldn't make her any more skittish than she was already.

"Jill, I was wondering if you ever gave that envelope from the lawyers in New York City to Priscilla."

"Lawyers?"

"I couldn't help but notice the return address. It was from a law firm in New York City."

"Of course I gave it to her," she mumbled.

"Was it important?"

"I'm assuming it was, since Priscilla had it over-nighted to you. She didn't share what it was with me."

"She was adamant that it be given to her as soon as possible. It must have been really important."

She shrugged.

"Where is the package now? Did one of the sheriffs take it?"

"I don't know. I don't know where it went," she mumbled.

She spoke so quietly, I had to ask her to repeat what she'd said.

"Why are you so interested in the package, Trixie?"

"I thought it might have something to do with Priscilla's death. Maybe it was her will or a real-estate sale or something else that might help us figure out why someone would want Priscilla dead so badly."

"Priscilla always received things from lawyers. She had several working for her. I'll keep an eye open for the envelope."

"Thanks, Jill."

We were silent again. Finally we were at her motor home, and I said good-bye.

"See you tomorrow morning after breakfast, Jill."

"Tomorrow?"

"For the grocery-shopping trip with Ty. Remember?"

She grunted. "Oh, yeah. I remember now. A shopping trip with my three guides. Life can't get any better than this."

Boy, she sure was acting strange, but with her job as Priscilla's assistant gone, maybe she was counting on a big score with this last cookbook of Priscilla's.

"Good night, then."

"Good night, Trixie. And I'm sorry that I was so rude about getting your recipes without permission. I was just . . . in a hurry and forgot my manners."

"It's ancient history. Don't worry about it. See you tomorrow."

I let out a deep breath as I walked toward the Big House. Jill was intense, and it seemed that her cheese had slipped off her cracker—at least tonight it had.

I couldn't wait to talk to Antoinette Chloe. That's how desperate I was for normal conversation! Well, ACB conversation anyway.

Antoinette Chloe was waiting for me, coat on. "We have to go back to my house."

"Now? It's eleven at night."

"Megan Hunter called." ACB closed the door behind her and stepped onto the stairs. "Milt got to know Walton DeMassie and Kip O'Malley while they were visiting at their place. They were playing cards in the Hunters' rec room, and then they took off in a van. Apparently Milt shared a couple bottles of Lord Calvert with them, and they got to talking crazy. Megan is pretty sure that the two chefs are headed to my house to shake down Peter McCall. Seems like they have a gripe with him. She doesn't want to call the cops because she doesn't want bad publicity for the contest and any more bad publicity for Sandy Harbor . . . blah . . . blah . . . blah."

"But the contest is over."

"Seems like there's still some animosity brewing over it."

"Why?" I asked, holding my breath.

"Megan blathered something about how they both thought they were going to win for sure. Anyway, I warmed up your car. Let's go!"

The last thing I wanted to do was go back to ACB's house tonight.

I remembered how Ty had told me to stay out of the investigation. Well, I was. I was just going to ACB's house—again. She simply must have forgotten a special pair of flip-flops.

"Ty will have a moose if he finds out we're sneaking out again to investigate," she said. "How about if we tell him I forgot a special pair of flip-flops? It isn't really a lie. I should have packed the sequined black ones, too. But I thought the sequined blue ones would be sufficient."

I laughed. "Great liars think alike, Antoinette Chloe."

"I hate to lie to Ty. He's such a good guy."

"Yeah, I know what you mean. But with any luck, he won't find out."

Soon her house came into view. It was all lit up, and a black van was parked in her driveway. We parked in our same spot on the road, but when we walked in this time, we could walk in the valley of the van's tire tracks.

As we got closer, I could hear shouting and swearing coming from inside. I looked at ACB. "I don't know if we should barge in on that, Antoinette Chloe."

Something thumped, then shattered. Like glass being thrown against the wall.

"What on earth was that?" She threw open the door and stomped in before I could stop her. "What on earth are you men doing to my house and to my things?"

She screamed so loudly, they could hear her at the International Space Station.

I followed her and then moved to her side to present a united front. Her living room was a mess. Some kind of glass vase was lying in pieces on the floor. Lamps were upset, the rug was rumpled, and three men were wrestling on the floor: Walton DeMassie, Kip O'Malley, and Peter McCall.

"Knock it off!" I yelled when one of the candy dishes on the end table hit the ground and rolled in a circle.

"Fix up my house. Immediately!" ACB screamed.

They all froze as if they were concrete statues. Blood leaked out of Peter McCall's nose, and one of his eyes was already starting to swell shut. The other two men looked fine.

It was two against one. Peter McCall should be grateful we arrived when we did.

"What are you two doing back here?" Peter said.

Not only was blood dripping from his nose; annoyance dripped from every word.

So much for gratitude.

"Apparently we are saving your face from getting beaten to a pulp!" ACB said. "And I'm picking up my pair of black sequined flip-flops."

Antoinette Chloe pulled out a pack of tissues from her cleavage—I call it her cleavage purse—and tossed them at Peter.

"Take a seat immediately, gentlemen. Peter, you sit on the wing chair. You two bullies, sit on the couch," ACB ordered, pointing her fingers at the furniture.

"What's going on here?" I added.

"Are you two cops?" said the one with the bushy mustache, who I remembered was Walton DeMassie, from New York City.

"They're not cops. They were in the contest, Walt. Remember that atrocity with the salsa and kielbasa—"

I felt the heat rush to my face. "Atrocity? My mac and cheese is delicious! I serve it at my diner and everyone gobbles it up and asks for thirds. What do you know, Mr. O'Malley?" I remembered the third-place winner, Kip O'Malley, the guy who cooked in the kitchen at the prison.

"At least I used real cheese. Not that fake stuff like this one did," Walton scoffed, gesturing toward ACB. "She used that fake orange cheese, and it was overloaded with fish. Ugh! Can you imagine?"

"Look, we lost and you won, and we're not cops," I said. "But that's not the point here. Antoinette Chloe here owns this house. The house that you're destroying."

"That son of a pup." Walton pointed at Peter. "That sucker cheated me out of first place."

"He cheated me out of first place, too," Kip said.

"There can only be one first-place winner," I pointed out, not that either of them saw the logic.

"And it was supposed to be me!" Walton said. "Not the chick who worked at the soup kitchen. Appearing on Priscilla's show was going to be my comeback."

"It doesn't matter now. Jean Williams won fair and square."

"That's what you think. She must have just paid Petey-boy over here more than we did!" Kip O'Malley pointed at Peter.

"Paid him? Peter?" I asked. "What do you mean?"

"Ask him yourself!" Walton shouted.

Peter looked at the floor and shifted on the chair. We stood in front of him.

"What do they mean, Peter?" I asked as my stomach sank to my shoes. "Talk!"

"I don't have to tell you two anything," he said. "I already talked to the cowboy cop."

"Oh, yes, you do have to talk, or I'll kick you out of my home," ACB said. "You can sleep in a snowbank for all I care, since there is no place else for you to sleep in little Cabbage Patch—or should I say 'Podunk'?"

Peter looked at ACB. "I—I might have taken some money from them to get Cilla to pick them for first place."

"Cripes," said ACB.

"How much did these two pay you, Peter?" I asked. He didn't answer.

I looked at Walton. "How much?"

"Five thousand," he replied.

"Kip?" I asked.

"Five thousand," Kip said.

"I don't get it." I pinched the bridge of my nose because I'd heard that it would stop a headache. "Why on earth would you pay that kind of money to win a little contest?"

Walton snorted. "Your little contest would have been my gateway back into television. I could have outshone Priscilla, and legions of my fans would remember me and petition to get me back to my own show." He grinned. "At least, that was my plan."

"Kip, what about you? Was five grand worth it?"

"Worth it? Oh, yeah. Then I could kiss the jail good-bye and work around my peers, not criminals who are learning a trade. Mostly they are just stealing and selling food. A win would have legitimized me as a real chef."

"Priscilla didn't pick either one of you."

"That's because Petey never told Priscilla," Kip said. "And she picked Jean Williams."

"So Jean never paid you anything?" I asked Peter. He shook his head. "She refused."

"Then she won fair and square," I said, relieved. Then it hit me. "Peter, how many other contestants paid you?"

He shrugged.

"Tell me, Peter! This was my contest, and my good name is on it!" Okay, it was mine, the town's, Megan's and a zillion Tri-Gams', but I was here, and I was tired and mortified at what they'd done to my friend's house.

Peter shrugged. "About two or three more chefs."

"And you promised all of them they'd win?"

"Yeah, but I never figured that anyone would squeal," Peter snapped. "It's like admitting they'd bribed a judge."

I looked at Antoinette Chloe and she looked at me. Her eyes grew wider than mine.

"I don't get it," she said.

"Must be we don't think like crooks," I replied. Not true. If we got caught by Ty, we were going to lie to him. There had to be some kind of penal law crime that covered that.

"So, Peter, why don't you give these gentlemen their money back?" I asked.

"I can't believe that I'm sitting here and taking this."

He stood to leave, but I whipped out my newly charged phone. I smiled. "Why don't I just call the Sandy Harbor Sheriff's Department and let them sort this all out?"

Peter swore under his breath, but he sat back down.

"Answer the woman, Petey-boy. Where's our money?" Kip said.

He swore again. "It's gone."

ACB raised a black penciled eyebrow. "Ten grand plus more, give or take *a lot more*? All gone?"

"There's no way you can spend all that in Sandy Harbor in four days," I said. "There's nothing here to buy for that kind of money. Not even Barney Pardo's roving car lot has cars for that much money."

"He gambled it away," Walton said. "Or it went to pay the debts he already had."

"My ex-husband had a gambling habit," ACB said. "He's in state prison now. Well, actually, he's not exactly in there for gambling, but he had a gambling problem—and a girlfriend problem."

I nodded to Antoinette Chloe, and she nodded back. Then I decided that her statement deserved a high five.

And a low five.

And a butt bump.

And snapping of fingers.

When we were finished, we turned back to the chefs and Peter.

I scanned the three of them. "How about picking up and cleaning up Antoinette Chloe's house? Then you can each contribute . . . um . . . fifty dollars for the damages." I turned to ACB. "Is that enough?"

"Thirty dollars each should do it," she said.

"Just like I said. I want you each to pay *fifty dollars*." I held out my hand. "I'll collect the money."

"What about our money from Peter?" Kip asked.

"I told you that when Priscilla's estate is settled, I'll pay you back," Peter said through gritted teeth.

"And what makes you think you're going to get money from her estate for sure?" I asked.

He didn't answer.

"Tell her what you told us, Petey-boy," Kip said, making a show of cracking his knuckles.

Petey-boy definitely noticed and heard the knuckles cracking, just like Kip meant him to.

"Cilla told me I was her sole heir and that I was going to be CEO of her company when she passed away."

"So you mean that when Priscilla died, it was all going to be yours?" I asked Peter.

"That's what he told us when we were beating the snot out of him."

"This conversation is over. Let's get out of here, Kip."

"Yeah. Let's go. Let Petey-boy clean up."

They handed over fifty bucks each and scurried out of ACB's house as fast as they could.

I stood in front of Peter, hands on hips. "Being in debt as much as you are because of gambling and you wanting to hurry and settle your *stepmummy's* estate makes you look kind of guilty, doesn't it?"

He stared at his hands.

"What about you answering that question, Peter?" ACB said.

"As I told that cowboy cop, I liked Cilla. I'd never kill her."

"Not even for her estate?"

"Of course not." He stood and straightened out the

rug. Then he stared at me. "I've been in worse straits, and I've always managed to come out smelling like a rose."

"Roses do grow best in manure," ACB mumbled.

"Look, Priscilla was my father's third or fourth wife. Who can keep track? But she was by far the richest. And she was very generous to us both. You see, neither my father nor I liked to work, but we have several vices, and Priscilla didn't mind bailing us out. All we had to do was treat her good. That's about all she wanted, and she showered us with money. It was a mutually beneficial relationship."

Ugh!

I couldn't believe he'd said that. Even though Priscilla Finch-Smythe wasn't my favorite person, she didn't deserve that kind of talk.

That was another reason to hurry this investigation: to get Peter out of my sweet town.

Chapter 11

I couldn't sleep all night. Who can sleep when there's a murder to solve and scenes from yesterday keep playing over and over in his head?

Of course, just as I closed my eyes, I awoke to Antoinette Chloe singing a country-western song—something about a bar, and drinking beer, and dancing the night away to a sad tune.

Seems as though I've heard that one before.

I dragged myself out of bed, stood under a cold shower, and got dressed. As we were drinking coffee and making toast downstairs, I realized that I was kind of nervous to meet Stan the Bookie at the Silver Bullet.

But I didn't have to worry.

Stan the Bookie was sitting in the fifth booth from the front. I knew it was him because he didn't look anything like what I expected him to look like—which was a black-suited, heavy man wearing a fedora with a red carnation in his lapel and a wet cigar stub in his mouth.

Instead Stan wore a royal-blue jogging suit with

black stripes down the sleeves, and he was drinking a large glass of orange juice.

"Stan, I'm Trixie, and this is a friend of mine, Antoinette Chloe—"

"Brownelli," he finished. "How ya doin', Ant'net Chloe?"

"Hi, Stan."

"How's the old man doing in Auburn Pen?"

She shrugged. "Okay, I guess."

"He shouldn't have tried to kill you."

"No kidding, Stan."

"Sit down, ladies. Breakfast is on me," he said.

"Did you place my bet, Stan?" I asked.

"Not yet."

"Then don't do it. I don't really want to bet. I wanted to meet you and ask you a few questions about Peter McCall."

He shrugged. "Go ahead. He's scum in my book."

"He owes you half a mil. Who else does he owe?"

"Too many to count. From what I know, he's cut off from the biggies."

"That's a lot of money," I said, winking at Nancy, who poured ACB and me coffee.

Stan declined. "No coffee for me, miss. I'm not putting any chemicals into my body."

"Are you ready to order?" Nancy asked.

"I'll have the eggs Benedict," I said.

"The lumberjack special for me," ACB said. "With the eggs over light and rye toast."

"Oatmeal with granola and a banana," Stan said.

Nancy flipped over her pad. "Thank you very much. Coming right up."

"What else can you tell us about Peter?" ACB asked.

"He keeps telling everyone that they'll get their money back when his stepmother's estate is settled. She's Priscilla Finch-Smythe, you know."

"I know," I said.

ACB stirred her coffee. "Can you tell us anything else about Peter? Do you know him well?"

"Well enough. Enough to say that he's desperate. Very desperate. And a desperate man will do anything to get out of the bind he's in. My pals want their dough, and Peter had better produce it, and soon."

"Or?" I asked, as Nancy arrived with our orders.

He picked up a spoon. "That's all I have to say on the subject."

Stan kept up a nice chatter throughout our breakfast, and it seemed as if we'd known him forever.

"By the way, why are you so interested in Peter?" he asked as we were finishing up the last bites on our plates.

"Just curious," ACB said. "He's staying in my guest room because he was told not to leave town."

"Ah, I did hear he was a suspect in Priscilla Finch-Smythe's murder."

ACB nodded.

He shook his head. "Poor woman." Standing, he peeled off some bills from a folded wad of money.

"Oh, no, Stan. It's on me. I own the Silver Bullet."

He grinned. "I know." He tossed the bills on the table anyway and left.

I looked at ACB. "Whew! I'm glad that's over."

"He's an interesting man. I wonder if he's single."

Back at the Big House, ACB and I were greeted by Ty beeping the horn of his black monolith of a SUV. Time for grocery shopping, I guessed.

Jill and I and ACB emerged from our dwellings. More snow had fallen—about two more inches—and Max and Clyde hadn't yet worked their way down to Priscilla's motor home or to the Big House.

I hadn't had a chance to make them the pies they liked yet, but I'd given them a winter raise, which they would see in their next paycheck.

If Ty hadn't glued me to ACB, I'd have made a break for it to do some retail-shopping therapy. Or maybe I'd find a quiet corner in one of the several bedrooms of the Big House, and sleep, read, or do one of the several things that I needed to catch up on.

Maybe I could bow out of the grocery-shopping expedition and ask ACB to come clothes shopping with me. We could sneak out while Ty was busy working on the case.

I kept thinking of what Peter said the night before, and I desperately wanted to ask Jill about Priscilla's estate. Jill was Priscilla's assistant, after all, and was on the front line of her business and personal activities, so I needed to talk to her again.

But I didn't know how much I could get out of her with Ty around. If Jill was hiding something or had good information, I was sure she wouldn't talk with Wyatt Earp pushing a grocery cart next to hers.

I was positive that Ty had already officially questioned her. Not that he'd tell me anything, of course, so I'd just have to glean interesting tidbits from Jill myself.

If the grocery trip was a bust, I'd invite Jill over for a nice visit with ACB and me.

Ty was in good spirits as we climbed in. ACB and I immediately took the backseat, careful not to spill our thermal coffee cups, which left the front seat for Jill.

Ty was pouring on the cowboy charm this morning, and Jill just loved it.

"Ladies, it's a pleasure to be around such beauty on this fine morning."

"Why, thank you, Ty," ACB said.

"Yes. Thank you, Ty." Jill's fresh face glowed under her perfect makeup. She licked her fuchsia-stained lips. She was really a perfect ten.

"Giddyap, Ty. You're burning daylight," I said.

"Aww . . . Trixie. Always a ray of sunshine in the morning," he chided.

Did my crankiness show?

I was usually sleeping in the morning due to cooking the graveyard shift. This morning I felt like a vampire. And the sun was giving me a headache.

I took a gulp of coffee. Maybe I just needed more caffeine.

Let Ty live with the always-cheerful, constantly chatting, flip-flop-snapping, perfume cloud of a person, Antoinette Chloe Brown.

The sooner I solved this mystery, the sooner my friend would hit the road and the sooner Jill Marley would remove that forty-foot rock-star motor home from my parking lot.

Then maybe I could stop getting sideways glances from some of the villagers who thought I'd choked Priscilla with her own scarf.

Ty turned onto Route 3. The Gas and Grab was straight ahead about six miles down the road.

It was a small grocery store with a terrific deli counter in the back, run by Adam and Gail Bolton. They had a good variety of cold cuts and salads. In the front were the usual grocery items. Around the perimeter there were clothing, household supplies, feed and grain for every barnyard and domestic animal, knick-knacks and souvenirs with the Sandy Harbor logo, and a post office.

While I ordered from Sunshine Foods, a local wholesale place, for the diner, I loved to support small-business owners for my personal needs as much as possible.

Ty, ACB, and I grabbed royal-blue plastic shopping baskets, whereas Jill pushed a grocery cart, loading it up with cans of veggies, soups, and fruit. She had a couple loaves of artisan breads and rolls, butter, cream cheese, and the like.

"Jill, if you're in the market for local cheese, this

Salmon River Fishermen's Cheese is delicious." I showed her the label on a brick of cheese covered with jumping orange salmon. "It's made right here."

"Okay. I'll take it."

I tossed a brick into her cart. Then I headed straight to the back and had Gail hopping around getting my luncheon meat order ready. "Antoinette Chloe, do you like bologna?"

"Love it. Especially fried with eggs in the morning."

Mmm. That reminded me of my childhood breakfasts at home. Mom would make some cuts in the slices of bologna to get it to lie flat as she was frying it.

"Yes!" I said enthusiastically. "Let's have fried bologna for breakfast tomorrow."

I ordered a lot more deli items and periodically asked ACB if she liked a certain item, since she was staying at the Big House.

"Don't forget that I invited Marylou and Dottie over this afternoon. I can't remember if I invited them for lunch or just coffee and sweets."

"I think you told me lunch." I'd certainly remember if she mentioned sweets, which were my downfall.

Then I was groceried out.

After taking a seat in the mini-café, I poured myself a large cup of pumpkin-spice coffee and waited with my loaded basket until everyone else was done with their shopping.

There had not been a single opportunity so far to ask Jill any of the questions that had been bouncing around in my mind all night. So when she sat at the café with me, I was more than happy to make small talk with her.

"Where are you from, Jill?"

"Prairie, Wisconsin."

"Wow. That's pretty far away from California and Priscilla's TV show. How did you two meet?"

"I was an intern at her station. Before that I worked for a small publishing company that specifically published cookbooks. So, you see, I was the natural choice to become Cilla's assistant." Jill tossed her full, rich chestnut hair with reddish streaks.

Involuntarily, my hand went to my hair, which was enhanced every six to eight weeks to my natural blond by Clairol. No gray for me!

"So you interned for her, and she hired you. That was so perfect. I remember you told me that you don't cook, but did anyone test any of the recipes that went into Priscilla's cookbooks?"

She looked at the items in her cart and moved them around. "Some of them. Uh . . . most of them. Priscilla did."

"Did she test any of the recipes from her *Comforting Comfort Food* cookbook—the one the Church of the Covered Dish ladies accused Priscilla of stealing?"

"Trixie, I don't know why you are asking me these questions."

"Just killing time," I said. "And making small talk." Taking a sip of coffee, I slouched in the white plastic chair, trying to look casual. "But I'm sorry if my questions seem too nosy or have offended you. Really."

She nodded. "Yes, they do bother me."

"Sorry, Jill." I put my hand over hers. "Can I buy you a cup of coffee? It looks like Ty and Antoinette Chloe are buying out the place."

"I'd actually love something cold. How about that red stuff that's dripping down that plastic tank?"

"You got it!" I jumped up, poured her a tall red drink of unknown content, got her a straw, and placed it down in front of her. "It's your liver!"

She laughed, which cleared the air.

"So, did you like working for Priscilla?" I figured that was a safe question.

"For the most part. Sometimes she could be quite demanding."

"I could tell that about her."

She took a sip of the red stuff and seemed to like it.

"And you were her personal assistant? Her confidante?"

She shrugged. "I'm sure that there were some things that I didn't know about Cilla's business, but yes, I pretty much was her personal assistant and confidante."

"Did you like her?" I asked.

She narrowed her eyes. "I didn't kill her, if that's what you are asking."

"Oh, no! Not at all. I just thought that she was a bit

of a diva. You know, like she thought most of the world revolved around her."

"It does revolve around her. She's very popular, you know."

"I don't know if I'd ever want to work with her. You must be a saint, Jill."

"Not a saint." She looked around. "When are those two going to be done? I have some things in my cart that are melting."

But I had yet to ask the big question. I took a deep breath. "Peter McCall seems to think that he will get all of Priscilla's estate. He's been telling a couple of guys that he's going to take over as CEO of Finch-Smythe Enterprises because he's related to her."

I thought she was about to turn her head in circles as if she were possessed and barf up her red drink.

"I don't think a stepson from a long-ago marriage should actually be considered a relative. I worked hard for many, many years and covered for her and . . ."

"Covered for her?" I pushed.

"Yes. Cilla was . . . um . . . scattered sometimes."

"Scattered?"

Jill looked around, and her gaze settled on a display of fluorescent fishing lures.

"She wasn't as focused on her career as she once was. She was talking about retiring."

"And you think the business should be yours?" I prodded. "Because you've covered for her and helped her?"

She smiled. "Not only with her professional life, but her personal life, too." Jill took a big gulp of the red stuff. "Besides, she doesn't have any real relatives anymore, and I've been with her through thick and thin. I was the one who helped her publish triple the number of cookbooks and booked her for numerous talk shows and other events—like your mac and cheese cook-off—for more publicity. I was the one who steered her toward lucrative investments. I was the one who encouraged her to leave her last husband and told her to stop funding Peter's gambling addiction," she said quietly.

Standing, she pulled her cart toward her with a white-knuckled grip. "I'm going to check out. Thanks for the drink, Trixie." She looked around the store. "Do you think we could leave soon? I have a lot of business to take care of."

"I'll give them a five-minute warning."

"Good."

And then she was off. But I believe that I got the information I wanted. I surmised that Miss Jill Marley was ticked over the fact that Peter McCall may—*or may not*—get the business that Jill had worked hard for.

Would that be reason to kill Priscilla?

No. That would be a reason for Jill to kill Peter McCall instead, wouldn't it?

Until I could narrow down my list of suspects, everyone was a suspect. That meant all the players in Priscilla's life. Peter; the church ladies who seemed more than incensed; the two very vocal and combative chefs who thought that by giving Peter money to bribe Priscilla, their careers would skyrocket.

Who else?

I didn't know quite yet, but I at least was able to rule myself out!

Twenty minutes later we were headed back home. Ty talked nonstop about Cousin Ronnie's Pepperoni, which he'd finally found at the Gas and Grab. Apparently he'd been searching for it for forever. He said that he'd first had it as a kid when his father and grandfather rented one of the cottages here for a salmon-fishing expedition.

Fishermen's cheese, Cousin Ronnie's Pepperoni, crackers, and birch beer soda were part of their happy-hour ritual every day.

I kept nagging Ty to invite his parents to the point. I'd reserve their old cottage for them, and they could re-create their memories and make new ones. Although his grandfather had passed on, Ty's mother had never been here.

Besides, I would just love to meet both of Ty's parents.

Antoinette Chloe chatted about the fishing lure she'd found that would look perfect on the new fascinator she was going to make. She debated whether or not to take off the large glow-in-the-dark rubber worm which was on it.

She decided to keep the worm.

Jill was silent for the whole ride and just stared silently out the window.

I thought about our conversation. If she was expecting to inherit Priscilla's zillions and her business, she might be out of luck.

But maybe I was jumping ahead of myself and just assuming what Priscilla's wishes were. Maybe she had split everything equally between Peter and Jill. Maybe she'd left it all to charity.

On the way back, I typed *Orlando, Biltmore, Orlando and Fischer* into the Google search app on my phone, to see what kind of firm they were. But of course, I couldn't get an Internet connection. I swear, if Sandy Harbor didn't get good cell service soon, I was going to start my own company! Trixie Talks, Inc., or Sandy Harbor Speaks.

Well, it seemed like no estate lawyers were ready to act on Priscilla's will yet. I was certain Peter would've blabbed about it if he had received word about the will.

I decided to invite everyone on Ty's "don't leave town list" to the Big House for some food, wine, and talk. There was nothing like a cold night in front of fireplace of the Big House, chatting and sharing a gooey pizza and wings and enjoying a couple bottles of wine or ten.

I wondered how far Ty had gotten in his investigation. Maybe I should invite him to pizza, wings, and wine night, too. Maybe liquor would loosen his perfectly fine, delicious-looking lips.

Not that I'd noticed.

I had to get Ty aside and see what information I could get from him. Oh, and Joan Paris, too. She'd spill information about Hal Manning's—the coroner's—findings. And then there were the church ladies and the two chefs. I might as well have a big pizza party and see what happened.

What a great idea!

Ty let us all out in the parking lot on the side of the motor home.

"I can help," he said.

"Antoinette Chloe and I can manage. You help Jill. She has the most."

He lifted up the tailgate, and Jill pointed out which grocery bags were hers. They both were loaded down, so ACB and I helped, too. I was dying to see the inside of the motor home anyway.

My parents have a motor home—way smaller than this one—and were, in fact, in Tucson right now in a trailer park, soaking up the sun, playing golf, and "shuffling," which is code for shuffleboard.

Priscilla's motor home was magnificent. In a motor-home magazine, this would be the centerfold. It had marble countertops, recessed lighting, and a glass cabinet to display china. It even had a king-size bed in the back. A small desk had stacks of paperwork and books, mostly cookbooks, falling all over everything, even onto the floor.

It looked as though Priscilla and Jill had been behind on her work.

All the while, I looked for the bubble mailer with the lawyer names on it. It had to be here somewhere.

And there it was, on the floor, under the desk.

My fingers were itching to take it and see what the contents said.

But I couldn't. Jill was right behind me.

I needed a plan. It was already formulating in my brain. And I'd execute it the night of the pizza party.

"What a beautiful motor home, Jill. I can see why you wanted to stay here," I said.

"I love it!" Antoinette Chloe raved. "I could sell my house and Brown's Four Corners Restaurant, buy one of these bad boys, and travel."

"Wouldn't you miss Sandy Harbor?" I asked.

"Not in the winter. It's not good for my flip-flops, as you've pointed out several times, Trixie," she said. "Remember how I was going to open a drive-in?"

"Yes, I do. You wanted it open in the winter so people could drive their snowmobiles in and watch the movies outdoors." I tried not to smile.

"Maybe I'll create a mobile-home park on my land instead and park my motor home here in the summer and drive somewhere warm in the winter. Sandy Harbor needs some extra places for people to stay, so a trailer park is definitely needed. I can have some of those cute cabins brought in, too."

This was a better idea than her drive-in, but her boyfriend's body had been found on that land. I wondered if the memory was still too fresh for her to handle.

"I'll put a memory garden where we found Nick," she said, as if reading my mind.

"You know, Antoinette Chloe, that sounds like a fabulous idea. Your heart hasn't been in the restaurant business lately."

"I could sell my restaurant to Fingers, my chef. He's doing an excellent job. My business has tripled ever since he took over as the manager."

"Then why wouldn't you keep your restaurant? You have all that money coming in, and you don't have to do a thing. You don't even have to be there," Jill said, putting her groceries in a cabinet.

ACB shrugged. "But Fingers is the one who deserves the credit, not me."

"I don't get it," Jill said abruptly.

"It'd be like you taking the credit for something that Priscilla did," I said.

"Thank you all for your help," Jill said quietly. "I appreciate the ride to the grocery store. It was an . . . um . . . interesting trip."

Guess that was our cue to get out.

Ty led the way down the stairs and helped us both down the last step.

I went back up the stairs and said to Jill, "I'm having a pizza party at my house later this week. It'll be nothing special, but I'd love it if you'd come. How about it?"

"Oh, I don't know. I have a lot of work to do."

"C'mon, Jill." I took her hand and gave it a squeeze. "You'll be glad to get out of this tin can by then. You can socialize, have a lot of laughs, and have great food and wine."

She was ready to protest, but I insisted. "I'll expect you. If you aren't here, I'm just going to have to drag you out of the motor home."

She smiled weakly. "Sounds like fun."

"Great."

We all went back to Ty's SUV. ACB and I got our groceries, and Ty helped us lug everything up the sidewalk.

Blondie greeted us like long-lost friends, jumping around us and whimpering. She'd missed us. Ty let her outside, and she rolled in the snow, then pranced like a gazelle.

"I'll come back in about an hour and take Blondie for a run," Ty said.

"She'll love that. She's been cooped up inside too much lately."

"Wish I could say the same. It seems like I haven't been in my apartment in days. This case has me hopping."

"How so?" I asked, knowing that he wouldn't tell me a thing.

"How about another cup of coffee first?"

"Sure." I put in a K-Cup.

ACB was still putting groceries away and half singing and half humming "Oklahoma," a tune she was way too fond of.

Finally the coffeemaker stopped, and I slid a mug of black coffee in front of him.

"What's going on, Ty?"

"Hal Manning's report came through. Of course, you know that Priscilla was strangled with her scarf, but it appears that she hit her head on the fire hydrant first. Hal figures that she was pushed. She must have been groggy. And the scarf was knotted in the front, so the murderer was face-to-face with her."

"That's cold-blooded."

"I'll say."

"Got any suspects who are in the lead?" I asked.

He shrugged. "They all had somewhat of a reason to kill her, but not good enough to commit murder."

"You're probably going to have to let some of them leave town soon, huh?"

He took a big gulp of coffee. "I'm getting a lot of hassle from our illustrious mayor to let them go."

"Does that include me, too? Can Antoinette Chloe and I part ways?"

He laughed. "You two are doing fine. Like two Tri-Gams in a pod."

"I'm not an official Gamma Gamma Gamma member," I pointed out. "I didn't attend Sandy Harbor High."

"Neither did I," he said. "I guess we're the two outsiders."

"You know it. And lately I've been given a wide berth."

"Trixie, that's your imagination. I don't think anyone seriously considers you a suspect."

"Then why am I chained to ACB? And why did you tell me I can't leave my property?"

"Because I wanted you to leave the investigating to me, and I wanted to keep an eye on you. I know you, Trixie."

"For heaven's sake!" I wasn't sure if I should be happy at this revelation or mad at the man. "Tell me, are you at least getting close to an arrest?"

"I just need one good break. We're still looking at Priscilla's phone contacts, but we haven't found anything exciting yet." He drained his coffee and got up to leave. Ty rarely lingered over his coffee if he was working on a case. "Thanks, Trixie. I'll be back to pick up Blondie for a run later."

I walked him out and waited as he put on his boots. I caught the scent of his aftershave—pine and musk.

Nice.

For some reason I always looked forward to seeing him. He'd be back in his winter jogging attire, but it was his summer outfits that made my heart palpitate— shorts and a tank top. On hot summer days, he didn't wear a shirt at all.

I lived for those days.

Watching him walk to his SUV was a treat, too. He had on a leather bomber jacket, and his tight butt was encased in perfectly faded jeans. Spectacular.

Not that I noticed.

Antoinette Chloe was sitting at the table when I got back to the kitchen.

"What's your next plan, Trixie?" she asked.

"I want to put a pizza party together. Here at the Big

House. If we get some of the suspects together, maybe we could get some clues," I said. "This may be like fishing in the dark, but what the heck?"

"You already took care of Jill. I'll contact Peter and invite him and the church ladies. We might as well throw in the two chefs. If nothing else, maybe we can find out more about Peter's gambling from those two. Who else?"

"Let's see if Joan Paris is available, too, although Ty told me what I needed to know about Hal Manning's findings. I think that's good. Let's leave out Ty. Maybe then everyone will talk."

"Leave everything to me. I'll take care of ordering the food, too. I love Cindy Sherlock's pizza and garlic wings."

"Thanks, Antoinette Chloe. I think I'll talk a walk over to the diner and see how things are going."

"Go ahead. I'll take care of getting a nice assortment of goodies ready for our lunch with the church ladies. I bought a lot of nice treats at the Gas and Grab."

How could I forget about that so soon? Senility, thy name is Trixie.

I noticed the lights on in Priscilla's motor home and could see Jill's silhouette. It looked like she was on the phone and was shouting. Taking a little detour, I walked closer to hear what she was saying.

It was a clear, quiet afternoon, and her voice traveled. It helped that she was loud.

"I don't care. Just settle the reading of her will already. I can't have things in such a state of flux."

Yes. I needed to execute my scathingly brilliant plan on the night of the pizza party.

And I'd need ACB's help.

Chapter 12

*T*he next morning I found that the media had mostly disappeared from their headquarters at my diner. There was only Joan Paris, the editor of the *Sandy Harbor Lure*, sitting in a booth with Hal Manning, Sandy Harbor's full-time funeral director and part-time coroner.

They lived together and were a wealth of information, and they were just the two people I wanted to see.

Hal Manning loved to talk about his cases—unlike Ty Brisco—and I was glad that he loved to talk to me. All you had to do was toss him a topic, and he'd be off and running.

I waved to them both, and Joan motioned me over. "How are you doing, Trixie?"

"I'm just plain pooped. The Miss Salmon Contest led to Christmas and then right to the mac and cheese cook-off. With my shift at work, I was just sleepwalking everywhere. I'm taking a mini break now, though, and Linda is cooking for me."

"She's doing a great job. This food is delicious," Hal said.

It looked divine and it was nicely presented on the plate. My waitresses were smiling and having a nice time while going about their duties, which made for a fun experience for my customers.

Everything was going just fine without me.

"Sit down. Join us." Joan winked and shifted her eyes toward Hal. I smiled at Joan's code. Hal had news and was ready to share.

She moved over on the red vinyl seat, and I sat down. Bettylou came over with a glass of iced tea and placed it in front of me. From behind her back, she pulled out a dish. On the dish was a peach hand pie.

How did she know that was *exactly* what I wanted?

Bettylou grinned. "Sarah Stolfus made a big delivery. I saved this peach hand pie for you. All her baked goods are going fast, really fast."

"Remind me to give you a raise, Bettylou."

"Oh, I will!"

"So, Hal, how have you been? Busy?" I asked.

"Yeah. I've been getting calls left and right about Priscilla Finch-Smythe."

"From?"

"Mostly the media. And several from Peter McCall and Jill Marley. They are both anxious to have Priscilla's body released for her calling hours and interment. I have a theory myself. I think they just want to hurry everything up so they can have the reading of her will."

I raised an eyebrow, and he chuckled. "It's common

to hold off the reading of the will when foul play is suspected."

"Hal, honey, tell Trixie what you told me about Peter and his debts," Joan instructed.

"I was talking to my old pal Jimmy Bosworth, from the State University of New York at Albany's forensic science program. Jimmy's now a lieutenant with the New York State Police in their Bureau of Criminal Investigation. We talk frequently since Sandy Harbor sends all their lab work to NYSP headquarters in Albany. Anyway, Jimmy told me that Peter's in hot water with a big-time loan shark and bookie by the name of Stan LaVolney. They're keeping an eye on Stan so he doesn't do anything to Peter. Peter has promised Stan full payment once Priscilla's estate is settled."

Of course, LaVolney was "Stan the Bookie"!

And now I had official verification of everything that Stan told me at breakfast.

Sometimes I had to lead Hal in the direction I needed. "I wonder what BCI verified about the Saint Dismas cookbook."

Hal leaned back on the red vinyl cushion. "Jimmy said that Priscilla's version was definitely lifted from the Church of Saint Dismas."

"Is there proof?"

"A used bookstore in Saratoga remembered Priscilla coming in and saying that she was buying the old cookbook to donate it to the Sandy Harbor Library. The bookstore even took a picture of Priscilla with the cookbook, because she was a celebrity. It was the Saint Dismas one. Then Priscilla and Jill had a fight. Jill wanted to keep it, but Priscilla insisted that she had no use for it."

"Well, that doesn't prove that Jill did anything wrong. Besides, after Priscilla died, Jill accused Priscilla of copying it."

Hal's eyes lit up. He was waiting to deliver a punch line. "But a computer was confiscated by BCI. It showed extensively that Jill was the one who copied it, changed a few things, and sent it by e-mail to the publisher. There was nothing to indicate that Priscilla was in any way involved. Jill finally admitted to Jimmy and Ty that Priscilla hadn't been entirely involved in the last several cookbooks. Jill wrote them. And when I did Priscilla's autopsy, I discovered Priscilla was borderline middle-stage Alzheimer's."

If I had false teeth, I would have dropped them. "Hal? What did you say? Priscilla had Alzheimer's?"

He nodded. "And she was taking a cocktail of meds."

"I can't believe it." An overwhelming sadness came over me. Poor Priscilla. No wonder Jill told me that Priscilla couldn't concentrate at times. Jill probably was helping Priscilla with her cookbooks, and later, as Priscilla got worse, maybe Jill got a little overwhelmed with everything she had to do to cover for Priscilla.

Priscilla had had Alzheimer's disease! Whoever killed her wouldn't even let her die in peace in her own time.

"The church ladies want the profits from the cookbook donated to the church, and it appears that Jill is going to do that," I said. "That's a good thing."

"I heard that, as well," Joan said.

"Hal, did the lieutenant say anything as to who had a strong motive to kill Priscilla?" I asked.

"Jill toiled in the salt mines for Priscilla. From what Jimmy told me, Jill *was* Priscilla Finch-Smythe, because at times Priscilla was too sick to work. She tried to save her energy for her TV show, since it was taped and they could do a lot of takes. On her good days, Priscilla insisted that they tape more than one show. Sometimes they did three."

That was just what I'd concluded.

"Interesting," I said. "Priscilla must have been exhausted most of the time."

I wondered if she'd broken the news to Peter about a year ago. That might explain his sudden appearance back in her life. Maybe he figured if he could ingratiate himself with his ailing stepmother, he could gain control of her finances before she passed.

"Probably." Hal leaned over and whispered, "I know you won't tell anyone that I told you all this, Trixie, particularly Ty. He likes to play his cards close to his vest."

"My lips are sealed." I raised my hand as if I were swearing to silence.

Joan gave me a big smile. "And I found out that one of the ladies from Saint Dismas used to live here."

"No way!"

"Oh, yeah. I ran some checks on against the *Lure*'s

database," Joan said. "Dorothy 'Dottie' Spitzer and her husband, Sidney, ran an ad every summer and fall in the *Lure*. They advertised U-pick berries, apples, pumpkins, and squash."

"Well, I'll be . . ." This information hit me like a bolt out of the blue. "She must have known Priscilla back in the day."

"It's very likely that she could have. They graduated in the same class—Dorothy was Reinhardt back then, Priscilla was Mabel Cronk back then, and your aunt Stella and uncle Porky were themselves. Oh, and Antoinette Chloe was in the same graduating class."

"Antoinette Chloe never said anything about knowing Dottie!"

"Maybe she didn't recognize her. It's been years, after all," Joan said. "And I can't cross-check Dorothy Reinhardt against the Sandy Harbor yearbook, so I really don't know if she's changed a lot. The yearbook isn't online, of course, as it's too old, and all the yearbooks were lost when the library's roof collapsed. I haven't gotten around to digging up a yearbook from the locals yet. Things have been kind of hectic with all the press bugging me for background information and old issues of the *Lure*."

"I know just where to find a yearbook. Aunt Stella has a whole collection of them in her office, off the kitchen."

I hadn't gotten around to making Aunt Stella and

Uncle Porky's office my own. There was too much history in it, and their history was my history.

This information was invaluable.

Then I had to pause. Maybe, just maybe, in her own way, by taking the Saint Dismas cookbook and putting Priscilla's name on it, Jill had really been trying to help Priscilla and keep her on track. From what I knew about the disease, stress could bring on forgetfulness—and having a stressful job in television could have made the situation worse. Personality changes might ensue also. I wondered briefly if that was why Priscilla had acted like such a diva while she was judging the contest.

Joan gave me a slight smile. "I can't print a lot of this just yet, but I will. Just as soon as an arrest is made, I'm ready to go. I'm going to get the scoop on everyone!"

I nodded. Joan worked hard, and if a scoop was to be made, Joan deserved to make it. But Joan did more than scoop. She always wrote sensitive, caring pieces.

"Is her body going to be released soon, Hal?"

"In a couple of days. Just as soon as I get the word from Jimmy and Ty."

"Is there going to be a service?"

"Peter and Jill are supposed to be arranging something, but I think they're bickering about it. Last I knew, they were planning to have something at my place due to the fact that all of her old friends are here."

"The Tri-Gams?"

"Yeah."

I'd like to think that Priscilla knew this might have been her last trip to Sandy Harbor. Maybe she wanted to revisit her roots and be surrounded by her friends one more time.

And maybe I hadn't been fair to her. Maybe she acted like a cranky diva due to her illness.

I vowed yet again that I'd find out who'd pushed her into the fire hydrant and strangled her with her own scarf. And bring her some belated justice.

Hopefully, my plan to do some investigative work during the pizza party tomorrow would work. I shuddered, thinking about what might happen if I got caught.

But right now I wanted to hurry back to the Big House and check out Aunt Stella's old Sandy Harbor yearbooks.

Then, as luck would have it, ACB and I were going to entertain two church ladies, one of whom I was almost positive was the former Dorothy Reinhardt.

"Antoinette Chloe, do you recognize this young lady?" I pointed to a picture in the black-and-white yearbook, where each student photo was in alphabetical order.

"Dorothy Reinhardt. I haven't seen her in decades. She married . . . um . . . ." She leafed through the pages. "He farmed out on Mile High Road. What was his name? Sidney . . . Sidney . . . uh . . . Spitzer! That's him." She pointed to a fairly good-looking guy. "He was the captain of the football team. All the girls had a crush on Sidney, and we were all astonished when he asked skinny little Dorothy with an overbite to marry him."

"Was she a Tri-Gam?"

"No. Her mother wouldn't let her hang out with us. She said that we were a cult of the devil."

I grinned. "What?"

"True." ACB nodded. "If she only knew that three of our members became nuns. And that the worst thing we did was paint 'Tri-Gam' on the water tower in red. But we were caught and had to paint silver over it."

"Well, I think that Dottie, who we are entertaining any second now, is actually Dorothy Reinhardt Spitzer."

"Naw. That can't be her. I would have recognized her when I was talking to her, wouldn't I? Although we didn't associate very much in high school—she didn't like me. She was fairly dull and quiet and I was . . . um . . . loud and colorful."

"And, Antoinette Chloe, I'd bet you a hand pie that you were the one who painted the water tower."

She put the palm of her right hand against her heart. *"Moi?"*

"Yeah, you!"

The doorbell rang, and I put the yearbook away in a drawer. "Make sure you take a good look at her. And then maybe we can ask her some pertinent questions."

"Absolutely."

We both went to answer the door.

"Welcome to my home," I said, opening the thick

oak door for Dottie and Marylou while trying to keep Blondie away from them at the same time. She wanted to lick them to death. "I think you remember me as the cochair of the mac and cheese cook-off, Trixie Matkowski."

"Of course we remember you, Trixie. Thanks for inviting us," said Marylou. "I believe that Megan and Milt are going to enjoy a break from us for a while."

"I'm sure you both need a break, too," I said diplomatically. "Welcome, Dottie."

We all shook hands.

"Let me take your coats," ACB said.

Dutifully, they pulled off the coats and handed them to ACB, who tossed them unceremoniously over the banister. Then they unlaced their winter boots, which looked a lot like L.L.Bean's rubber boots, and put them on my boot tray.

I knew immediately by their winter etiquette that they came from a four-season place.

"Where are you ladies from?" I asked.

"Downstate. Poughkeepsie."

Bingo!

"Another tropical place at this time of year," joked Antoinette Chloe. She was wearing a muumuu with little palm trees sprinkled between massive purple hibiscus flower heads.

When they were both dewinterized, I escorted them to the kitchen. "I hope you don't mind sitting around the table. It's my favorite thing to do. And lunch is ready."

I'd heated up the pea soup Antoinette Chloe had made and stirred in a hint of cream. I figured that it would be the perfect meal on a cold winter day like today.

"Can I fix everyone a bowl of split pea soup?" I'd poured the soup into a tureen that matched my Syracuse China pattern and brought it to the table.

"Absolutely."

"Count me in."

"Me too."

As I ladled the soup into bowls, ACB pulled out the tray of tea sandwiches we'd made earlier with the luncheon meat we'd bought at the Gas and Grab.

"I made us a pot of tea," ACB said. "Cranberry spice. Is that all right?"

The two church ladies nodded.

"Dottie," ACB began. "You look so familiar. Do we know each other?"

Dottie hesitated, then said, "Dorothy Spitzer, formerly Reinhardt. I went to Sandy Harbor High School. I believe we were in the same class."

"Small world," ACB said. "But you look very different, Dottie."

"It's probably my wig—my hair is very thin—and I've gained a lot of weight since high school."

"Haven't we all?" ACB laughed. "And I don't remember you wearing glasses."

"Old eyes."

"I hear you. Luckily, I've avoided them so far," ACB said.

"Dottie, did you know Priscilla back in high school, too?" I asked.

"I did. Back when she was Mabel Cronk, that is. I followed her career throughout the years with interest." I handed Dottie the platter of sandwiches, and she reached for ham with maple mayonnaise.

"Did she remember you, Dottie?" ACB asked.

"Of course she remembered me. We used to be very friendly. She'd always come to my parents' farm during U-pick season and work for them. She was maid of honor at my wedding to Sid. We kept in touch years after we graduated." Her smile turned into pinched lips. "Then, after a while, things turned ugly between us."

"Oh. That's too bad. Do you mind me asking what happened?" I pressed, dying to know.

"I don't particularly want to talk about it right now. Let's just enjoy our lunch." Dottie smiled dimly.

"Please, have as many sandwiches and helpings of soup as you want, but I should warn you to save some room for Sarah Stolfus's hand pies," I said. "I apologize, ladies. I would usually bake something special myself, but lately time has been flying. And her hand pies are simply delicious."

We chatted for a while about nothing special, and I was enjoying their company. However, after too much idle chitchat, I felt that I should try to get more information out of them, but of course, ACB beat me to turning the conversation around.

"Marylou, how about you? Did you know Priscilla before now?"

"Not really. I felt like I sorta knew her from watching her show on TV, but I can't say I knew her. Then, when the cookbook scandal broke, Dottie and I were elected to represent the Church of the Covered Dish. She was the original editor of the cookbook. I was in charge of finances.

"And we did a ton of work on it," Marylou said. "Everyone in the church had participated and sent in their family recipes and anecdotes. We sold a lot of cookbooks, and the money all went to the church. We even copyrighted it. Priscilla violated our copyright."

"Can you copyright recipes?" I wondered.

"Well, no. Not the actual recipes themselves. But all the stories and text around it can be copyrighted!" Marylou said. "And Priscilla stole everything from us, word for word."

She was spunky, whereas Dottie seemed to be quietly seething.

"Did you manage to speak with Priscilla about the copyright violation at all before she died?" I asked.

"Briefly." Marylou nodded. "The three of us went outside at the cook-off to talk in private, but we talked quickly because it was cold, and we weren't dressed for it. Anyway, Priscilla asked us not to talk about the cook-book to the press and said she'd talk to us more after the contest."

Dottie fished in her purse and pulled out a tissue. "Priscilla also said that she didn't know anything about our cookbook and that she didn't plagiarize from us, but I find that hard to believe. She was in the cookbook business, for heaven's sake."

"Dottie, calm yourself. You said yourself that Priscilla didn't seem like the same person you'd once known."

"She wouldn't be the same after the thirty-something years since I'd last seen her."

"Why didn't she seem the same to you?" I asked.

"She kept losing her train of thought during our conversation," Dottie replied. "She fished for words constantly. Just like my aunt Patty used to."

"Did your aunt Patty have Alzheimer's?" I asked.

"Yes, she did. Oh! Priscilla seemed to have a touch of it, too." Dottie put her hand on Marylou's. "I wonder if she had Alzheimer's, Marylou. Oh, my! When Aunt Patty was under pressure or experienced some kind of emotional upheaval, she usually got kind of scattered. And sometimes she got obnoxious."

Scattered. That was the word Jill had used.

Obnoxious. That was the word I had thought.

We sat in silence for a while, sipping our tea and en-joying our soup and sandwiches. Big flakes swirled out-side, and it was pretty to watch.

Blondie was curled up in front of the door that led to

my wraparound porch. If anyone from outside saw us, it would look like we were a gathering of friends, not suspects. Well, only three of us were suspects: Marylou, Dottie, and me.

Dottie fidgeted in her chair. "Later, we went back outside in the frigid cold and talked again. In exchange for our silence, Priscilla promised to give us some money for our church. It's in terrible shape and in need of extensive repair, and fifty thousand dollars would go a long way."

"Wow! Fifty thousand!" ACB said.

"Well, I'm sure she made millions with *our* cookbook! Still, that was a lot of money. That's why we backed off Priscilla and sat nicely in our chairs for the contest," Marylou said. "Even though Dottie was upset about it and made it known to Priscilla in no uncertain terms."

Dottie looked ready to bolt, but instead she took a deep breath and reached for a roast beef sandwich with horseradish mustard.

"Let's compare the cookbooks, shall we?" I said. "Antoinette Chloe has Priscilla's."

"I have ours right here," Marylou said, pulling a yellowed, dog-eared book out of her purse.

"I'll be back in a minute," ACB said. "Priscilla's cookbook is upstairs." ACB's flip-flops faded; then their slapping became louder as she walked up the stairs.

"You two are good friends, aren't you, Trixie?" Marylou asked.

"Yes. She was the first person who became my friend when I bought the restaurant. Then we became closer as certain things . . . unfolded."

Dottie's eyes began to tear, and I handed her tissues and paper napkins that were handy. Marylou and I sat quietly until she composed herself.

"Dottie, if you feel like talking, please do," I said. "You're among friends."

ACB plodded into the kitchen, and I held up a finger so she wouldn't speak. She nodded slightly, then took a seat.

But Dottie wiped her eyes, cleared her throat, and gave a slight smile. "Let's compare those books, shall we? Then you can see why we at Saint Dismas are so upset."

Dottie took the books and opened them both. Priscilla's cookbook, *The Countess of Comforting Comfort Food*, was opened to page ten; the Saint Dismas cookbook to page four. "See? Grandma's Apple Betty, with an introduction by Grandma Allister of Poughkeepsie, New York. It's word for word! Only Priscilla called it Aunt Betty's Apple Betty with an introduction from Betty Smudler of Glens Falls, New York. On page eleven, there's the same story and recipe with Cousin Diane's Chicken Marinade from Poughkeepsie and Cousin Barbara of Aspen, Colorado, in Priscilla's cookbook, page five. Cousin Diane writes about her chicken barbecues around her pool. Same goes for Cousin Barbara."

We all hunched over, comparing them both, until I was convinced. It was plagiarized.

"Mabel stole everything from me. Don't you see?" Dottie began to sob in earnest. "I used to be one of her closest friends in Sandy Harbor. Sid and I and the kids would visit her in California all the time. Then Sid, my husband of fifteen years, ran off with her and left me to raise Louise and Mark alone." I handed her several sheets from a roll of paper towels, and she paused to blow her nose. "Priscilla stole him away from me. I loved Sid, and Priscilla knew that. They both broke my heart." She sniffed. "And the worst part about it is that she was my friend."

Oh, my! I wondered if Dottie held a grudge against Priscilla after all these years.

I swallowed hard. "What happened after you found out, Dottie?"

"I moved away from Sandy Harbor to avoid all the embarrassment and small-town chatter such a scandal would cause, and moved my family to Poughkeepsie to live with my cousin."

We waited patiently for her to regain her composure. ACB put an arm around her.

"That stinks, Dottie. I'm so sorry," I said.

Dottie blew her nose. "I—I didn't know Sid and Priscilla were having an affair behind my back until Sid said that he was moving to California to be with her. I was shocked, and then I fell apart."

"You don't have to say any more, sweetie," Marylou said.

"Strangely, I feel like a weight is being lifted off my shoulders, sitting in this warm kitchen and enjoying the lunch." She dabbed at her eyes. "I can say it now: I tried to kill myself with sleeping pills. My daughter found me and called nine-one-one." Dottie smiled weakly. "But as you can see, I lived to tell the tale."

"Priscilla must have divorced him later. She had a handful of husbands, didn't she?" I asked.

"No. They never got married. Their relationship didn't last very long after he left me for her. After Priscilla was done with him, I took him back, but things were never the same. I—I tried everything I could to make us into a happy family, like we were before Sid abandoned us, but I couldn't please him. You see, he kept reminding me that I was no Priscilla. *Can you imagine that?* After a while, I wanted to kill him, but I wanted to kill Priscilla even more. I was angry. Angry for many, many years. I ended up hating Sid. And Priscilla . . . Well, Priscilla got richer and richer. Even though she destroyed my family and my life."

There was dead silence.

Dottie took a break to catch her breath. "And then, to add insult to injury, she plagiarized the Saint Dismas cookbook. *My* cookbook! I was the one who compiled it. I was the one who sold it on behalf of the church. And she stole it. She took my husband, and she took my cookbook. To top it all off, my cookbook was much better than anything she published throughout the years."

I exchanged glances with ACB. It seemed that we were both wondering if Dottie had acted on her anger.

Marylou look stunned, and I assumed she didn't know Dottie's entire story. She'd probably thought she was just taking a bus trip with the Saint Dismas group to demand recompense from Priscilla for the lost revenues.

Marylou had gotten more than she'd bargained for.

Dottie might have gotten just what she wanted. Revenge.

"I'm so sorry." Dottie shook her head. "I don't know what came over me. What on earth possessed me to carry on like that?"

"Don't you give it another thought," I said. "There's nothing like sitting around the kitchen table for baring the soul, huh?"

What else was I supposed to say?

ACB nodded so hard that I thought the glow-in-the-dark bait worm would break off of her fascinator and take a swim in my pea soup.

Marylou and Dottie must have been thinking the same thing, as we all giggled at the same time.

When the luncheon was over, ACB and I walked Dottie and Marylou to the front door.

"Remember the pizza party about seven o'clock tomorrow." I had invited them earlier, while we were eating dessert.

"We'll be there," Marylou said. "I've heard that the pizza at the Silver Bullet is fabulous."

"It can't be missed," I added. "Cindy is a sculptor with her pizzas."

ACB adjusted her muumuu. "See you tomorrow at the pizza party. We can catch up more. Right, Dottie?"

"I'll be there."

As I shut the door behind them, I felt like taking a nap. I was mentally exhausted. But I'd gotten a lot of good information and filed it away in the back of my brain to act on later.

And Dottie had jumped to number one on my suspect list.

Chapter 13

I was running on empty. I wanted to take a nap, or just sleep outright, but I couldn't, so I resorted to pacing in my bedroom and picking out the squeakiest boards to play "Chopsticks."

The suspects were twirling around in my head like Blondie chasing her tail. I picked them out one at a time to think about.

First there was Dottie. If anyone had a reason to kill Priscilla, she did. Her husband, who she loved dearly, had run off with Priscilla, her old friend. Priscilla, the nice gal that she was, sent him back to Dottie when she was done with him, but things were never the same, and poor Dottie had to move away.

But why now?

Why would Dottie kill Priscilla after all those years? Had the recent cookbook trauma finally sent Dottie over the edge? Was it because their paths had finally crossed in Sandy Harbor and the opportunity was there?

And then there were the two chefs. Walton DeMassie had already lost his TV chef job, and he'd lived to tell the tale. He'd had high expectations of a return to fame by appearing on TV with Priscilla.

Maybe that was just speculation on his part, or wishful thinking.

DeMassie was a hothead, but I ruled him out. There didn't seem to be any reason for him to kill Priscilla. Peter was the one he wanted to beat up so he could get his bribe money back.

Now, Christopher "Kip" O'Malley, the jail chef who took a cooking correspondence class, had more to lose—especially if Priscilla told his employer about his criminal record. He wouldn't be able to work in the jail, and then he wouldn't be able to pay back the thirteen thousand dollars he owed in child support.

But all his dreams of fame and fortune and credibility as a chef died when Priscilla did. Even though Jill vowed to find another chef who would be willing to put the winner on TV, no one matched the caliber of Miss Priscilla Finch-Smythe.

Then again, when Priscilla died, his secrets were safe and sound.

Peter McCall was a wild card. He'd come back into Priscilla's life a couple of years ago and started battling with Jill, like Godzilla versus King Kong. Priscilla's favorite person to inherit her empire was anyone's guess at this point, but maybe Peter and Jill were slated to share it.

I had to get ahold of that envelope from the lawyers.

Maybe that would answer the question as to who would reap the benefits of Priscilla's lifetime of work!

And then there was yours truly. I had shot my mouth off and would have loved to win the contest and appear on TV, too, but I didn't kill anyone, and Ty knows it!

His telling me not to leave the house was his way of helping me to get some rest and of having ACB keep an eye on me.

As if I'd listen to him and stay put!

Okay, four suspects. How do I narrow them down?

I'd love to bounce things off Ty, maybe exchange information with him, but that wasn't going to happen. As he kept telling me, he was bound by law.

But I wasn't.

And neither was my partner in crime solving, Antoinette Chloe Brown.

"Antoinette Chloe?" I knocked on the wall that separated our rooms. "Are you awake?"

"How can I sleep with all that infernal squeaking? You must have walked a hundred miles. What's bothering you?"

"What isn't?"

"Let's talk," she said. "Your place or mine?"

"I'll meet you in the kitchen. I'd like some tea and donuts."

I slipped into my old reliable pink chenille bathrobe and my slippers and went downstairs to put the teakettle on the stove. I liked nothing better than a late-night tea party with lively conversation, and ACB could always be counted on to provide lively conversation.

ACB appeared in a floor-length muumuu covered with sleeping birds—or dead birds, depending on your point of view. On her feet were glittery flip-flops with a huge sunflower covering most of her toes.

She was fascinator-less, but she wore her hair up in a ponytail on top of her head, secured with a leopard-print elastic band.

"Here you go, Antoinette Chloe." I poured boiling water into a tall mug and pushed a flowered china bowl containing an assortment of tea bags over to her. Then I put a bag of sugar donuts between us, along with some paper plates, paper towels, and plastic spoons.

I didn't have to be fancy during a late-night tea party.

"So, what do you think of everything's that's been going on?" I asked, dunking my Earl Grey tea bag.

"You've been thinking a lot about what's going on. I can tell."

"There are four good suspects."

"I know." She loaded her tea with sugar and stirred. "Kip, Dottie, Peter, and Jill."

"Who can we eliminate, Antoinette Chloe?"

"Beats me. Maybe Peter. He wouldn't want to off his cash cow, if you will pardon the expression."

"But with Priscilla gone, he could get at least half of everything—that is, assuming he has to share it with Jill—not just get it doled out to him piecemeal.

"And what about Jill?" I asked. "She has access to all of Priscilla's accounts. As her personal assistant, she must know all of Priscilla's business details, along with all the skeletons in her closet. Jill covered for Priscilla as she dealt with Alzheimer's. Jill seems like a good egg, but maybe she wanted more power. Wanted to *be* Priscilla." I dunked a cinnamon donut into my Earl Grey. "Am I making any sense? I guess I'm just brainstorming, but my brain is failing to storm."

"Brainstorming is good. Let's take on one person at a time. Let's investigate Kip. What do we know about him? Like his whereabouts on that fateful day?" ACB said.

"From what I remember, and I was people-watching, Kip stayed pretty close to his mac and cheese entry. He fussed over it, turning his pan every which way and putting it under various pretty napkins for a nice display. He chatted up the judges, and when Priscilla was talking, he sat intently in the audience. There was only one time when I couldn't find him, and he was in the men's room with Chef DeMassie. I know that because I was looking for someone. . . . Oh, yeah. Peter McCall! I asked Ray, who came out of the men's room, if Peter was in there, and Ray said that both chefs were in the men's room complaining that the contest was rigged."

"So all of their time was accounted for?"

I shrugged. "At least as far as I saw, Antoinette Chloe. They could have slipped out and killed Priscilla without me knowing it, but I think I would have noticed their absence. No, I guess I can't say that. I didn't notice them go into the men's room." Frustrated, I pushed my bangs back. "This is going nowhere."

"We'll come up with something. Hang on, girlfriend."

"I got it! I have a scathingly brilliant idea!"

ACB fished out a donut chunk from her tea with a spoon and posed with it not far from her mouth. "Do tell."

"I'm going to invite both chefs to cook with me at the Silver Bullet. You, too. You're a chef. We'll do something special for . . . what? The library! You, me, Kip, and Walton—we'll put on a special buffet for a set price. And we'll find out what makes them both tick. We can ask some special questions, like 'Hey, Kip, did you think that you were going to lose your job if Priscilla ratted on you? Did that make you want to kill her?'"

ACB chuckled. "Do we have anything on Chef De-Massie?"

"Not really. We have to feel him out, too."

"I wouldn't mind feeling him out! He's kind of hot."

We giggled like two teens.

"Trixie, the buffet is a brilliant idea, but you do realize that you are doing another fund-raiser, don't you?"

"Call me crazy, but I have to find out who did this. I want to get my little town, my life, and my diner back to normal."

"Let's call a planning meeting at the diner tomorrow

and invite the two chefs and tell them about the fund-raiser buffet."

"And we can get the word out quickly. *The Lure* goes out in two days. First thing tomorrow I'll get Ray to work up a nice ad and drop it off to Joan."

"This is going to work, Trixie. We'll either rule them out or put them at the top of our suspect list. I feel it in my bones, and my bones never lie."

"Think we can get some sleep now?" I said, draining my tea.

"No way. Let's plan the menu for the buffet."

The morning of the buffet, the four of us were prepping the buffet items. Juanita, my day cook, handled the regular diner orders, and we positioned ourselves on two long steam tables near the pizza oven.

We made aluminum steam pans full of kielbasa and kraut, meat loaf, baked ziti, goulash, steak fries, mashed potatoes, steamed veggies, and—you guessed it—macaroni and cheese. I decided to let Kip O'Malley prepare his own recipe. It wasn't that exciting. He just fried some burger, drained it, and added a hint of chili sauce to his melted-cheese mixture. That was okay, but at least ACB's and my food had more interesting ingredients.

We all talked and joked as we worked, and I found out that I really liked the two chefs.

But I tried to remain neutral. ACB flirted shamelessly with Chef DeMassie, so she wasn't much help in talking to Kip, but ACB usually came through with something good.

"So, Kip, were you a big fan of Priscilla's?" I asked.

"She was okay. I took a class from her way back when, and she took a shine to me. I think she wanted to be my mentor, but when I brought it up, she looked at me like I was speaking Latin with a French accent."

I chuckled. "Did you read her wrong?"

"Obviously, I did."

"Priscilla was a bit of a diva. Maybe you didn't fit her mold of a TV chef."

"Probably not." He cut up the steak fries faster than anyone I've ever seen. His correspondence class must have come with videos unless . . . "That's fast, Kip. Did Priscilla teach you that?"

He laughed. "One of the criminals at the prison taught me that. He went by the name of Knifeman."

I shuddered. "It must be tough to work at the prison day after day. You must feel like you're doing time yourself for the sins you've committed."

I was proud of my excellent lead-in!

"Yeah," was all he said.

I took a deep breath and blurted, "Have you ever been arrested, Kip?"

That was real smooth—not!

He flipped the knife into a potato, and it stuck. "Knifeman taught me that trick, too." He hesitated, then let out a long breath. "If I have an arrest record, I can't work at the prison. Dumb rule, isn't it? I mean, the place is loaded with criminals, and I can't have any arrests myself."

"That's pretty unfair."

"You said it."

"If you have any arrests, you'd better keep it quiet or you'd probably lose your job, huh?"

"Yeah, but that's no great loss. I have another job to go to. Matter of fact, I sent in my two weeks' notice."

"No kidding?" That was interesting. "What are you going to do?"

"I'm going to work at Syracuse University in their maintenance department. My brother-in-law is the supervisor, and he keeps telling me—very strongly because I owe my ex-wife a lot of child-support money—that I have a job waiting there for me. I'll be painting dorms and that kind of thing. I'll have great insurance, and my kids can attend college there. It's a win-win for me and my family."

"But you won't be a chef anymore!" That was too bad. For a correspondence chef, he knew his way around a kitchen.

"I'll cook at home."

"Sounds like your new job is a better deal. Does SU know about your record?"

"They don't care. Too bad Priscilla did. She was going to squeal on me. She told me that after she judged the contest. She said that it would be a big scandal if I were to appear on her TV show and the public found out about my record. She didn't want that to reflect on her."

"I'll bet that made you awfully mad at Priscilla." *Enough to kill her?*

"Naw, I understood. I just want my money back from Petey-boy. I borrowed it from a coworker at a high interest rate. It was a shot in the dark anyway. Besides, it pushed me to finally accept the SU job. The old broad did me a favor."

I was satisfied. It all made sense to me. It didn't sound like Kip cared enough to kill Priscilla. He had a better job to go to all along.

I looked over at ACB and Chef DeMassie. Her face was shiny and sweaty as she stirred a twenty-gallon pot full of macaroni. Her fascinator was about to make a dive into the boiling pot of water, and Chef DeMassie was trying to pin it to her hair.

I walked over to help. "Let's go into the ladies' room, Antoinette Chloe, and repin your hat. And you should probably cool off a bit. You're looking flushed."

She grabbed me around the waist and pointed me toward the ladies' room. Whispering into my ear, she said, "He's totally hot, Trixie. I never realized what a hunk he is."

"Antoinette Chloe, be careful. His show got canceled because he put the moves on a coworker and there was a scene. He seems like a player."

"And a player is just what I need. No strings. No melodrama. Just fun and maybe a little hanky-panky."

I chuckled. "You are too much." I found the bobby pins holding her fascinator and made some sense out of her hair without a brush or a comb. "Do you want this back in?"

It was a conglomeration of minuscule plastic forks, tiny plates, and a set of miniature books. I got her theme immediately: library fund-raiser.

Impulsively, I hugged her. What a sweetie she was. Unless you looked into her heart, all you saw were wildly printed muumuus, crazy hats, sequined flip-flops, and wild jewelry and makeup.

"Did you manage to find anything out about Chef DeMassie other than that you're hot for him?"

"I don't think he did it, Trixie. He's so arrogant, he thinks he's better than Priscilla, and soon the world will know it. He has other plans of a comeback, but winning the contest would have fast-tracked him. His biggest beef was directed at Peter McCall. He wants his money back."

I nodded. "I can't blame him. Or Kip either."

"Me neither."

"Are we ruling DeMassie out?" I asked.

"I'd like to, but you know my past record with men."

"Yeah, I do. Your judgment is lacking when it comes to believing criminals."

"I know, so maybe we shouldn't eliminate Walton just yet."

Dottie was next on my list to be investigated, and she had the biggest pile of axes to grind with Priscilla.

Judging by the number of people sitting in my diner, the mini fund-raiser was already a great success. I loved watching everyone, and there were certain people I'd picked out especially to watch.

It was interesting to see Jill and Peter make eye contact across the crowded diner, glare at each other, and then sit in separate corners of the room.

Peter sat with none other than Stan the Bookie.

They huddled together over a table for two and were oblivious to anything around them. Finally Nancy, one of my evening waitresses, offered to make them each up a plate of food from the buffet. They shook their heads, and a good half hour later they left together without eating.

I wondered what they were up to. I hurried to the front door, making like I was going to seat some customers, but instead I watched the two of them out the window.

Stan the Bookie took off in a slick black car, and Peter walked back into the diner. He took his old seat, ordered a soda from Nancy, and then heaped his plate at the buffet.

He ate in silence and periodically sneered at Jill.

I craned my neck and saw that Jill was busy in conversation with a couple of the Tri-Gams—Megan and Connie.

I walked around with two coffeepots—regular and decaf—and tuned in to their conversation.

"I sure hope they find who did it soon. It's not good for Sandy Harbor," Connie said.

"They will. Our sheriff's department is very good,"

Megan said. "And speaking of our sheriff's department, here they are. I wonder who's minding the shop."

Connie laughed. "Everyone's here, Megan! They can watch us all at the same time."

I turned to see Ty, Lou Rutledge, and Vern McCoy walk in—our entire Sandy Harbor Sheriff's Department.

And there was a line beginning to form of people waiting for tables. I had to get people moving out of the diner so others could be seated.

Karen Metonti, one of the snowplow drivers, walked in, looking half frozen and hungry. She made a face when she noticed the line.

Ty walked over to me. "Trixie darlin', you have a very successful event going on here, but I believe you've exceeded the maximum capacity of your diner."

"Ty darlin', how do I get them up and out? They are mostly just talking."

"Hmm . . . watch me clear out the place." He stood in the front of the diner and called for attention. "Sorry for interrupting your meals, folks, but don't forget to pick up your fifty-fifty raffle tickets at the Gas and Grab for tonight's drawing for the library. The drawing is in about an hour, and I hear there's a lot of money in the pot. Route 3 is cleared, but don't speed, please!"

That worked. Half of my customers got up and moved toward the door. Others, who were waiting in line, hurried to the vacant seats.

"Ty, you're brilliant."

He grinned. "I know."

He settled onto a stool at the end of the counter. "How about some of that coffee, Trixie? I need—"

"I know. Coffee strong enough to float a horseshoe." I poured him a hot, steaming mug and one for myself. Then I made more. My waitresses were going to need it.

"Are you here for the buffet, Ty?"

"You bet. I heard that four of the best chefs in town cooked for this event."

"You heard right."

He took a sip of coffee and raised a perfect black eyebrow. "What are you up to, darlin'?"

"It's a fund-raiser, Ty, for our library. The same library that is now an ice and snow storage facility because the tarps that were covering the roof have blown into Canada."

"Yeah, but what are *you* up to?"

I turned and straightened the coffee cups behind the counter to gather my thoughts. I had to be careful with Ty. If he thought I was investigating on my own, he'd watch me like an eagle, and I'd rather he work on solving the murder than babysit me.

I had ACB for that.

"Ty, we all decided to pool our talents and do something good. The chefs can't leave town, and they are getting bored. I came up with this idea."

"Uh-huh."

"You don't believe me?"

"I believe that you came up with this fund-raiser

and that you all worked together, but I'd bet my badge that you wanted to pump them for information related to Priscilla's murder."

I swallowed. "We talked as we chopped, baked, and boiled."

"Did you find out anything I should know?" His brilliant blue eyes peered over the rim of his coffee cup.

"Just that I don't think either of them had *enough* motivation to kill Priscilla."

"Why do you say that?"

I lowered my voice to a whisper. "Because they were madder at Peter than Priscilla. Peter took five grand from each of them to fix the contest, but I'm sure you know that."

"I do. So does all of Sandy Harbor about now. What else do you have?"

"Kip was worried that Priscilla would squeal to his employer about his criminal record, but basically, he has another job to go to. A better job. Long story short, they both took a shot at TV chef stardom, but it didn't work out. And neither of them is really that mad about it. Chef DeMassie is regrouping, and Kip is heading to Syracuse University to paint dorms."

He held his coffee cup up for a refill.

"So, Ty, what do you have on them?"

He smiled, that cute—but annoying—cowboy smile complete with one stray dimple and brilliant white teeth.

Not that I noticed.

"You don't have anything on them!" I concluded. "You're going to have to let them go!"

"I sure am starving. Time for me to go to the buffet." He got up and walked toward the tables.

I watched as he walked away. Nice view.

But I had more important things to do than to watch Ty's butt.

Chapter 14

*T*he next evening, our pizza party guests arrived right on time, and we were ready for them.

There were six bottles of wine and a case of beer chilling in a big galvanized tub filled with snow. If six bottles weren't enough, then I had more. We had the fixings for mixed drinks if they didn't want beer or wine.

I had a couple liters of ginger ale for those who didn't imbibe, which I hoped wasn't anyone tonight.

ACB and I were ready to rock and roll and to pour drinks freely.

Because liquor loosens the lips!

"Ladies and gentlemen," I announced, holding up a basket. "I will be collecting everyone's keys, and Antoinette Chloe and I will be the designated drivers tonight and will drive you back home. Your vehicles will be safe in my parking lot overnight, and I'll give you a ride back here in the morning to pick up your car. Just remember that this is *your* party. We know how hard it has been, staying cooped up, so this is your time to cut loose. And remember, whatever happens at the Big House stays at the Big House!"

ACB added, "Heather Flipelli, our local weatherperson, said that tonight was going to be clear, so expect a blizzard. We don't want anyone to drive in it after they've been drinking, so one of us will be driving each of you home."

I held the basket in front of every guest. "Drop in those keys."

Kip O'Malley dropped his keys into the basket. "I drove me and Walton."

"Peter, how did you get here tonight?" I asked, remembering that he'd originally arrived in Priscilla's motor home.

"I rented a car from some guy who was selling and renting cars out of the parking lot of the Spend A Buck. I hope he's legit. I'm in enough trouble as it is."

"That's Barney Pardo and his roving lot. He's legit."

"What kind of car did you rent?" I asked, just making small talk.

"A red Mini Cooper."

That was the car Linda Blessler wanted to buy. "I hope you're taking good care of it."

Peter McCall nodded absently, gulped down two fingers of whiskey, and tossed his keys in. ACB was already refilling his drink.

The two church ladies, Marylou Cosmo and Dottie Spitzer, already had the giggles from the Riesling.

"Milt and Megan Hunter let us use their car again.

They practically pushed us out the door," Marylou said, laughing. "When Dottie went back to get something she forgot, she said they were running upstairs hand in hand like two kids!" She dropped the keys into the basket. I saw that there was a big *M* on the chain.

I went on to Jill. "Your turn, Jill."

"Don't be silly. I walked here." She threw back a half glass of Merlot just as ACB came flip-flopping toward her to refill her glass.

"But you must have keys to the motor home," I said. "Drop them in, Jill. We wouldn't like you to take a motor-home tour of the countryside while over the legal limit on wine, would we?"

She didn't seem to like it, but she dropped in her keys. I noticed that they had a tag on them that said P's MOTOR HOME in red print.

I put the basket on top of my china cabinet, right behind an ornate fleur-de-lis carved out of the same mahogany as the cabinet.

After more drinks and chatter, Ray Meyerson, the high school senior who was my computer guru and dishwasher, delivered four large pizzas along with dozens of garlic, mild and "atomic explosion" chicken wings and several containers of blue cheese dip.

ACB continued to pour freely, making sure that they all had enough liquid to "wash the food down" with.

As the time ticked by, the volume of the conversation got louder.

"I miss Priscilla," Jill told the church ladies. "She

was my mentor, and she gave me a lot of freedom to do things."

"I'll bet she did," Peter snapped. "And I wonder if she knew exactly what *you* were doing."

Jill took a sip of wine and mumbled, "Leave me alone, Peter."

"Oh, my," said Marylou, shifting on the couch. "I'm getting light-headed. I'd better eat. Are there more garlic wings?"

"Sure. I'll get you some more," ACB said, flip-flopping over to the table to open a foam container.

"By now everyone knows that the contest was rigged, don't they?" asked Kip O'Malley.

"What? Are you serious? I didn't know any such thing," said Jill, immediately looking at Peter. "What did you do?"

Walton DeMassie smoothed his mustache. "Petey-boy here took five thousand bucks from each of us. One of us was supposed to win and get on Priscilla's TV show. It would have been a real boost for my career."

Peter shrugged. "Well, the best recipe won, and that was Jean Williams's mac and cheese with lobster meat."

"Did Priscilla find out what you did?" Jill asked Peter.

"Yeah. She found out. She overheard one of these two dopes on their phone, calling their lawyers." Peter pointed at the two chefs. "Priscilla was grilling me about it when, thankfully, she lost her train of thought."

The two dopes stood up. They looked like they were

ready to pick up where they left off on Peter's face, but ACB and I stepped in front of them.

ACB was trying to draw Peter out of his bottle of Jack Daniel's, but Peter was tight-lipped tonight.

So far we weren't getting any information we didn't already know.

Suddenly Marylou let out a long, ungodly sound. I took the wineglass from her hand. This was going to be epic. "At the contest . . . Dottie, we shouldn't have yelled at Priscilla, should we have? And then, when you went back to apologize to her, it was too late, and . . . and she was already dead!"

Dottie stood and snapped at her friend, "Marylou, that's enough."

Nothing like a scene at a party. Mouths dropped. Eyes grew wide. All the air left the room.

Marylou had just let it spill that Dottie had gone back alone to talk to Priscilla. Or had she gone back to kill her?

"Ladies, please. Relax. We are here for fun," ACB said.

Dottie held up her glass, and it swayed in the air. "I suppose we should have a toast to Priscilla, the husband-stealing, book-plagiarizing, superstar TV chef."

All eyes focused on Dottie, and we wondered what she would do next.

I couldn't wait!

ACB broke the silence first. I figured she would. "Did you ask Priscilla why? Why she had to have Sid?"

"Of course I did. She said that she couldn't keep Sid away from her, but that she was doing me a favor. She said that after a little time with her, he'd come running back to me. And he did. But things were never the same. He always carried a torch for her. She couldn't extinguish that."

"So she thought she did you a favor?" I asked. "By sending Sid back?" I just wanted to make sure where she was coming from.

Dottie laughed. "I suppose she did." She laughed harder and held up her glass. "To Priscilla!"

"To Priscilla!" everyone said.

"And to Dottie," ACB said. "You poor thing, Dottie. Your life was never the same after Sid died."

"Hell, no! It was better! Soooo much better!" Dottie held up her glass again. "Here's to Harry Harvy, the love of my life!"

"Harry?" I asked.

"My husband of fifteen years. After Sid died, I met Harry at the cemetery. He'd just buried his wife. We talked, went out for coffee, went to his house for a little romp, and eloped to Vegas thirty days later. Harry owns a chain of pet-supply stores, and we're rich! We have a house in Palm Beach, a condo on the Strip in Vegas, and we keep the Poughkeepsie house as our headquarters."

Marylou giggled. "I've visited their house in Palm Beach. Oh, my! They have a . . . a . . . yacht floating in the front yard."

Dottie stifled a hiccup. "Harry is going to match

Priscilla's donation for the church's roof. He's also going to remodel the rectory and add on a community center."

"So, after all you've been though, you've done well, huh, Dottie?" I asked.

"Priscilla did me a favor. She sent Sid back to me, and after a while he had the decency to die. And then I met Harry."

"But, Dottie, what about your speech about how she stole your husband and your cookbook and all that!"

"Well, she did."

"But you were distraught. You were a mess. You were falling apart."

"I know. But they were old memories and not great memories. It kind of hit me at once. We could have stayed friends, Mabel and me, and that made me sad. It also made me sad when I saw her. And then to find out she had Alzheimer's, well, it broke my heart." She wiped the tears from her eyes. "And it made me realize that I have to live each day to the fullest and spend as much as I can of Harry's money while I have my health. At least I am enjoying fifteen years of happiness—and counting! Mabel had a bunch of boyfriends, fiancés, and husbands, but she never was truly happy. God rest her soul."

I was mentally kicking myself that I didn't own a chain of pet-supply stores.

I made eye contact with ACB. That was quite the heartwarming speech, and now all of my guests were swarming over Dottie, congratulating her with hugs and kisses.

And I just crossed Dottie off the top of my suspect list. She'd been a great candidate, too.

After her remarkable toast I concluded that she had no reason to kill Priscilla. She was over Sid and what Priscilla had done and had been living it up for fifteen years with Harry Harvy. She'd just wanted to see Priscilla and tell her off for stealing from the church, get some restitution, and maybe gloat a little. Instead, when Dottie had met Priscilla, Dottie had felt sorry for her.

Now it was time for me to institute my plan.

"How about some dessert?" ACB asked. "We have fruit hand pies and a white-chocolate cheesecake. Who's in?"

That was my signal to leave. Hurrying, I ducked out the back door, grabbing a little flashlight on my way out.

There wasn't time for a coat or boots, so my sneakers would have to do. After two steps, I already felt them leaking.

I fingered the key in the pocket of my jeans—the key to Priscilla's motor home, which I'd palmed when I'd collected everyone's keys.

Feeling like Nancy Drew with my flashlight, I opened the door with the key and went in. I knew exactly what I wanted to look at: the contents of that vanilla bubble mailer from the New York City lawyers.

I hurried to the bedroom. The mailer was in a red tote bag under the small desk.

Just as I was reaching for it, a hand clamped over my mouth and I was pulled against a hard body. I screamed, but nothing came out.

"Trixie, what the hell are you doing?"

I relaxed so much that my knees wouldn't lock in place. I slumped to the floor.

Nancy Drew I wasn't.

"Ty?" I whispered. "Wha—"

"I saw a light moving in here, and I thought I'd investigate. Now, let me repeat: What the hell are you doing?"

"Searching for the package that Priscilla sent in care of me. I want to know what was so important in it."

"Have you lost your mind?" he asked.

"Ty, just pretend you're not a cop for a while. Or you'd better get out of here, because I'm going to commit a crime."

"You already have, darlin'."

I shined my flashlight around the items on the floor.

There it was! I pulled out the mailer from a tote bag and slid out a stack of papers. "I, Mabel Elizabeth Cronk Connors McCall Foxworth, do hereby . . ."

"Obviously, it's Priscilla's last will and testament," Ty said. "I've been in contact with her lawyers. Jill gave me their names, as did Peter."

"Do you want to know what this says?" I skimmed the document.

"I know what it says. I talked to Priscilla's estate lawyer."

"This says that everything goes to Peter. It's not signed, and I know why: because Jill never gave it to her. Then Priscilla was murdered."

Ty didn't say anything, but I could tell by the look on his face that he knew the answer.

"I'd bet a couple of my housekeeping cottages that there was a prior will and that Jill was the beneficiary! No wonder she doesn't like Peter. And she had to be totally angry at Priscilla for excluding her."

"Stay out of it, Trixie, and get out of here. Or I'll arrest you right now! And be careful!"

"I have to tell you a couple of things that I found out about Dottie Reinhardt Spitzer Harvy, the church lady."

"I knew there was some kind of grudge, but Dottie wouldn't give it up to me. She'd said it was old news and didn't pertain to the death of Priscilla, but I'm going to interview her again," Ty said.

"I don't think you have to interview her again after what I have to tell you. What about Marylou, Ty?"

"I can't find a motive for Marylou."

"I think that Dottie has been holding a grudge against Priscilla for a very long time, ever since Sid, her husband, left her to be with Priscilla years ago. Dottie knew that Priscilla was going to be here, and she gathered up a busload of church ladies to come with her. I mean, they were all rip-roaring mad about the cookbook, but Dottie also had a real 'frenemy' relationship with Priscilla."

"I'll question Dottie about it, but we'd better get out of here."

"Ty Brisco, this is the most that you've shared anything with me. I'm not letting you go anywhere. What about the two chefs? Are they still suspects?"

"I can't answer that."

"What about Peter?"

No answer.

I looked up at him, and in the glow of my flashlight, I could see his bright blue eyes and the dimple on his left cheek, which sometimes made an appearance. Those lips of his always made m . . .

I grounded myself. "We gotta get out of here. Now," I echoed him. "Go!"

I raced down the steps, and Ty followed behind me. Locking the door, I turned around and he was gone.

Hi ho, Silver! Away!

I walked around the Big House to the back door, which actually faced the water. The wind had picked up, and grainy snow blasted against my face.

I brushed the snow off myself before I slipped into the kitchen.

"You were outside?" Jill asked, meeting me at the door. "In this weather?"

"I—I . . . uh . . . was calling for Blondie. I can't find her."

"She's been in the front room since the party started. She's been sleeping at the side of your chair." Jill raised an eyebrow.

"I . . . um . . . guess I was so busy with the party that I didn't see her."

"You were feeding her some chicken," Jill said.

I laughed. "I was? Imagine that!" I took her arm. "Let's go back and join the party. It's just getting started."

"I think I've had enough. I'm headed back to the motor home. Thanks for the party, Trixie, but I'll take my keys now."

In a brilliant move that even David Copperfield would be amazed at, I cupped her keys in my hand, took down the basket, and made like I was pulling them out of the basket.

Now, for my next trick . . .

Peter McCall walked into the kitchen and leaned against my sink. "So, Jill, I've been meaning to tell you how impressed I was that you blamed the cookbook fiasco on Priscilla and offered to give a cut to Saint Dismas church. For a moment I was worried that it would screw up the dissolution of Priscilla's estate."

I could see a stain of red creeping up her neck. "What are you talking about, Peter?" Jill said through gritted teeth.

"It was you who copied their cookbook, not Priscilla. You know it, and I know it, and you blamed poor *stepmummy*."

As he said *stepmummy*, he paused and grinned, knowing that Jill hated it to the core when he called Priscilla that.

"And, darling Jill, Priscilla finally figured out why the cookbooks were still coming out and she wasn't writing them. She shared her concern with *me*, and I checked it out. We both know that she wasn't herself, that the Alzheimer's was getting worse. That's why you got away with so much."

"But you didn't care when those royalties started pouring in, did you, Peter? It was more money than you could take from Priscilla."

"She gave me money. Priscilla was very generous."

"When you asked her for it, she was generous. She shared with *me* that she was worried about your gambling debts."

"And you know that I'm the executor of her estate, don't you, Jill? That's something that I'm sure Priscilla told you, too."

"I have to go. I can't stand listening to him anymore." She pointed her chin at Peter. "Thank you for the invitation, Trixie."

The party started to break up after Jill's exodus. Antoinette Chloe volunteered to take everyone home, leaving me on cleanup duty.

Well, I'd rather do that than hit the snowy roads.

I drained the aluminum tub, put the wineglasses and the dishes in the dishwasher, and dusted the end tables. I folded up the pizza containers for recycling and then took the recycling and the trash out.

This time I put a coat on and mittens, but I didn't slip into my boots. My sneakers would do. I wouldn't be long. The trash containers were behind the Big House—which was really the front because it faced the parking lot. Trash pickup was tomorrow.

The snow pummeled me. I pushed the snow off the trash containers so I could open them. Since my little party had started, we must have received four inches of snow—the thick, heavy stuff.

I hoped that Antoinette Chloe would make it back safe and sound. When it was dark out, the falling snow could be hypnotic, especially in the path of headlights.

As I walked back to the Big House, I pinched the bridge of my nose to stop a headache that was hovering at the corners of my temples.

My list of suspects grew, than shrank, then morphed into a mushroom cloud. I put their names in order, then changed the order, then changed it back again.

I'd never been so confused in my life.

Oh! Hold everything!

I took several deep breaths and let the cold air sweep out the used cells from my brain.

I hadn't ruled out Walt DeMassie. It was the lust-struck ACB who had, but I wasn't quite sure yet.

Great. Just great. I was back to two suspects.

Wasn't I?

Chapter 15

I called Ray and asked him to shoot over to the Big House.

"Ray, could you do a quick search on Walton De-Massie?" I asked.

"Sure, Trixie." He pulled out his laptop from his backpack and set up on my kitchen table, just like he'd been doing a lot lately.

He typed and typed and finally said, "There's tons of stuff on him. Oh! A scandal!"

ACB laughed as she entered the kitchen. "I love scandals, as long as they aren't mine."

Ray skimmed the articles. "It looks like DeMassie had an affair with Tessa Martin. She has a show called *Cake Lady* on Channel Fifteen, and it was on just before his show. DeMassie's wife, Ruth, found out about it and tried to rip Cake Lady's hair out by its roots. Now they're divorced, and he's moved in with Cake Lady." Ray laughed. "And get this: The article quotes Priscilla. She said, 'Ruth DeMassie and I were having lunch together at the restaurant in the Savoy North Hotel when

Ruth saw Walton and Tessa come out of one of the nearby rooms. It was obvious that they were engaging in a tryst. Well, Ruth was just so terribly heartbroken and hurt.' "

I laughed, too. "Wow! That's a biggie."

"Sounds like Priscilla set them up to me." ACB grinned. "But I don't like cheaters, and that's based on my own experience."

"I'll ditto that," I said. "But if Priscilla set up De-Massie and got him fired, he'd certainly be fighting mad. I'm going to call the channel to see if I can find out anything."

I looked up the number before I lost my courage.

"Channel Fifteen. We are here to entertain you."

"Hi. Can you just tell me if Chef DeMassie, Priscilla Finch-Smythe, and the Cake Lady all worked out of your studio?" I asked. "I know it's a strange question, but I'm such a fan, and I have a little bet going with a friend. A steak dinner depends on your answer."

"Why, yes. They did."

"And obviously they must have known one another."

"Oh, yes." She laughed. "They sure did."

"You're laughing," I said cheerfully. "How come?"

"There was no love lost between them. And it's so quiet now with only the Cake Lady."

I laughed with her. "I do miss Chef DeMassie. Is there any chance he'll be back on TV?"

"Funny you should ask. Now that Priscilla is . . .

um . . . deceased, God rest her soul, we have recently asked Chef DeMassie back."

"Thank you so very much," I said. "Bye now."

"Thank you for letting Channel Fifteen into your home."

I shut off my phone. "You'll never believe this. Now that Priscilla is gone, Walton DeMassie will soon be back on Channel Fifteen."

"Oy," ACB said. "Motive!"

"I wonder if he knew that he'd be able to come back if Priscilla was gone, or was that just a recent perk?" I said.

"I don't know if he could have predicted that."

"Maybe he could have. There would have been only one show—a cake show—and no cooking shows."

All during my conversation with ACB, Ray was typing. He grinned. "DeMassie's cooking show—*Cooking Around the World with Walton*—was pretty successful before the scandal. There was an Internet campaign going to get him back. It had six thousand signatures, but Channel Fifteen was still balking."

"Walton DeMassie had to know how popular he was. And with Priscilla gone, he probably figured there would be a really good chance he'd be asked to come back!" I said. "Now, that's really a motive!"

"Maybe, but Chef DeMassie never left the cook-off, did he?"

"I didn't see him at the end, after he stormed off."

"I did," Ray said. "Remember? He was in the men's room with Kip."

"And this was about two o'clock, the time of Priscilla's death?" I asked.

"Yes. I remember checking my watch because I had to work here at three o'clock."

"Hmm . . . I think we can rule out Chef DeMassie," I said. "Thanks for all your help, Ray."

"Anytime, boss."

When Ray left, I turned to Antoinette Chloe. "Feel like making more calls?"

"To whom?"

"I want to see what we can find out about Peter and Jill."

"How?"

"I don't know yet."

"Maybe we should have another pizza party!" she joked.

"No, thanks!"

"Trixie, do you mind if I take a trip to the drugstore while you make your phone calls? I'm running out of blue eye shadow, and I want to get another bottle of Sock It to Me nail polish."

"Oh, sure! I can make the calls myself."

The important package was still tweaking me, so I decided to call Orlando, Biltmore, Orlando and Fischer. I checked my list of contacts from the phone Peter had. Jake Orlando was the man he kept calling.

I punched in the number.

"Orlando Law Firm."

"Jake Orlando, please. This is Miss Kowski calling."

All right, so I lied.

"One moment, please."

"This is Jake Orlando."

"Mr. Orlando, this is Miss Kowski. I represent Peter McCall, and I was wondering when you plan on settling Priscilla Finch-Smythe's estate and whether we need to meet."

"No. We don't need to meet at all. Peter isn't in the will. Jill Marley is the entire beneficiary. Cilla was going to change her will and leave everything to her stepson, but she never signed the paperwork and returned it, so I'm assuming she changed her mind. I will be releasing Priscilla's assets just as soon as there is an arrest and a conviction, so we're in for the long haul on this one, Miss . . . Miss . . ."

"Kowski." I took a breath. "So let me understand you—you're not going to release the assets to Jill until there's an arrest and a conviction? Is that customary, Mr. Orlando?"

"It is when I'm the lawyer."

"Okay. Thank you, Mr. Orlando. Have a nice day."

Holy crap! Jill was the beneficiary. It was official!

Now I was absolutely positive that she never gave the new paperwork to Priscilla. And then Priscilla was murdered.

All things considered, Jill had the most to lose if Priscilla changed her will and gave it all to Peter.

I had to find Ty and tell him. I looked out my bay window at his apartment over the bait shop next to the Silver Bullet, but there weren't any lights on.

I was making chicken salad when the phone rang. It was Antoinette Chloe.

"Trixie! Oh my! You're never going to believe this!"

"What's up?

"I decided to go to my house and pick up my flip-flops—you know the ones that I lined with fleece? Well, I figured that since it was below zero and you were nagging me, I should—"

"Antoinette Chloe, what's going on?" As Ty said on numerous occasions, sometimes you just had to corral that gal.

"Okay . . . okay . . . Well, I turned the corner, and in front of my house there's two sheriff's cars with their red lights flashing. I swear my neighbors are going to petition to get me out of there, and Mayor Tingsley will—"

"Antoinette Chloe!"

"Okay! Anyway, I saw Vern McCoy and Lou Rutledge bringing out Peter McCall in handcuffs! Yes, handcuffs! And Peter didn't look very happy in the least, but Vern and Lou did."

"Wasn't Ty there?" I asked.

"I haven't seen him, but maybe he's inside gathering more evidence. I hope he locks the door when he leaves."

"He will." I let out a deep breath. "Peter? Arrested!

And just when I decided to cast my vote for Jill, the overlooked worker who covered for Priscilla for years."

"Nah. I thought Dottie had the real motivation, though I don't know if she could have done it in the end. But it's Peter!"

"Thanks for the information." I breathed a sigh of relief that a killer wasn't running around lose in Sandy Harbor anymore.

She lowered her voice and tried to sound like a TV announcer. "This is Antoinette Chloe Brown, coming to you from in front of a beautifully painted Victorian home, the scene of Peter McCall's arrest for the murder of Priscilla Finch-Smythe. Now back to our studio for a wrap-up with Trixie Matkowski."

I chuckled. "See if you can find out anything more from Lou or Vern."

"I'm on it."

I hung up. "Well, I'll be a dieting vegan! Peter McCall did it."

Deciding to take the recycling and trash out for pickup tomorrow, I got the bags ready and quickly slipped into the sleeves of my parka. I didn't get all winterized as I was just going out around back—which faced my parking lot.

But something tweaked me. If Peter wanted to kill Priscilla to get his inheritance and to pay off his gambling debts, he could have done it long ago—not now. Not in Cabbage Patch, as he called Sandy Harbor.

Since he was living and working with Priscilla, he

could have arranged a fatal fall at her California home or a drowning in her pool.

Jill's lights were on in her motor home, and I thought I'd pay her a visit. Maybe she'd invite me in for coffee. I could tell her the news about Peter being arrested. It would be interesting to see her reaction.

I knocked on the door, but Jill didn't seem welcoming. She stood on the steps and blocked the way in. She was wearing her coat, boots, and hat. "I'm really busy, Trixie. Did you need something special?"

"No. I didn't mean to bother you, but I was just looking for some company, and I thought I might beg an invitation from you for coffee or tea."

"Um . . . I am really busy. I'm loading up my car."

I looked past her and gestured to the floor of her motor home. "I see that you have a lot of things packed. Are you going somewhere, Jill? I hope Ty knows, or he'll think you're skipping town." I said that with a smile on my face, but she knew I really meant that she'd better not incur Ty's wrath.

"I'm not going anywhere. These are donations. I'm just getting them in my car and out of the way so I can have more room in here." She sighed. "But I could use some help, if you don't mind. Just a couple more trips, and then I'm done and we can sit and talk."

I wasn't born yesterday. These weren't things to be donated. This was luggage, and there was her red tote bag, which used to contain Priscilla's unsigned will, but the will was gone now. Maybe she'd destroyed it.

I casually walked up the stairs of the motor home and leaned against the counter.

"You have a car, Jill? When did you get a car?"

"I borrowed Peter's car. He isn't going to need it."

"Why won't he need it?"

Jill remained silent and looked away. Something smelled fishy here on the shore of Lake Ontario, and it wasn't fish.

I made my move and knocked over the trash can with my knee. "I am so sorry. I'll pick everything up."

Kneeling on the floor, I scanned the contents as I returned the trash can to its upright position. Bingo! There were pieces of paper with numbered lines on the side here and there. It was the will, torn up. Oh, yes.

"The cops arrested Peter, but I think you know that already." I had to tread carefully; she had crazy eyes. "Peter didn't kill Priscilla. You did. It was as simple as you wanting her money," I said, looking up from my position on the floor.

"I wanted to be famous like she was. I wanted to be iconic. Her money would be the means to help me do just that."

"And you were tired of living in her shadow?"

I stood, looking around for something to defend myself with, just in case. I'd had enough experience to know that you could never be too prepared in situations like these. I inched toward the door.

"Funny. Antoinette Chloe's money was on Dottie or

Kip. I couldn't decide between you and Peter. By the way, how did you know he wouldn't need his car?"

"Because I called and ratted on him. I said that he was planning on skipping town because he killed Priscilla and that he'd booked a flight to Dubai with Priscilla's credit card."

"But *you* booked him that flight, didn't you?"

She shrugged. "It was easy."

"How about turning yourself in, Jill? Antoinette Chloe redecorated the women's cell at the jail. It's really comfortable now. There're plush rugs. The toilet's behind a Japanese screen for privacy. And there're some menus there for takeout."

I was almost to the steps. I just had to turn quickly.

Then something whacked the back of my head. A frying pan. Luckily, it was a light one—maybe a non-stick one, not cast iron—but it still knocked me to my knees.

"Don't move an inch, Trixie!" I felt the cold touch of metal right under my ear. "Put your hands behind your back!"

"Jill? A gun? What the heck are you doing with a gun?"

"Shut up! I am so sick of hearing you talk. You are one nosy busybody. You and that nutcase you call a friend."

"Don't you dare call Antoinette Chloe a nutcase! You're the one holding a gun on me." And it was longer than life. "Is that a silencer?"

She rolled her eyes.

I tried to think, but it was a little hard when my life was flashing before me.

"Come on. Let's go, Trixie. We're going for a ride."

"But there's a snow advisory in effect. No unnecessary travel."

"Shut up! If you make a sound, or if you move a muscle, I'll shoot. I don't have anything to lose. Now, let's walk. And make it casual, or I'll shoot you where you stand."

My gloves were stuffed in the pockets of my parka, but I didn't dare put them on. As we hit the snow-covered ground, more water seeped into my sneakers.

Behind my favorite pine tree, I heard ripping, and then my hands were pulled together. Duct tape.

"Jill, don't. Please don't. Just turn yourself in before you make things worse. I won't say a word about this."

"That's right. You won't. We're going to take a little drive." She pointed to Peter's red Mini Cooper rental from the roving car lot. "Let's walk."

When we got to the car, she shoved me into the back-seat and tried to tape my ankles together. I didn't make it easy for her. I kept moving around, and then I slammed my foot against her chest.

She paid me back with a whack of her gun across my temple.

Ouch!

As I was trying not to cry from the pain, she taped my knees together. I was trussed up like a Thanksgiving turkey.

"How'd you get Peter's keys?" I asked.

"I asked to borrow his car before I framed him."

"Why, Jill? Why are you doing this to me?"

"I realized that you were in my motor home during your pizza party—and you've been awfully nosy. What were you looking for in the motor home, Trixie?"

"It's still Priscilla's motor home, not yours."

"Not for long."

"Deputy Brisco is here, Jill. He's not going to be far behind when he realizes I'm gone."

"That's what you think," she said. "He's in no condition to help you."

My heart started to pound like a drum. "What did you do to Ty, Jill?"

"I told you to shut up." She slammed the door, then went around the car and plopped into the driver's seat.

"That little frying pan isn't going to keep him down," I snapped, thinking of the gun she had with the silencer. "Did you shoot Ty, Jill? Oh, please, tell me you didn't." Tears stung my eyes, and I let them fall.

She laughed, started up the Mini Cooper, and did wheelies and spins out of the parking lot.

"Be careful with this car. Linda Blessler is working hard for it!"

"Shut up, Trixie."

But I couldn't shut up. I was surprised she hadn't duct-taped my mouth, but I wasn't going to give her any ideas.

"If you're going to kill me, I have a right to know what you did to Ty," I said.

"You'll never know. You'll go to your grave thinking that I killed your boyfriend."

I didn't correct her about Ty and me.

"When you found out that Priscilla was going to change her will and leave everything to Peter, that was kind of a slap in the face to you, huh?"

Jill started to cry. "How could she do that to me?"

"Did you talk to her about it?"

She sniffed. "She accused me of being a liar and a cheater, and that was why she was going to change her will and leave everything to that fool. And she fired me. Can you believe that? After all I did for her, she fired me!"

"And that sent you over the edge. When she told you that, you pushed her, and she fell and hit her head on the fire hydrant. And when she was stunned, you choked her with her red silk scarf."

"I told you to shut up!" she screamed, and I thought the windows were going to explode out of the Mini Cooper.

"Did you kill Ty, too, Jill? You'll get the electric chair for killing a cop." I held my breath, wanting to know if Ty was dead or not, but on the other hand, I didn't want to know.

She threw her head back and laughed. I wished she'd watch the road before she killed us both.

I could see that she was driving me to the dead-end area where the village snowplows make U-turns. The snow piles here looked higher than the Rocky Mountains.

"How did you find this place?" I asked. "Only villagers know about this turnaround."

She sighed. "Don't talk."

"Jill, if you're going to shoot me, I'd like to spend my last minutes talking to someone—even if it's to a no-good killer like you."

"We made a wrong turn with the motor home on our way into town and got stuck here!" Jill shouted. "I thought it would be a good place to drop you off. The plows will be here in a while and will be covering you up with a fresh load of snow. With any luck, no one will find you until the spring thaw."

She got out of the car and walked around to the passenger side. Why hadn't I brought my cell phone?

It probably wouldn't work out here anyway.

With all the anger I could muster over her killing Ty, I tossed myself backward over the seat like a pole-vaulter and stepped on the gas, but all I did was stall the car.

Sheesh!

Why on earth would my substitute cook Linda want a standard car? They were more trouble than they were worth.

And what criminal in their right mind uses a standard shift as a getaway car?

She pulled me up by the lapels of my unsnapped parka, but I kept on talking.

"Jill, how could you look at Priscilla's face and choke her with her scarf? How could you?"

"It was easy. I wanted to shut her up, just like I want to shut you up."

Jill pushed me out of the Mini Cooper, and I fell onto the snowy road.

"Get up!" she screamed.

"Like how? It's not as if I'm physically fit, and this duct tape certainly doesn't help. Unwrap me, Jill. Come on. We shared a beverage at the Gas and Grab. We had a nice meal at the Silver Bullet together. I invited you to my pizza party. I thought we were friends." I was stalling.

"Friends? Are you crazy?"

"Would you mind snapping up my parka, please?" I asked. "I'm cold."

She laughed. "You're going to be a lot colder."

She pushed me, and I hopped like an overweight, out-of-shape rabbit. I fell a couple of times, getting my T-shirt and jeans wet. My sneakers were already big, wet blocks of ice.

My mittens were in the car, too. Not that I could put them on over the duct tape.

I was getting madder by the second.

I hoped that Karen Metonti would see me here before she plowed and would help me. If she didn't, I'd be buried ten feet under. That is, if the steel of the powerful snowplow blade didn't strike me first.

My heart broke when I thought of Ty being shot. He was a tough Texan, but even Ty was no match for bullets.

"I have a last request," I said, stalling for time.

"Shut up, Trixie. You're giving me a headache."

"Jill, would you mind letting me live?" I asked. "I owe my aunt Stella a lot of money."

"She'll get her property back when you're dead," Jill replied. "Don't worry."

I heard the sound of duct tape ripping. Jill was going to cover my mouth.

Oh, no!

"Are you going to shoot me now? Here?" I asked.

"No. My gun jammed as I emptied it into Ty Brisco's chest. Can you imagine? He was watching the motor home, but I was too smart for him." She sniffed. "I have something else in mind for you."

Tears dripped down my face. I figured they'd turn into icicles if I stayed out here long enough.

"You're a coward and a cheater and a killer."

She slapped the duct tape over my mouth, and my eyes watered even more from the pain.

"Like I care what you think."

She pushed me, and I fell like a giant redwood into the mountain of snow. Then she rolled me into the valley, where no one would see me.

As if that weren't enough, she buried me with more snow. I struggled like a beached trout in order to breathe. Then I tried to flip over onto my back and sit up, but with my parka half off my arms and me being duct-taped more than any ducts in North America, I couldn't move.

I screamed in frustration, but nothing came out.

The ignition fired on the Mini Cooper, and I heard it drive away. Then there was deafening silence.

I don't like death, and I didn't like to think about it. I can't really handle it—well, who can?—but I didn't want to die frozen in a glacier of filthy road snow and then bashed by the blade of a snowplow. I struggled to get out, but I was like a giant turtle trying to slosh through quicksand.

The only things moving were my teeth chattering.

If there's ever a *Jeopardy!* question that says, "Believe it or not, your teeth can chatter through this sticky substance," the answer is: "What is duct tape?"

But somehow I was able to breathe—not much, but I could breathe. I didn't know for how long.

And then I saw lights flashing and heard the unmistakable noise of the snowplow getting closer and closer.

I swear, if Karen Metonti hit me with her snowplow, she would never get free donuts and coffee from my diner again.

My eyes were closing, closing. I was just so tired and cold and sleepy. I couldn't keep them open, couldn't think.

Far away I heard a dog bark. It sounded like Blondie, but that was crazy. My Blondie was home. Home. I'd never see my pup again. I'd never see the Big House again or my cottages. Or Lake Ontario. I'd never cook at my diner again.

I didn't fight the sleepiness, but closed my eyes and let it wash over me. It felt as if I were floating. There was no cold . . . no shivering.

And there was silence.

All except for that infernal barking dog.

I heard whimpering and scratching at the snow. It sounded like Blondie.

Leave me alone. I'm tired.

It *was* Blondie! I heard digging and scratching at the snow. Then she licked my face, my neck, back to my face. She barked several times, and then I heard the low, deep voice of Ty Brisco.

Ty was alive! He was alive!

"Trixie, thank God." He paused. "You're safe now, Trixie. You're safe." With his bare hands, he dug me out more.

I cried with joy. Ty was alive! The extra moisture turned my face into an iceberg. I shivered like crazy.

"Good job, Blondie," he said. "Trixie, I'm going to call you an ambulance—just as soon as I cut this duct tape."

He pulled out a big jackknife from the recesses of his navy blue uniform jacket and started hacking away at the tape on my wrists.

I felt the relief immediately on my shoulders and rubbed my wrists to get the circulation going again. Then I stood still as Ty quickly got rid of my parka and had me put on his jacket.

He hugged me close to him. Nice.

The coat might have been toasty warm, but I couldn't feel it yet. It did have the scent of his aftershave clinging to it, which I couldn't enjoy since my teeth were back to chattering and my whole body was shaking. I pulled the tape off my mouth, and I chattered and shook in stereo.

I hugged him close to me. "I am so glad you're alive, Ty. Jill said she shot you!"

"She did. Four times. Then her gun jammed. She got the jump on me as I was doing surveillance on the motor home. I figured she was ready to skip town, so I was watching her. She shot me as I got out of my truck to stop her from leaving. Dumb mistake. Luckily, I was wearing my Kevlar vest, but the shots knocked me out for a while. I hit my head on a rock or something. Long story short, Linda Blessler happened to be looking out the kitchen window and saw her future Mini Cooper doing wheelies and spinning out of your parking lot. I followed the car tracks in the fresh snow to here. Blondie did the rest."

I was still unsteady on my feet, so he half carried me.

Out of the corner of my eye, I saw Ty's black SUV blocking the road, a red light clamped to the roof of it, spinning. One of the town's snowplows had stopped, and Karen Metonti was running toward us.

"Trixie?" she asked.

"Call an ambulance, Karen. I'm sure she has frostbite."

"You got it, Ty."

"What about the b-b-bad guy?" I tried to ask.

"Jill is in custody."

"H-how?"

"Get in my truck and get defrosted, and I'll tell you about it."

We got into his car, he blasted his heater, and he hugged me close to him as I shook. It took too much energy to do that, and I just wanted it to stop.

"She was easy to find in that red Mini Cooper. On these snowy and icy roads, she could go only about twenty miles an hour."

I yawned. I was fading—shaking, chattering, stuttering, and slurring my words. "Blondie's a great dog, Ty. We share a great dog."

"You did a great job figuring all this out, Trixie. Too bad you almost turned into roadkill in the process. Why won't you ever just let me handle things?"

"She planted Peter's cell phone. Then she booked him on a flight to Dubai and Vern and Lou arrested him."

"I know. We'll sort it all out later."

I heard the siren of the ambulance getting close. "You know, Ty, I feel really sorry for Priscilla. She had Alzheimer's and wanted love from Peter, but all he wanted was to keep gambling. And Jill used her."

I could barely get the words out, I was shaking so hard, but I had to fill Ty in.

The ambulance driver, Lonnie Cancillo, called Ty on

his radio. "Ty, I just got word from the State Highway Department that Route 81 and Route 11, both north and south, are closed due to the blizzard. So is the Thruway. We can't get to the hospitals in either Syracuse, Watertown, Oswego, or Utica, Ty."

"I'll take her in my SUV to Syracuse," he said. "Go back home, Lonnie. I'll take it from here."

"Ty, no. Just take me home. I'll snuggle under quilts and drink hot cocoa. I'll swim in my tub in hot water."

"I'm taking you to Syracuse. There are three major hospitals right off the interstate. This monster will get through anything, and it has four-wheel drive."

So he drove us in his monster of a car through a monster of a blizzard on a closed interstate highway. I slept most of the way except when I heard Ty swearing under his breath.

I remember being cranky with the bright lights of the emergency room and got even crankier when a needle went into my arm for an IV.

The next thing I remember is ringing my buzzer to go to the bathroom and seeing Ty asleep in a chair next to my bed. He stayed with me for four days straight.

I insisted that they take a look at Ty's chest and his head. If bullets hitting a bulletproof vest can knock him down so hard that he hit his head, he should be checked out.

So the doctor checked his head and eyes and looked at his chest, and I got a nice look, too. It made me feel a whole lot better.

Thankfully, he was okay, other than four angry-looking black-and-blue marks marring his sculpted chest.

And I was going to be fine. All my fingers and toes were nicely recovering.

And after what I'd gone through and worrying about my toes, if my pal Antoinette Chloe didn't get herself some socks and a pair of boots, I'd get them for her and duct-tape them onto her feet!

I did find it interesting that I was almost within spitting distance of Jill. She was in the Syracuse Public Safety Building Jail due to the fact that Sandy Harbor didn't want the likes of her in their jail.

After all, Antoinette Chloe had decorated the two cells there with her very special decor: a salute to red, white, and blue polka dots and purple cabbage roses for the women's cell, and "Let's go to NASCAR and along the way let's stop at the WWF" for the men's cell.

Jill just wasn't suitable enough to enjoy the comforts of the superbly decorated Sandy Harbor Jail.

Epilogue

I hope this e-mail finds you well. If I remember right, I think you're on another cruise. I figure you'll get around to reading e-mail sooner or later.

Winter has come early to Sandy Harbor, and with it, a lot of fun and a lot of craziness.

The craziness came when the library's roof collapsed from snow, sleet, and whatnot. What a mess. All those beautiful books—gone! I was named cochairperson of a fund-raiser to help replace the books, along with Megan Hunter. We decided on a macaroni and cheese cook-off (because everyone does chili!).

Megan Hunter asked Mabel Cronk, your old Gamma Gamma Gamma sorority sister (who was none other than the famous Priscilla Finch-Smythe), to be the judge of the contest since she's a TV personality and cookbook author. She graciously accepted.

We had a delightful parade through town for her. She was a hoot in my friend Sara Stolfus's Amish wagon. We had the high school's marching band along with the Scouts, the Elks, our one fire truck, Hal Manning's vintage hearse, and our two snowplows.

You know how much Sandy Harbor loves their parades—even in the middle of winter!

Then Priscilla came over to the Big House for a tea party in her honor. The Tri-Gams and I made it special for her with your silver trays and fancy punch bowls and exquisite crystal. We had three different types of punch and lots of hors d'oeuvres and whatnot. The house looked beautiful.

Priscilla also asked for a breakfast and a dinner special at the Silver Bullet to be named after her. I did a dinner special named for her along with "Priscilla's Potato Pancakes" for the breakfast. She seemed happy about that.

Priscilla brought her assistant, Jill Marley, and her stepson from one of her marriages, Peter McCall, along with her in her huge motor home.

Those two are another story. Someday I'll tell you all about it.

When you get a chance, you'll have to come and visit so we can catch up on all our adventures. I have lots to tell you, but it would lose something if you just read it in an e-mail. Besides, I miss you. I know you get a subscription to the *Sandy Harbor Lure* in Boca Raton, so try not to read it or get too upset until we've talked.

Like I told my parents, I'm fine, really. Oh, and all my body parts are still intact. HA!

As for the library, there's a committee to write up grants, and more fund-raisers are scheduled. Because of the historic value of what's left of the building, there are strict guidelines that must be followed to restore it to its former glory.

And, yes, I'm a member of the committee— but not the chairperson!

Oh, all right, I'm a cochair along with Antoinette Chloe Brown. Someone has to stop her from decorating the library with polka dots and cabbage roses.

In your last e-mail, you asked about Ty Brisco. Well, Aunt Stella, he's turned out to be quite a good friend. He drove me to the hospital in a raging blizzard and he never left my side while I was there. He even did his follow-up reports from my room. Actually, we both had to do a lot of report writing.

But don't worry about me.

All my love,

Trixie

P.S. I was inducted into the Tri-Gams!

*Family (and Friends'!) Recipes
from the Silver Bullet Diner,
Sandy Harbor, New York*

Aunt Gen Bielec's Christmas Eve Punch

Aunt Genevieve Bielec loved to entertain and loved it when people stopped in for the holidays. This punch was always on her counter for every event: showers, weddings, baptisms, birthday parties, and cocktail parties. Everyone was always welcome at Aunt Gen's house, especially on Christmas Eve!

I served this punch at Priscilla Finch-Smythe's tea.

2 quarts "real strong" tea
1 32-oz. can pineapple juice
1 12-oz. can frozen orange juice
1 12-oz. can frozen lemonade
1 2-liter bottle ginger ale
Wine (if desired)—"must be Manischewitz" according
  to Aunt Gen!
maraschino cherries

Make tea a day ahead and chill it. Thaw the frozen juices/lemonade and mix with the tea.

You can freeze some of this mixture in ice-cube trays and decorate the cubes with maraschino cherries.

Add the wine (if desired) to the punch. Add ginger ale to taste.

Darlene's Pink Champagne Punch

Darlene was an avid reader and could always be found with a book in her hands. I had lunch with her several times when we worked at the same place. She was the nicest person you'd ever want to meet. Darlene passed away much too early, but I always make her punch on special occasions and drink a toast to her.

1 750-ml. bottle pink champagne, chilled
1 2-liter bottle ginger ale, chilled
1 6-oz. can frozen lemonade, thawed
1 qt. raspberry sherbet (or any kind of sherbet)

Mix first three ingredients together.
Let sherbet float on top.

Cheese-Olive Puffs

Sue Lewandowski Szmanoski, who is a Tri-Gam, serves these simple puffs at cocktail parties. She says she makes a triple batch and freezes them, pulling out what she needs for parties.

She brought them to Priscilla Finch-Smythe's tea, and Priscilla begged for the recipe. Sue wouldn't part with it, but she'll share it with you!

2 cups grated sharp cheddar cheese
½ cup butter, softened
1 cup flour, sifted
½ tsp. salt
1 tsp. paprika
48 stuffed green olives, drained and dry

Blend cheese with butter. Stir in flour, salt, and paprika and mix well.

Wrap 1 tsp. of mixture around each olive, covering it completely.

Freeze firm on baking sheet, then place in at least two plastic bags. Return to freezer for at least one more hour.

Bake frozen for 15 minutes at 400 degrees F.

Ann Williams's Quick Coffee Cake

Ann loved to bake and created this recipe in case friends or family dropped in on her unexpectedly. At a moment's notice, Ann would make this cake.

1 cup flour
1 cup sugar
1 Tbsp. baking powder
crack 1 egg into a measuring cup and add milk to make
    one cup
pinch of salt
1 Tbsp. butter
½ tsp. vanilla or other flavoring
cinnamon, to taste
sugar, to taste

Mix all in bowl and pour into an 8"x8" pan sprayed with Pam.

Bake at 350 degrees F for 25 minutes.

Sprinkle top with cinnamon and sugar when done.

Michele Goldstein's Luchen Kugel

Michele is a Tri-Gam who used to live by the Gas and Grab on Route 3 in Sandy Harbor, but left for the balmy weather of Syracuse, New York! Michele says that this recipe is sort of a Jewish mac and cheese, and it's definitely a comfort food! She serves it as a side dish to break her family's fast on Yom Kippur.

  1 lb. wide egg noodles, cooked
  1 cup sour cream
  1 lb. small-curd cottage cheese
  ½ lb. cubed Velveeta (yes, Velveeta!)
  ⅓ cup plus ½ cup sugar, plus additional for topping
  1 stick butter, melted
  4 eggs
  1 tsp. vanilla
  1¾ cups milk
  cinnamon, to taste
  sugar, to taste

Mix together egg noodles, sour cream, cottage cheese, Velveeta, ⅓ cup sugar, and butter.

  Place mixture in a greased 9"x13" pan.

  Beat together eggs, ½ cup sugar, vanilla, and milk.

  Pour this over the top of the noodle mixture.

  Sprinkle a cinnamon-sugar mix on top, if you'd like.

  Cover with foil.

  Bake at 350 F. degrees for 75 minutes.

Apikian Family's White Bean Salad

This recipe is from my friend's (Donna M. Coyle's) Armenian family. Donna said her mother always made this salad by eye and taste and that most Armenian cooks pass down their recipes by watching food being prepared and by word of mouth.

In fact, Donna revealed that this is the first time her mother's recipe has ever been written down!

2 8-oz. cans great northern or cannellini beans (rinsed
    and drained)
1 small sweet white onion, chopped
2 to 3 Tbsps. chopped parsley
juice of ½ lemon (more or less, no seeds)
¼ cup extra virgin olive oil (more or less to taste)
salt and freshly ground black pepper

In a medium glass or ceramic bowl, combine the rinsed beans, onion, and parsley. Add the squeezed lemon juice, olive oil, salt, and pepper. Mix carefully so as not to crush beans.

Chill before serving.

Juanita's Baked Macaroni and Cheese

Juanita likes her mac and cheese spicy hot. She adds jalapeños and chili peppers when no one is looking!

2 Tbsps. oil
1 lb. dry macaroni (16 oz.)
8 Tbsps. plus 1 Tbsp. butter
½ cup Muenster cheese, shredded
½ cup mild cheddar cheese, shredded
½ cup Monterey Jack cheese
8 oz. processed cheese food
1½ cups half-and-half
2 eggs, beaten
salt and pepper

Preheat oven to 350 degrees F.

Bring a large pot of lightly salted water to a boil. Add the oil and the pasta and cook for 8 to 10 minutes (or until al dente if you like it that way), drain well, and return to clean cooking pot.

In a small saucepan over medium heat, melt 8 tablespoons butter; stir into the macaroni.

In a large bowl, combine the Muenster cheese, mild and sharp cheddar cheeses, and Monterey Jack cheese; mix well (feel free to try other cheeses—like Mexican or other blends!).

Add the half-and-half, 1½ cups of cheese mixture, cubed processed cheese food, and eggs to macaroni;

mix together and season with salt and pepper. Mix into the macaroni.

Transfer to a lightly greased deep 2½-quart casserole dish.

Sprinkle with the remaining ½ cup of cheese mixture and remaining butter.

Bake in preheated oven for 35 minutes or until hot and bubbling around the edges.

Trixie's Baked Macaroni and Cheese

I add sliced kielbasa to mine and everyone loves it. I also add drained, mild salsa to my cheese mixture. ACB adds shrimp, scallops, or other types of fish. It all works!

8 Tbsp. butter
1 medium onion, diced
2 Tbsp. flour
1½ cups whole milk or half-and-half
salt and pepper
paprika or other preferred spices
1 Tbsp. mustard (optional)
3 8-oz. packages of whatever kind of cheeses you like
  (Velveeta is good, too!)
1 8-oz. package shredded cheese (reserve for top)
1 lb. macaroni, cooked and drained
2 Tbsp. margarine (or Pam spray) to grease pan

Preheat oven to 350 degrees F.

Melt butter in a medium saucepan over medium heat. Sauté onion for 2 minutes.

Stir in flour and cook 1 minute, stirring constantly. Stir in milk, salt, pepper, paprika, and mustard; cook, stirring frequently, until mixture boils and thickens.

Lower the heat. Add the cheeses to the milk mixture; stir constantly until cheese melts. Be careful that it doesn't burn.

Combine macaroni with the cheese sauce in a large baking dish (or aluminum pan) that is greased with margarine (so it doesn't burn); mix well.

Bake in preheated oven for 30 minutes on middle rack, or until hot and bubbly. Let cool 10 minutes before serving.

While it's cooling, sprinkle the shredded cheese on top.

Note: You can sprinkle buttered panko crumbs, crushed potato chips, crushed crackers, or just cheese on top while it's baking (about halfway through).

Trixie Matkowski's Split Pea Soup

There are many ways to make split pea soup. This is my favorite way and I make a bucket of it!

   2 bags split peas
   2 medium onions
   3 32-oz. cans chicken broth
   2 grated carrots
   ½ lb. cubed ham chunks (optional)
   ½ quart half-and-half or regular milk (optional)

Put all ingredients except half-and-half/milk in a five-quart pot.

Boil, then reduce temperature and cover.

Cook on low until peas break down. Stir frequently. When done, put some into a blender until entire contents are blended. You're going to have to use another pot.

Variation: If you like it *creamy*, use the following instructions:

When done remove from heat and add half-and-half/milk and pour some into a blender until it's the consistency and color that you'd like. Keep blending until entire contents are done. You're going to have to use another pot.

Grandma Bugnacki's Polish Potato Pancakes

My grandma, Sophie Bugnacki, used to grate the potatoes by hand and fry them in her big cast-iron frying
pan. Now people use a food processor. I don't think the
potatoes come out fine enough in a food processor and
they seem more like latkes.

> 6 to 8 medium-size potatoes, peeled (white potatoes work
>   well)
> 1 onion, peeled (optional)
> 1 egg, beaten
> 2 Tbsp. plain flour
> salt and black pepper
> oil for frying

Using the fine side of a box grater, grate the potatoes
and place them into a colander over a bowl with very,
very cold water. (The water helps keep the potatoes
from turning dark. You could also add a little vitamin
C powder or a crushed vitamin C tablet.)

If you like, you can grate an onion on the fine side of
the grater and add it to the potatoes. Grandma B didn't
do this, but you certainly can!

Really, really squeeze out the water when you are
done grating!

Put the grated potatoes (and onions) into a bowl.
Add egg and flour and season with salt and pepper.
Stir.

The mixture should be thick.

Heat a little vegetable oil in a large, flat frying pan. Drop three or four mounds of the mixture into hot oil and flatten to make small pancakes.

Fry for 2 to 3 minutes per side, turning once, until golden brown. Transfer the pancakes to a plate lined with a paper towel.

Repeat until all the potato mixture is used, adding a little fresh oil if necessary.

You can serve the pancakes immediately, or keep them warm in oven on low, wrapped in tinfoil.

Makes about 12, depending on size.

Read on for a sneak peek at what's cooking
in the next Comfort Food Mystery,

IT'S A WONDERFUL KNIFE

Available in February 2016 from Obsidian.

I just love Christmas.

At times, the holiday season might be stressful. Yes, there's never enough time to decorate, bake, shop, write out thoughtful messages on cards, entertain and enjoy the numerous events, but it's a busy, crazy and wonderful time of year.

I am a big list maker, and intentionally I write "Stop, sit down, relax and smell the cocoa," and I make my cocoa with real chocolate, milk instead of water, with whipped cream, and a sprinkle of cinnamon on top, and a candy cane for a stirrer. . . .

I was looking forward to making cocoa in a big mug, my special red Santa Claus mug that Grandma Bugnacki bought me one year when we visited Santa's North Pole Village. I'll sit down with a big plate of my mom's Snowball Cookies with a fresh dusting of powdered sugar, and wash them down with the cocoa and then maybe squirt some more whipped cream, and maybe heat up more. . . .

I looked around at all the boxes and bins that I'd just brought up from the basement and lugged down from the attic of my Big House. Now, where was my Santa mug?

But no matter how much I love Christmas and all that goes with it, I will *not* decorate until the dishes are in the dishwasher after Thanksgiving dinner and all my guests are either gone or in a recliner sleeping off the trypto-phan from consuming mass quantities of turkey.

Right now, on Thanksgiving night, all my guests are indeed gone. The only one sleeping in a recliner is my pal Antoinette Chloe Brown (who has recently shunned her married name of Brownelli).

So now I'm going to begin decorating my diner, the Silver Bullet, which is only a few hundred yards off the main road, Route 3, which splits Sandy Harbor, New York, in half—sort of diagonally, then a dogleg left to the right.

Speaking of dogs, I decided to take my sweet golden retriever, Blondie, for a walk in the thirteen degree tem-perature and three feet of snow on the ground. Mother Nature and Lake Ontario have gone easy on us so far, with only one blizzard, but this balmy weather won't last.

"Blondie, come!" I said, and she grudgingly lifted her head from a cozy spot under my thick oak kitchen table. "Let's go for a walk!"

She didn't hurry to get up. "Come on. You love the

snow." Ty Brisco, a Houston cowboy transplant who works as a deputy with the Sandy Harbor Sheriff's Department, and I rescued Blondie when she appeared half-frozen by the Dumpster in back of the Silver Bullet. Poor thing.

We share her, but I have primary custody. It gets lonely here at the Big House—my huge white farmhouse with green shutters and a wraparound porch.

I got winterized—puffy parka, hat, boots and gloves—and picked up a couple of plastic bins and a couple of boxes. I called for Blondie one more time, and she appeared at my side. Juggling everything, I opened the door, let her go out in front of me and then closed the door. Carefully, I felt my way with my boots across my back porch and down the five steps that would lead me to ground level.

Or was that *eight* steps?

I dropped to the ground like a cut Christmas tree. My packages soared through the air, and a box of lights landed on my head. I did a split that any gymnast would have envied, but I'd bet they'd never heard anything crack as loudly as a couple of my bones.

My teeth hit the snowy and icy sidewalk, and I tasted blood, salt, and snow and spit out a tooth. Oh, sure. I'd just paid off Dr. Henny, after a root canal, and there I went again. Shoot! I should have saved the tooth.

Where had it gone?

I quickly gave up. It was like looking for a tooth in a snowbank.

Blondie was barking, and I couldn't calm her down. I couldn't even calm myself down.

"Blondie, go get Ty. Go get Antoinette Chloe!"

She just stood there, barking. Then she peed in a fresh patch of snow, not far from my head. Then more barking.

"Get Ty, Blondie. Go get him!"

She stopped barking for a while, then tilted her head as if to say, "Trixie, I'm not Lassie, for heaven's sake!"

"Yeah, I know. Just keep barking. Maybe someone will hear you."

I tried to get up, but I felt like a manatee swimming through quicksand. Everything hurt, but mostly it was my right leg and ankle.

As I lay there, trying to catch my breath, I noticed my big Santa Claus mug, which I had been thinking of. It had fallen out of the box and was broken.

It was then I began to cry.

I don't like to cry, although I am a pro at it. I cry at sappy movies. When the channels start putting on their holiday movies, I am one big, blubbering mountain of tissues.

But now I was crying for myself, as I saw my Christmas season melt away before my watery eyes.

Who was going to decorate?

Who was going to finish my shopping?

Who was going to cater the rehearsal each evening for the holiday pageant at the Sandy Harbor Community Church? Most everyone was coming right from school or work during the three weeks before Christmas Eve, and they needed sustenance, so Pastor Fritz had hired me to provide food and drink.

And I was supposed to cater the town's annual Christmas buffet after the play in the church's community room.

And who was going to cater the approximate three dozen holiday parties that I'd booked?

I wasn't going to be able to drive to make deliveries. I wasn't going to be able to stand to cut, chop and cook, if all my bones that I thought were broken were broken.

I was getting pretty cold here, sprawled out in the snow and ice. My parka was the jacket type, but right now it was the midriff type, and I tried to pull it down. My jeans were wet and icy.

"That's it. Keep barking, Blondie."

Silence.

"Blondie, can you spell S-P-C-A?"

She ran off to jump like a gazelle in the snow.

Finally, finally, finally Antoinette Chloe appeared at the back door.

"Trixie? What are you doing down there?"

"Counting snowflakes."

"Interesting." She yawned. "Why was Blondie barking? She woke me up. Want any coffee? I think I'll have a cup before I drive home."

"Antoinette!"

She knew something was wrong because no one— and I mean no one—ever leaves off the "Cloe" in her name if they value their lives.

And no one calls me Beatrix for the same reason!

"What's wrong?" she asked.

"I need help. I fell. I heard bones snap, crackle and pop."

"Oh! I thought you were putting lights up around the sidewalk or stairs."

"By lying on the ground?"

"I thought you were being . . . creative."

"Not that creative." My leg and ankle were throbbing. "Antoinette Chloe, call an ambulance for me. I'm hurt pretty bad." I sniffed.

"I will! I will! I have to get my cell phone. I'll be right back. Don't go anywhere."

"'Don't go anywhere'?" I mumbled. "I thought I'd go Christmas caroling with the church choir, but I don't have my sheet music with me."

I waited, and waited, and finally ACB returned. "You're in luck. The ambulance drivers are at the Silver Bullet on a dinner break. Ty is on his way, too."

"Good. Thanks."

Under normal circumstances, I'd have to be half-dead to want to travel in an ambulance, but this wasn't under normal circumstances, and I felt half-dead.

The pain was so intense that it turned my stomach. It would have been a shame to waste a perfectly good Thanksgiving dinner.

I took deep breaths of the cold air and listened to ACB ramble on. She did help pull down my jacket, and I felt a little warmer.

Finally, I heard Blondie barking, and Ty's deep voice. Then I saw red lights flashing. I didn't know which made me feel better, but it wasn't ACB talking about the upcoming auditions for the Christmas pageant at the Sandy Harbor Community Church.

"Trixie, why on earth do they have auditions? Everyone who wants to be in the play gets to be in the play, for heaven's sake. I think that being pageant director has gone to Liz Fellows's head."

"It's her first pageant," I panted out each word. *Where was my ride to the hospital?* "She's finding her own way."

"Margie Grace's pageants were certainly entertaining. People are still talking about the shepherds tending their flock of salmon."

I shivered. "But people didn't get it when the shepherds did the tango with the salmon. It was a little over-the-top for Sandy Harbor."

"Margie is hopping mad. She wanted to be asked again."

"Trixie? What happened?" Ty finally arrived with Blondie, and I relaxed a little. "The ambulance guys are here."

"I–I . . . f-fell . . . down the s-stairs." My teeth chattered, and I tried to get them to stop. "My right leg and ankle hurt. Maybe my back."

"Don't move."

"I c-can't anyway."

"Here come Ronnie and Ron. Linda Hermann is with them."

"Good."

After much ado, I was wheeled into the back of the ambulance and covered with heaps of blankets.

"We are going to drive you to Syracuse," said Ronnie. "I checked, and they have the shortest wait in their emergency room."

"Okay, Ronnie. Let's go. I have decorations to put up!"

After an hour ride to Syracuse, two hours in the ER and another half hour getting trained on how to use crutches, I was headed home in Antoinette Chloe's delivery van from her restaurant, Brown's Four Corners. Her van couldn't be missed. On the side, it sported a colorful salami with a fedora dancing with a chubby ham in jogging shoes and a tennis outfit. Nearby was an assortment of cheeses watching the dancing and clapping to music that only deli items could hear.

I climbed into the van with ACB helping me or rather shoving my ample butt up and into the seat.

Exhausted, stressed and ready for a meltdown, I plopped into the seat and then tried to position my behemoth of a cast into a comfortable spot.

It didn't help that I had a couple of broken ribs.

"It smells like garlic in here," I said, taking a deep breath.

"Fingers just made a kielbasa run to Utica. Remember?"

"Oh. I forgot."

ACB and I love this kielbasa, which we can only find

in Utica at a certain grocery store. I turned ACB onto it, but I've been eating it for years. It's a Matkowski tradition at Christmas and Easter, and it's only complete with the fresh horseradish I make.

Fingers, who was missing a couple of them, was ACB's cook at Brown's Four Corners Restaurant in downtown Sandy Harbor. ACB was thinking of selling the place to Fingers and opening a year-round drive-in movie on land she owned adjacent to mine, but she hasn't figured out the logistics of snow and blizzard conditions on the drive-in screen or on the drive-in viewers, especially if they came in snowmobiles or Amish wagons.

That was my pal ACB. Her ideas were as wild as her couture.

I had given up nagging her about wearing flip-flops in the dead of winter. She had some kind of aversion to winter boots. She told me that she had lined her flip-flops with faux fur to shut me up.

But it hadn't.

"Do you want to stop for anything in Syracuse?" she asked.

"I'd like to go home and get some sleep. It's been a long day."

"While they were putting your cast on, I called Linda Blessler. She's going to work for you until further notice."

"Oh! That's so nice of her, and it's thoughtful of you to call her for me. Thanks, Antoinette Chloe. I'll call her later and tell her that I might be recovering for a while. The doctor said that I did such a number on my ankle that I couldn't have a soft boot. He had to put a cast on it."

"Oh, and I know you have a lot of catering coming up. Of course I'll help you."

"What about your own restaurant?"

"Fingers will shout if he needs me, but he never needs me. I should just sell the place to him."

"Does he want to buy it?"

"I don't know. I never asked him," she said. "Maybe I should."

"Yeah." I yawned. "I think the doc gave me something. I'm falling asleep."

"Go ahead, but first, tell me how to get to the highway."

"Go straight. Down the hill. You should see signs."

"I remember an Italian bread bakery around here?" she asked. "I love their bread."

"Antoinette Chloe, it's ten o'clock at night. It's closed." I pointed to the tiny store in an old shingle house by the highway entrance. "Closed."

"Too bad. I'm in the mood for warm bread. We could have shared it on the ride home. I'm starving."

As if on cue, my stomach growled.

Antoinette Chloe laughed. "I see a restaurant over there. No. It looks mostly like a bar, but they'd have bar food. Are you interested?"

My throbbing ankle and ribs yelled, "Are you nuts?" but my stomach screamed, "Let's go!"

"Do you think they have anything to go?" I asked, hopeful that I could stay in the van.

We both must have looked in the grimy window at the same time as ACB tried to pull her big van into a space only fit for my cook Linda Blessler's red Mini Cooper.

"It's a cowboy bar," ACB said.

The mechanical bull in the window with a cowboy type riding it and ladies in Daisy Dukes cheering for him was our first clue.

"You stay here, and I'll see if they have sandwiches to go," she said, reading my mind.

"Thanks, Antoinette Chloe."

"Yeehaw!" was her response.

I was going to point out that her dancing-salami-and-ham van was only half-parked, but she was already opening the door to the Ride 'Em Cowboy Saloon.

That was our other clue that this was a cowboy bar.

She came back to the car and opened the door. "Oops . . . Trixie, do you have any money?"

I went to reach for my purse, but came up with a handful of air. "Oh, no, I don't." It was the second time I reached for my purse, which wasn't there. The first was to hand the ER intake worker my insurance card. Luckily, they already had my insurance information from my recent late-in-life tonsillectomy.

"Don't worry, Trixie. I'll get us some takeout. Trust me." ACB slammed the door.

Yikes. We were headed for jail as sure as snow was falling.

The heat was on full blast in the big, empty van, but I still shivered. I closed my eyes for just a moment, and when I opened them, I saw my friend Antoinette Chloe Brown riding the mechanical bull in the window.

I could hear her yeehaws and laughter over the blasting heat and the highway noise. A couple of street people who were camping next to the highway in boxes and crates came to investigate.

"Someone being stabbed?" I heard one ask the other.

"I think it's that lady in the muumuu riding the bull. She's certainly enjoying herself."

My friend's orange muumuu with various green palm trees covering it was hiked up almost to her waist. Not a good look for her, or anyone, for that matter. Her rhinestone flip-flops caught the glint of the overhead lights surrounding the bull. I had to get her out of there, or we'd never get home.

I rolled down my window, and gave the horn a little tap. "Excuse me, sir."

One of the men pointed at himself, and I nodded. He came over to my side of the van.

"I just came from the hospital, and I have a cast, and it's hard to walk. Would you mind going in there and telling my friend"—I pointed to ACB in the window—"to come to the van, please?"

"My apologies, but I'm banned from going in there."

"What about your friend?"

He looked at the man standing not four inches from the window, looking at ACB. "He is also not welcome.

The owner said that we couldn't stare at the gals in those little . . . ahem . . . *shorty shorts* . . . because we were making them uncomfortable." He pointed at ACB, who seemed to be going for another eight seconds. "But that there's a real woman."

"Would you pound on the window then, and yell to her to that Trixie wants her?"

"Who's Trixie?"

"I am."

"Oh. Okay."

They both pounded on the window, got ACB's attention, and pointed to me sitting in the car. Reluctantly, she waved to me and slid down from the bull as her muumuu slid up.

Yikes.

I could hear the crowd hoot and holler, and Antoinette Chloe grinned and waved.

Whatever I was given in the hospital for pain and nausea was beginning to wear off. My body ached, my head was throbbing and my leg felt like I was dragging an anvil. I was hungry enough to search the pockets of my jacket for stray, lint-covered Tic Tacs.

I found only one.

Again, I was feeling sorry for myself. At least I wasn't living in a box by the highway in the middle of winter like my two friends who were staring at a platinum blond woman with a red sequined blouse and "shorty shorts" now riding the bull.

I looked up at the hospital I'd just left. It was sprawled

on top of a hill overlooking Syracuse and glowing like a lighthouse in the crisp, dark night. I was much luckier than most of the people in that hospital, too.

Making a mental note to contribute to the hospital as my Christmas gift, I beeped the horn to my two street guys. My friends came over.

"Yes, Trixie?"

"Um . . . I don't know your name."

"I'm Jud and that's Dan."

"This is all the money I have right now." Pulling out all the change from the ash tray, I handed Jud around sixty-two cents. "Jud, if you and Dan ever get to Sandy Harbor, stop at the Silver Bullet and get yourself a nice meal on me. Okay?"

"We sure will." He smiled, and I wished I could get him some dental work.

"Merry Christmas, Jud."

"Merry Christmas, Trixie."

Finally, ACB shuffled out of the bar, carrying several white bags. She hesitated when she saw Jud and Dan.

Rolling down the window, I shouted, "They're okay."

She plodded to the car. Dan pulled off the navy fisherman's cap from his head and clutched it to his breast.

"You are my kind of woman," Dan said. "May I have the pleasure of knowing your name?"

"Antoinette Chloe."

"Antoinette Chloe," Dan repeated. "It rolls off the tongue like a song . . . or rather a poem by Emerson." He cleared his throat. " 'She walks in Beauty, like the night/Of cloudless climes and starry skies; And all that's best of dark and bright/Meet in her aspect and her eyes. . . .'"

"'Climes'?" ACB's eyes grew wide. "Don't you swear at me, mister."

Jud held his hands up. "It means weather. Climates," he said. "Dan and I were both professors of literature until we were downsized. Now we are writing a book about living with the homeless."

"That's got to be sad," I said.

He looked over his shoulder to the mess of boxes and crates. "It'll be even sadder as Christmas gets closer."

My heart sank. "I wish I had my pocketbook, but I'll be back as soon as I can."

Antoinette Chloe was busy searching in her bosom purse. That's what I called the depository in her cleavage, which held just . . . everything. She pulled out a roll of money.

I looked at her in astonishment.

"I won it. Over two hundred bucks. Apparently, no one thought a full-figured woman in a muumuu and flip-flops could ride Cowabunga. That's what they call the electric bull."

She handed the money to Dan. "I am counting on you to make sure that they get whatever they need for the *clime*—blankets, soup, coffee. . . ."

"You have my word, my lovely Antoinette Chloe." Dan kissed the back of her hand, and she giggled like a fifth grader.

Jud nodded like a bobblehead. "Darling ladies, the charitable goodness you promulgate is beyond reproach."

"Who said that?" ACB asked. "Shakespeare?"

"Judson Volonade."

"Is he famous?"

"Not yet. He is I."

We waved good-bye to the professors and headed north to Sandy Harbor.

I felt bad for dragging ACB out of the saloon. She had just been having fun and earning us some dinner. And I was cranky from pain.

"So, Antoinette Chloe, do you think that Jud and Dan are legitimate?" I asked, taking a bite of a chicken tender. It was still half-frozen, but I could eat around the frozen part.

She shrugged. "I'd like to think so."

"I just hope they are really professors doing research and that we didn't just give them a drinking binge that would last until Christmas," I said.

"Yeah."

"Oh, I'm being negative, and I just vowed to stop being negative and not to feel sorry for myself."

"Trixie, you'll still have a great Christmas, and we'll all help you fill your orders and deliver them."

Tears stung my eyes. I did have great friends and a great staff at my diner. I knew they'd help, but my Christmas season wasn't going to be the same this year.

Maybe it would be even better!